ABOUT
MIND CHRONICLES TRILOGY

This series is based on the Hermetic principle "As above, so below." Its goal is to experience and chronicle the story of humankind since the primeval fireball, as found in the depths of one human mind—my own. The Hermetic assumption is that all places, times, and beings we have ever known exist now in the memory bank. If the key can be found to unlock this primordial memory bank, then light can shine into the records of time.

There have been many times in our history when it seemed that the end of the world was upon us. These potential End Times often came at the end of an astrological age or millennium. Perhaps this twentieth-century period is unusually threatening because the end of an age coincides with the end of a millennium. In times past, we have thought the disaster was caused by moral depravity, war, or catastrophe. What is essential to understand is that all those fears *were a failure of the imagination*. Matter is never destroyed; it just changes form. In times past, we knew little about the planet as a whole, but our inner resources were richly developed. Now we know much about the whole planet, but almost nothing about our inner minds, which are creating inexplicable agents of destruction on the Earth. The Bomb, like the medieval dancers of death, confuses inner and outer. We thought our salvation was in knowing more about the world, so we did this. We must now explore the landscape of our inner selves.

Past-life regression under hypnosis and other altered states of consciousness for deep exploration are the methods I have used to obtain the material for this series. Ancient initiatory religions used these techniques to bring the initiate to his or her highest potential for living, and the techniques in these books are as old as the first human awareness. This series attempts to go even further, however. It recaptures the phylogenetic Earth-mind records, including all the influences on this planet from other galaxies and planets. We contain all this knowledge deep within ourselves, and this series recovers the long-forgotten Earth story.

We are now precessing from the Age of Pisces into the Age of Aquarius. Thirteen thousand years ago, Earth precessed from the Age of Virgo into the Age of Leo. The Age of Leo—when Atlantis flourished—was an age of creativity, and the Age of Aquarius will be the full expression of cosmic consciousness. This Golden Age will be aborted, however, unless we recapture our story, our myth. Knowing this great myth will awaken our souls. Like the initiated bards of old, I unfold my tale for you. Together, let us awaken to full planetary consciousness.

SIGNET OF ATLANTIS

Volume Three of
The Mind Chronicles
Trilogy

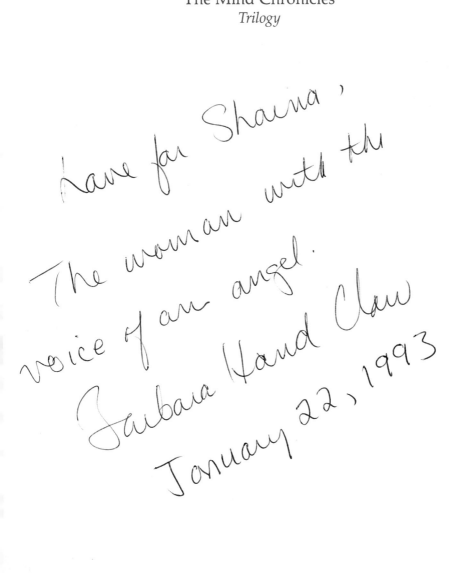

Love for Shauna,
The woman with the
voice of an angel.
Barbara Hand Clow
January 22, 1993

SIGNET of ATLANTIS

War in Heaven Bypass

Barbara Hand Clow

ILLUSTRATIONS BY
ANGELA WERNEKE

BEAR & COMPANY
PUBLISHING

SANTA FE, NEW MEXICO

LIBRARY OF CONGRESS CATALOGING-IN-PUBLICATION DATA

Clow, Barbara Hand, 1943-
    Signet of Atlantis : war in heaven bypass / Barbara Hand Clow :
illustrations by Angela Werneke.
        p.   cm. —(The Mind chronicles)
    Includes bibliographical references.
    ISBN 1-879181-02-9

    1. Occultism. I. Title. II. Series: Clow, Barbara Hand, 1943-
Mind chronicles trilogy.
BF 1999.C594 1992
133.9′01′3 — dc20   92-12392
                                          CIP

Bear & Company, Inc.
Santa Fe, NM 87504-2860

Cover & interior design & illustration: Angela Werneke
Author photo: Valerie Santagto
Editing: Brandt Morgan
Typography: Buffalo Publications
The Veiled Goddess and Time Calendar diagrams are adapted
from *Plato Prehistorian* by Mary Settegast.
Printed in the United States of America by R.R. Donnelley

1 3 5 7 9 8 6 4 2

To the Earth.

May she continue to be patient
with our journey on her surface.

CONTENTS

ACKNOWLEDGMENTS

I am in awe of Rick Phillips for his ability to help me access many dimensions and time zones while always maintaining the awareness that all of this is actually the One.

I am deeply grateful to Angela Werneke, who has made all three volumes of *The Mind Chronicles* much easier to access. Her ability to make visual what I have written is phenomenal, and she has been willing to draw on every resource she has to be able to create at the highest possible level.

I honor my medicine teachers: Grandfather and Grandmother Hand, Hunbatz Men, White Eagle Tree, Frank Aon, Pamela Adger, Alberto Ruz Buenfil, Gerry Clow, Matthew Fox, Nicki Scully, Robert Hand, Jeanne Relyea, Jim Berenholtz, Mazatl, Heyoehkah Merrifield, Brandt Morgan, Zuleika, Reno, Teri Weiss, Elizabeth Clow, Hawk, Veronica Basil, and the people of Hopi and Jemez Pueblo.

Many thanks to Brandt Morgan for his brilliant work as editor, and to Barbara Doern Drew and Amy Frost for the final polish on this book. Thank you as well to the other Bears, who have truly helped me on this journey.

Above all, I honor my family for their patience with a wife and mother who was driven by an unseen force for seven years.

FOREWORD

The inner world of consciousness is the ultimate frontier, waiting to be explored. Being the essence of creation, it holds the keys to self-knowledge and the only real solutions for the world's ills.

I have had the pleasure of watching this last book of *The Mind Chronicles* trilogy come into form, and it has been a fascinating experience, to say the least. In my psychospiritual work at the Deva Foundation, I have witnessed thousands of sessions over the years, and I can say without a doubt that Barbara Hand Clow's ability to reach deep inside herself and express her experiences is unique. Transcending space-time, she journeys into the mystical realms of creation, bringing us gifts of expanded awareness and new perspectives on human possibilities.

Acting as the facilitator for her inner session work, I used my knowledge of spiritual acupuncture to help her channel forth the information her Higher Self was ready to reveal. The sacred acupuncture points not only open the flow of energy in the body, they also have the ability to expand consciousness in various ways, carrying the person into the various esoteric realms of being. But with Barbara, it became clear immediately that my techniques and guidance were mostly unnecessary. The experiences were bursting forth on their own; she was merely the vehicle, and her skill of letting them come through her filled me with awe. As a result, I also experienced the energies and teachings that you will be touched by in this book. Make no mistake of the intellect: this book not only stimulates thought—it is an energetic experience of consciousness.

Signet of Atlantis opens the doors to the dimensions of pure emotion—we rediscover the sensitivity of true feeling within the human being. It challenges each of us to pierce through the programming of ages of ignorance, allowing a new reality to dawn.

The search for Atlantis is the symbol of the search for Self. Atlantis is a state of consciousness; it changes as global consciousness changes. At this point in time it represents the male psyche, that technological, ever-controlling need to create (or destroy) through the intellect, to use the Earth as if it were a collection of resources for us all to exploit. Fortunately, the times and, therefore, the consciousness of Earth are changing. The Goddess is rising from her imprisonment and is already express-ing her feminine divinity with a gift of empowerment for each of us. The symbol of Atlantis offers us that gift of knowledge of the male and female living in harmony, the communion of spirit that revitalizes the powers of Gaia. Atlantis is not a place that has been destroyed, but a consciousness that is being expanded and recreated. The lessons are being learned. What seemed to be a violation, a tragic mistake, now presents the world with new possibilities.

Barbara Hand Clow offers a vision. Each book of her now-complete trilogy has charted the territory through which humankind has journeyed in time. That mystical mindscape was mostly the painful emotional ex-periences that we have denied, repressed, or endeavored to project onto others. This in turn created the theme of the victim and victimizer. We have become addicted to this illusion, and being subject to the realms of ignorance engendered by our separation from God, we actively perpet-uate our disharmonies. In the drama of humanity's separation from the unity of all the laws of nature, Atlantis was the tragedy that arose from the misuse and abuse of power. The collective chose the punishment of their very own self-judgment, just as we today are so close to repeating that same karmic theme.

But Barbara gives us in this book a "signet," a key that opens the wisdom of the heart as a solution to the age-old patterns that we are now ready to shed. The empowered heart is not only the "signet," but the salva-tion for Earth and her creatures as well. As we empower ourselves with spirit, all of creation shares in our celebration.

Barbara's voice is one of many that are heralding the window of op-portunity for us all. She has shown the courage that can inspire us to manifest our destiny now. As she tells her story, we may now discover our own stories and know that our stories are one and the same. The pieces become whole, and our hearts no longer need to suffer the fragmentation of perpetual heartbreak. The healing within each of us heals the heart of the Mother, and her love will become obvious to us, expansive and dy-namic in this beautiful world we share. We come home again.

Rick Phillips
Valencia, New Mexico
April 1992

Rick Phillips is a teacher and psychospiritual facilitator for
the Deva Foundation, of which he is a cofounder. He is author of
Emergence of the Divine Child.

PREFACE

Writing *Signet of Atlantis* was a truly extraordinary experience. This is the third and last book of *The Mind Chronicles*, a trilogy written to explore all the facets of my inner world of consciousness. What follows is the story of how it was created, and I offer this remarkable story to you as a teaching in the value of unconditional trust.

The Mind Chronicles began in June of 1983 when two Jungian analysts reviewed my graduate thesis, "A Comparison of Jungian Analytic Theory and Past-Life Regression Under Hypnosis," and informed me that they thought it should be made into a book and published. I stored that thought in the back of my mind and left for a new job as acquisitions editor with Matthew Fox at Bear & Company.

One day in March of 1984, I was taking out the garbage and thinking about whether to publish a very violent but gripping novel I had just completed, when a stupendous God-like voice filled the garage with great sound. The voice boomed, "Destroy the manuscript and all the disks for your novel, and we will give you a trilogy. The first volume will be called *Eye of the Centaur*, and it will be published in 1986; the second volume will be called *Heart of the Christos*, and it will be published in 1989; and the third book will be called *Signet of Atlantis*, and it will be published in 1992."

I was shaking from the force of the sound as well as from the energy in the garage, which could only be compared to the Hebrew prophets hearing the voice of God as described in the Bible, and I wrote down the three titles and dates. I had always felt something close to contempt for Yahweh as God depicted in the scriptures, but I could not ignore this extraordinary experience. Being basically adventurous as well as very ambivalent about my novel because it had the potential to incite black/white tension in the United States, I destroyed all copies of it and began to imagine what *Eye of the Centaur* could possibly be.

I already had tapes of twenty sessions of my so-called past lives that I had experienced with Gregory Paxson, a past-life therapist in Chicago. These were filled with marvelous stories of a Minoan priestess, an Egyptian priest, a Druid, a Near Eastern prostitute, merchants from the time of the Roman Empire through medieval Europe, and even a past life as the prophet Isaiah. I had them transcribed by a typist, and when they were all done in 1985, I went into a deep meditation and asked for guidance. Magically, within six hours the structure of *Eye of the Centaur*, based on the seven stages of initiation at planetary sacred sites, formed itself.

I spent many months crafting the work using the image of a deep pond for guidance. My present self was the surface of the pond, and all the past lives became the weeds, mud, and creatures of the depths of the pond—the voices of my inner world. A love and passion for this trilogy emerged in me, and even though I am the author of books in other fields, this series will always be my favorite. As you will see, I became a whole person as I allowed it to come through me.

The next problem was how to get it published. Since I was an editor at Bear & Company, I felt I should seek another publisher. Carl Llewellyn Weschcke, president of Llewellyn Publications, decided to take a chance on me, and *Eye of the Centaur* ended up being published in May of 1986! I had had no control over this publication date, and so I began a process of taking very seriously the voice I'd heard in the garage. Honoring it was even easier when I began to understand the book's title due to another creative work that started to rush through my consciousness. This second book ended up being titled *Chiron: Rainbow Bridge Between the Inner and Outer Planets*. I saw that the "eye" in *Eye of the Centaur* was the Eye of Horus, my guide, and that the "centaur" was Chiron, the mythological centaur renowned for his skill as a healer.

When I had done the sessions for *Eye of the Centaur*, many of the historical dates and locations that came through contradicted conventional historical and archaeological data. But I made the decision to trust the information I had gotten under hypnosis, even if I made a fool out of myself. Then, after publication, some of my own information started getting verified in new research. For example, the date I got on the Exodus was about 1425 B.C. under Amenhotep II, and yet in the years 1983 through 1986, most researchers were dating the Exodus around 1220 to 1250 B.C. under Ramses II. Since 1988, however, many archaeologists have been revising their date of the Exodus to 1425 B.C. Archaeologists and historians still may not take my work seriously, but I began to see that my material was extremely accurate. Like Edgar Cayce, I had to assume I was reading records of time that were even more accurate than human attempts to record events.

So, in 1987, when it came time to begin sessions for the second book, I already trusted my right-brain skills to a high degree and had been developing my ability to shut off the left brain and go deeper and deeper into the subconscious. I chose Chris Griscom of The Light Institute in Galisteo, New

Mexico, as my facilitator because I felt that the book would tend to access the darker states of awareness; I sensed that the book would be very shamanic, and Chris is a wild and courageous healer who could take that journey with me. Also, I knew it was important to have no judgment about what I encountered. In fact, I became so trusting of the material attempting to move through me that I made a pact to publish *whatever* I accessed. I realized by then that I was a chosen vessel for this trilogy and that I must trust that gift above all else.

The book that became *Heart of the Christos* is a ferocious cauldron of human karma—involving sacrifice, sexual abuse, struggle with possession and Faustian pacts—and I now am very proud of my truthfulness, which was assisted by Chris. When I began the sessions in 1987, I did not know that I had been raped and beaten when I was less than two years old. I went back through all that pain, accepted it, and cleared it, and I found freedom from judgment and fear. I will always be grateful to Chris for her work with me, and also to Jamie Sams, author of *Medicine Cards*, for a session that enabled me to remember the early rape. They attempted to be true sisters in this time when women have been so alienated from each other by the male separatist modern world.

I had some control over the publication date of *Heart of the Christos* because it was to be published by Bear & Company; I was sure it would succeed with them as their newly developing line of books in alternative medicine and healing was thriving. The trilogy was perfect for this line, and Carl Weschcke of Llewellyn graciously gave me the rights to *Eye of the Centaur* because my second Llewellyn book, *Chiron: Rainbow Bridge Between the Inner and Outer Planets*, was doing so well for them. But I didn't have total control over the date of publication because of the incredible strain caused by writing three books in four years while handling a job and family. Mysteriously, *Heart of the Christos* came out in 1989, and its subtitle wanted to be "Starseeding from the Pleiades." I wondered if the source coming through me was Pleiadian, but I did not understand what that meant until meeting internationally known channel and teacher Barbara Marciniak in 1991.

Exhausted as I was after finishing *Christos*, as I call it, more magic started to happen. First of all, the book hit the bookstores just as the media and public were in the midst of a binge exposing the real truth about sexual abuse and violence. Suddenly thousands of brave individuals began telling their stories about what had been happening to them in these apocalyptical times. Few if any of these people had read my book, and yet it was voicing that need to expose and clear this festering inner wounding—else madness or planetary ecocide would overwhelm us all. I began to see very clearly something that I had always felt deep inside: *that the outer reality is a mirror reflection of our inner minds*. Little did I realize then that this next level of trust about our powers and perceptions would be needed just for me to even begin to create *Signet of Atlantis: War in Heaven Bypass.*

Next began the craziest and most impossible two years of my life. During 1990 and 1991, my work at Bear & Company increased in complexity, my personal life became more rich and wonderful with a teenage son and daughter at home while my marriage evolved into an ever more wonderful passionate journey, and then *another* book began flowing through me outside of the trilogy! Throughout all the writing and the busyness of my personal and professional activities, I had continued to be a counseling astrologer as much as possible. More than twelve years of research work on the key passages of life suddenly demanded to become a book to help prepare people for the powerful Uranus-Neptune conjunctions of 1993. So, in addition to everything else, *Liquid Light of Sex: Understanding Your Key Life Passages* had to be written and published by fall of 1991!

At this point, I got just plain mad at all the demands being put on me. I stayed up all night thinking and meditating when the United States invaded Iraq, and I asked, "Who are you and why do you ask all of this of me?" Magically, in response to my questions, I was gifted with a series of transmissions from the Pleiadians. They informed me that they had been communicating with me since I was four months old and that they loved me very much and highly esteemed my willingness to bring their teachings to people. I agreed to somehow go on and finish *Liquid Light of Sex,* then go out and teach it as well as create *Signet of Atlantis.* But this time I made a deal with them: my family was to be happy, safe, and fulfilled and was not to be stressed unduly by my work. Then I sat in my living room at about four in the morning while the room filled with an incredible vision of exquisite blue-white light. The Pleiadians showed me a vision of my four children, my husband, and myself all transmuting to white light as we were in the midst of total bliss. I began a phase of trusting even deeper, but that was only the beginning of my relationship with these beings.

I taught in Bali in May of 1991 where I set up a private session with Barbara Marciniak, who is the world's most factual and clear channel of the Pleiadians. There are many people who say they channel this source, but the individuals who seem to be receiving information from the same vibration that comes through me are Ken Carey, Timothy Wyllie, and Barbara Marciniak. I had decided to consult with Barbara because I wanted help on how to write *Signet.* At that time I was still finishing *Liquid Light of Sex* as well as teaching all over the world, and the manuscript for *Signet* had to be turned in at Bear by November of 1991 for the 1992 publication date!

I had been doing sessions with Rick Phillips of the Deva Foundation, in Valencia, New Mexico, and we had been accessing experiences of contact with other dimensions as well as enlightened masters. I couldn't imagine making this ethereal material into a book—it seemed it needed to be like the celestial work the *Paradiso* by Dante—and, anyway, how was I to create such a work in less than six months? Well, the news from the Pleiadians could not have been worse, and I found myself getting mad at them again. What were they? Cosmic slave drivers? The Pleiadians, speaking through Barbara Marciniak, responded: "You will publish *Signet of Atlantis* in 1992, and you cannot access the method until after the July 11, 1991 eclipse." Great! Now they were saying I couldn't do anything with it until mid-July, though I had to hand it in by October and I also had to work during that period. I felt an energy rush in my body that seemed to be rearranging something, and I instantly accessed a whole new skill: I just started laughing.

I admit that I tried to cheat and get all the session material together and make something of it sooner, but everytime I did that something would interfere—a child would call with an emergency, my husband would want to make love, I'd get sick, and so on. So, like an old dog lying in the sun, I just gave in. On Monday, July 15th, after the eclipse ceremony was finished and I was done with teaching all weekend, I went down to my office and made a holographic calculator out of quartz, an ancient Sekhmet (the Egyptian lion goddess), an ancient head of Egyptian pharaoh Akhenaton, an ancient head from Teotihuacan, an amber carving from Agua Azul, an ancient Thoth (the Egyptian god of wisdom) as baboon, a crystal from Knossos, and an ivory spirit guide from Tana Toraja. And I waited. Then I felt an urge to draw, and I drew a strange symbol with a triangle in the middle that connected three moving wheels. I could feel wind as I drew this; I was sure it was a symbol for the book.

Two days later at work, something amazing happened. My German publisher, Lutz Kroth, had known I was fascinated by the "crop circles." So, on July 17th, he faxed me a drawing of a crop circle first seen near Avebury, in England, on July 16th, and it was the same diagram that I had drawn as the symbol for writing the book! This raises some very interesting issues: (1) Was this symbolic form existing someplace like the fifth dimension and then imprinted in the third dimension in the field while I accessed it? (2) Was my thought imprint as I worked with the *Signet of Atlantis* holographic calculator so powerful that it imprinted in the field near Avebury as I drew the symbol? (3) Were the Pleiadians involved in the crop circles as well as with me? Whatever the answer, I knew I had to release my control over how this book would be created to a degree that was impossible for me to comprehend. Again, I just had to allow the process to occur.

I worked on the book in the summer a bit, but it seemed like wherever I turned, I got interrupted. I was scheduled to teach seminars about *Liquid Light of Sex* in a different city every weekend, and the most leave I could take from my job was an extra four hours a week. So, I finally became like a sleepwalker: my lungs kept getting dried out on airplanes, and exhausted by all-day workshops, I would come home and go right into the moment of family needs and carrying on my job at Bear & Company. I wrote about fifteen hours a week, and I barely remember doing it. There were many times when I stared at the magical calculator, fell asleep at my computer, and awoke to find myself sitting there with pages typed. It is only because of the incredible clarity of the session material with Rick Phillips and the excellent work by my editor, Brandt Morgan, that this book has come to us from the higher etheric realms.

Before writing this preface, I studied the manuscript once more. This book takes you on a multidimensional journey, and I am still amazed that it could be accomplished in written form. This is a gift from the Pleiades through me, and it has all the powers and keys to teach you that your thought determines where you are and who you are. Let it carry you to its dimension—the fifth—and do not be afraid because that is where divine consciousness exists, waiting for you to arrive. And if the Pleiadians ever visit you, make a clear deal with them first!

Chapter One

LABYRINTHIAN JOURNEY

Unity consciousness or God consciousness is to find myself in everything I perceive because everything is none other than myself. It is a journey without distance because that is where I started in the first place; that's where I was. There is no journey involved. The seer says, "My bliss is nearer to me than my mind. It is closer to me than my body, and it follows me wherever I go. I don't need to strive to find it because it is me."

—Dr. Deepak Chopra, Bali, 1991

It is summer solstice 1989 at the ancient temple of Knossos on the isle of Crete. I pass through a narrow, blood-red temple entry door, just tall enough for my head. Straight ahead, I see the horns of a great bull sculpted out of granite. My knees weaken as sobs well up from the center of my heart. Tears gush from my eyes as if they have been swelling the ducts, waiting for this moment all my life. In seconds, my face is wet and my chest heaves with trapped breath. I rush quickly into the first courtyard of Knossos, oblivious of the tourists. I remember the labyrinth.

Even though this temple is thirty-five hundred years old, I feel as if I were coming into my own house. I survey the scene to my left, noticing steps leading up to the central, open courtyard of the temple. A mural depicting a delicate Cretan youth amidst papyrus plants is visible through a hallway, but I turn right to stand in front of the great bull horns. Looking through these round, arching horns that reach for the sky, I see the familiar crystal mountain looming to the south. As though swirling in a gritty, sucking dust devil in the desert, I am swept back in time to 1569 B.C., when I was first initiated in the Cretan labyrinth.

My name is Aspasia, and I am fourteen years old. I am tall, with a solid body like a young oak tree. My thick hair is black and curly, and I am filled with crackling energy. I stand in the entrance to a labyrinth, a maze created by priests as a "journey form" that contains every thought my mind will ever think.

I move into the labyrinth feeling as though I have been put here by the priests so they can initiate me into their secret world, but I have actually entered so that I can move myself beyond fear. The great iron doors have just shut behind me. Cool air sucks from a deep center down tunnels somewhere in the distant darkness, and I breathe quickly. This initiation is the eternal test, arranged to see whether or not I have the capacity to escape the traps of the mind.

This dark place feels very solid and real, as if it were a physical labyrinth of rock walls with many pathways. As I enter into it, its reality is projected onto me by means of a mental image from the magician priest Didymus, and it all *does* become solid. I begin walking with determination down the stone passages. They are like catacomb tunnels, about six feet tall and two to three feet wide. My eyes become catlike, glowing in the dark and lighting up the corridors; my "lion self" is being activated.

My last contact with the outside world was when Didymus shut all the exterior doorways to the labyrinth. Now that I am inside, I am supposed to just keep on walking. I hurry as fast as I can without bumping into the walls created by the labyrinth's many turns and side chambers. I concentrate my energy in my third eye so that I do not turn off into any of the side hallways. Instead, I walk straight down the main pathway toward the center. I intuit that all the side rooms hold my own personal nightmares and painful experiences. I do not choose to linger and experience any wars, initiations, mystery plays, court intrigues, or love affairs. I want to walk into the center of myself—the center that is cosmic.

As I spiral around and around the labyrinth, getting closer to the center, I feel its great power. My arms begin to feel dense—especially my left arm—and my chest feels thick as my heart begins to pound. My fingers feel hot and my legs are heavy. Dark green, spongy light glows and throbs in the hallways.

I continue to walk, getting closer to the pulsating energy. This is animal energy, something very ancient, and I feel increasingly afraid. But I push forward, avoiding all the experiences of the side chambers. The closer I get to the central energy, the more I feel its power. It feels like something that could devour me, but I am walking straight into it.

Now the "ruby"—in the pineal gland in the center of my skull—begins to glow, and I can feel that its low red light will protect me. The only way out of this place is to go to the center first. I know that if I go anywhere else I will perish. This center is a block within me that I don't want to look at; it is the home of my personal dragon within.

I already know that there is a powerful bull at the center of the labyrinth, but I also hold the belief that if I *do* penetrate the center, I will find something ugly and faulty, some central flaw about myself. I know that everything from which I form my identity is made up of images encrusted around this hidden center—images I have created that I have chosen to believe.

When I was initiated, the grandmothers taught me to just keep walking forward if this challenge ever faced me. They said I would discover that my center is really a pearl enfolded in layers of soft mollusk flesh. However, I am confused because I have been put into this labyrinth by a priest. Up to this moment, all my tests have been created by my trusted grandmothers; the priests have only been allowed to toy with me—to challenge my imagination with their mystery plays, never to actually make me face fear. But I must go forward now.

In the mystery plays, I learned to observe the shifting of shadow between dark and light. Now, as I hear the pounding heart and the deep, sucking breath ahead in the corridor, I become aware of the monstrous shadows within me that were created by seeing those dramas. Now the voices of past chaos and mind-rending trauma clamor in my ears like a chorus of harpies. Often before, when I trance danced for the grandmothers in plays in which the dark forces emerged, their rasping voices were always pushed away by the sweet bliss rising in my body. But then, as I was drawn into mystery dramas by male teachers, Didymus and the other priests somehow pierced and got inside me. Now I am a wounded bird, but I did not know that until this moment.

Past, present, and future fuse as I walk through the Cretan labyrinth thirty-five hundred years ago. As Aspasia traverses the dark corridors, I, Barbara, remember the exact moment when my current life was shattered into monstrous shadows. As Aspasia approaches the center of the labyrinth, I return to a time in my childhood when I had a nurse who wore white uniforms.

I am four years old and have recently returned to my parents' home from a foster home where I was kept during World War II. I am "home," but I am extremely confused. I don't really know what home is.

I have a nurse—or the nurse has me. She is always dressing me, making me sit, making me eat, making me go to sleep, making me walk around. I am crazy inside, like a wildcat. I am exploding with energy. But my nurses are always trying to cram my excitement into restrictive clothes—black patent leather shoes and tight, tailored coats, gloves, and hats. They are always trying to get me to stand there and look nice. When I sit at the table, I'm not supposed to spill anything. When I go to sleep, I'm not supposed to wet my bed. I'm not even supposed to yell when I feel like it.

But I don't know where I am! Nobody around here realizes that I don't know I am home. They keep talking about home as though it is someplace where you are. They seem to be telling me that home is where I am.

I suppose I must be the person who is crammed inside these shoes and clothes, but I am more familiar with myself as a person who flies every night. I know myself as the wind and as the brown water that courses in the river behind my house. I know myself through the voices of my teachers, who talk to me as I stare with wonder at their blue-green, luminous forms that pop into existence before my eyes. They used to come to me wherever I was—Long Island in New York or Bay Port or Saginaw in Michigan. But then came the day when I got shocked by that terrible accident, and after that I accepted the definition of home that was said to be mine. I suppose I can tell you about it.

My nurse never gave me any love or warmth; I only felt such things from my dog when he snuck into the house or when I got outside with him, which was rare. My nurse never spoke to me in a pleasant voice, either. She never hit me or hurt me—she just made me get dressed and stand up or sit down all the time. I always felt so huge, crammed into those shoes and clothes. My only escape was in the night in my bed when my teachers came to me.

I didn't hate my nurse, and I didn't love her either. But then one morning she fell down the back stairs. She was old and heavy, and they made her cram herself into a white uniform and thick-soled shoes every day. That morning, she slipped. She fell down the back stairs, hit her head, and broke her back. Soon I heard a siren screaming. The ambulance came while I was still in the kitchen, standing quietly by the back door. I always remembered that moment feeling her back breaking as though it were my own. I remembered it especially when I lamely sang with other little girls, "Skip to my loo, skip to my loo; if I step on a crack, I break my mother's back."

Oh, my left arm hurts! Somebody is clutching my left arm. I don't know who it is. I think it is one of the people who work around here—maybe the gardener, or maybe one of the men who came here with the ambulance. He is pinching my arm and shaking me, trying to get me to describe what happened to my nurse.

I remember now: he is the iceman. He says, "This is your home, and you were in this room when she fell down the stairs. You left your rain boots over there at the top of the stairs. The water and ice made the floor slippery, and she slipped and fell. This is your home, *where the nurse broke her back."*

I never saw my nurse again, and nobody ever said anything about her that I remember. That was my home, where her great spine cracked like a rifle shot. That was when I discovered home, *when I was four years old.*

As Aspasia, I was feeling a suffocating fear of something in the center of the labyrinth. This fear was almost identical to what had happened inside me when the iceman clutched me and made me feel like I had done something bad. *I thought back, trying to remember what really happened.*

The iceman had speared a block of ice with his great iron pincers and placed it temporarily near the top of the back stairs. Then he had gone into the bathroom. While he was in there, the nurse had slipped on the melted water and fallen down the stairs. Returning to the kitchen, he realized what had happened as he heard the nurse screaming at the bottom of the stairs. He had quickly hauled the ice outside by the back door. He had seen me cowering there, so he had picked up my wet rubber boots and placed them in the puddle from his block of ice. Then he had grabbed my arm and jostled me. The pain in my right arm had revived the same feelings I had once felt when Didymus, the high priest of Knossos, had grabbed me and taken me to a mystery play. Both the priest and the iceman had been trying to blame me for something terrible they had done themselves.

For some reason, the pain in my right arm is the entrance to the secret keys of Atlantis, but until now it has been hidden by the blame imprinted on me when my nurse fell down the stairs and broke her back. Let us return to that formative mystery play for the secret inner key.

Again I am Aspasia, but it is years before my labyrinthian initiation. I am in a room in the west temple complex above the Knossos bull keep. I have never been allowed into this section before, even though I could always hear the bellows of the bulls echoing through the temple. I have been brought here by the elder priest, Didymus, and he is rough and authoritarian with me. As the future high priestess of this temple, I have never had this kind of treatment from anybody. His demeanor makes me feel as though I have done something wrong, as though I am *bad.*

Didymus clutches my arm as we stand before the stage in the hidden theater watching the play. A maiden dressed in diaphanous white robes appears. She stands with her legs solidly planted and her pelvis thrust forward as if expecting an assault. An agile male dancer, playing the role of a bull, bounds out from a high ledge in the back like a visitor from the sky. His face is obscured by a heavy lapis lazuli and gold bull's head attached to a bull hide hanging over his back. The front of his body is hairy and naked. He bounds into the room like an animal/man, rotating his pelvis and thrusting his erect phallus outward while bracing his hands on his knees.

I am lost in a swirl of feelings. Nudity is common at Knossos, but I have seen erections only on animals. The walls of the theater are painted with murals of bulls with erections and of maidens holding vessels intended to capture bull semen. The vessels are painted with brown spirals and surrounded with papyrus flowers releasing pollen grains into the wind — pollen grains that create dotted pathways tracing the motion of Venus in the sky.

The bull/man writhes his taut body obscenely, and his erect phallus makes me feel breathless. As he dances, he bobs his great blue bull head up and down. For a long time, the bull/man dances around the maiden, who seems to be in a trance. He does not inseminate her, but I wonder what might be created if he did.

After the male dancer has left the stage, the maiden in white undulates her body and waves her arms and hands like a plant in the wind. Her belly begins to balloon outward as if the moon were rising from her womb. Her body shivers with waves of energy, and she laughs as a child—half human and half bull—emerges from between her legs. Suddenly I notice that the grandmothers are grouped in the darkness toward the back of the stage, and they begin a chorus of lamentation. Didymus points to the new child and tells me that this monster is the Minotaur, the one who lives in the center of the labyrinth.

As though moving out of a dream, I move forward in time. Again, I, Aspasia, find myself walking in the labyrinth. The ruby in the center of my skull glows intensely. I know that the Minotaur is in the center. I am experiencing exactly the same confusion that the iceman created in me the day my nurse broke her back. The great moment has come again. Somehow these belief systems are the same. I *must* know why, so I keep moving forward.

I come to the last turn in the spiral, a sharp whiplash turn. As I come round this last curve, a green luminescence with flecks of gold begins to form on the pathway and on the cave walls. At this moment, the ruby within my pineal gland begins to activate, emitting a bright ray of white light, I feel heat and hear breathing and snorting in the tunnel ahead. I know the rasping breath must be the monster, but my intuition already knows that the monster is a chimera, an *illusion* inserted into reality by Didymus. However, as I walk forward, my body and mind still believe that I am about to encounter the monster. Which is real? Walking forward on intuition only, I feel like I might be coming to my end, but I have to know the answer to my question: why is all this drama created around what somebody else says is *me*?

Finally, I come to the center chamber. There I find nothing but a great, empty space with a column of white light reaching from the floor to the ceiling. My heart rips open. I feel dense levels of pain. In this place of nothingness, I am also in the center of my mind. This is the place of purity and wholeness that existed in myself before any judgments or identities were projected on me. Greenish white energy moves up and down from my head to my feet. I don't feel solid. This place feels timeless and empty, like the Dreamtime where I go flying at night. This is the center of my intuition, and it is wordless.

When the iceman was clutching my arm, telling me I was home, the inner power of the Goddess left my body. I have seen as the Goddess sees and felt as the Goddess feels, but because of this block, I have not yet *become* the Goddess. I see the illusion now: the magician Didymus tricked me. He put me into the labyrinth and imprinted me with a thoughtform of fear. But by being able to walk to the very center of that fear, I can now walk out of the labyrinth with my *own* awareness.

As I move back around the tight curve of the spiral, the light is very intense. Like a beacon, it shines from the center of my skull. Now I am going back to the point where I got stuck before—and also the point where Barbara got caught.

The iceman was afraid my family would think he had caused the nurse's fall. Clutching my arm, he transferred the blame to me by hurting me. In his mind, I was just a dumb kid, too small to get into big trouble for anything yet. The iceman shook me until the back of my neck hurt. Then, as I listened to her moaning, I felt I had hurt the nurse. It was easy for the iceman to use me, since I had already been abused and was generally terrified most of the time. When the police and my parents questioned me later, I told them I had left my wet, icy boots on the back stairs and that the nurse had slipped on the puddle. Now, of course, I realize this is not true! Even so, when the nurse fell down those stairs, I could feel her back breaking in my own spine.

Now, as Aspasia in this welcoming labyrinth of inner nothingness, I move the traumatic energy out and release it. In its place, I imprint a new perception of being *home,* a perception beyond that of the broken child that I was. The iceman and the nurse were great teachers for me in this life. They opened the wounds that accessed memory pathways leading to the center of the labyrinth.

Walking out of the labyrinth now, I have exploded Barbara's belief that *home* on this planet is within the broken child. My body is coursing with joyous energy. The white light intensifies in my head as my Goddess body awakens, for the grandmothers have taught me how to illuminate my inner crystalline fields. Now I walk back through the labyrinth with my white light shining. My light illuminates pictographs, symbols, paintings, and niches with statues and sacred power objects all along the walls. I encode all of their messages into the crystalline matrix of my being. These symbols, I know, are secret holographic keys to cosmic and solar cycles, and they have been guarded by the *Keepers of Tradition* from the stars. Now it is time to release them from the mythic mind, for they are the records in the library of the signet of Atlantis. I imprint these symbols into my inner mind.

As I walk along, the light intensifies. I am hurrying, for I am sure that the priests do not want me to get back out. I see the gate ahead. As I emerge from the last hallway, I know the metal gate must open. Didymus is waiting. He looks very sober as he sees my eyes and skin glowing. A blue aura radiates ten feet out from my body. I have integrated the Blue Lady of the Pleiades. I have been able to go through the darkness and come out with the light.

Didymus is surprised—my accomplishment is most unexpected. This feat means that I am in direct resonance with the Pleiades and that I have earned the right to be placed in certain teaching and power roles at Knossos. I will be able to reactivate this inner light in any other soul incarnation. This activation of my diamond body is an Atlantean skill for which Didymus did not realize I possessed the recessive gene. This skill is much desired by him, and he will attempt to control it when it emerges again.

I walk out the gates and glance at the magician, but I do not accept his projection. I am completely free of his control mechanisms in this or any other lifetime. Didymus will remanifest after Harmonic Convergence in August 1987 as dance chiefer of secret lineage holders. I look into his eyes and walk away, free of his control forever.

As I contemplate the question "What is the signet of Atlantis?" I note that a signet is a seal of authority. Along with the titles of the other two books in The Mind Chronicles *trilogy,* Eye of the Centaur *and* Heart of the Christos, *the title and publication date for this book were given to me by the Pleiadians in 1985. Now that we have come to this last book, it is time to share with my readers that I have never known what these books would be about in advance. It was only in 1988 that I exactly identified the Pleiadian voice that had given me the three titles and forever changed my life. The "Pleiadians," as they call themselves, are extremely anxious to have me reveal this information, and that is why I have opened myself to record their messages. So it would seem that this book is some kind of authoritative teaching about what was or will be Atlantis.*

To write Signet, I did twenty sessions under hypnosis as I had with the other two books, this time with the central questions being, "What is Atlantis, and what does it mean to us?" There are hundreds of books about Atlantis that are very technological, obsessed with locating Atlantis as well as with determining the date it submerged and why. Anybody who has done a deep and liberal exploration of ancient artifacts and mythology is aware that there was an advanced, ancient global civilization that might have been called Atlantis. I decided that the path to take was a deep journey into why we incessantly dwell on this archetype and what about it is relevant to our future.

As soon as I managed to re-embody the Goddess by going to the center of the labyrinth, a wondrous cast of characters appeared. From behind the scenes of male Atlantis I gained new insights into the great technological island with a crystal in the center that sank because of the human obsession with power and control.

Like contemporary science fiction, the techno-historical image of ancient Atlantis actually tells us more about who we are now, including what we fear and where we assume we are going. Just as much as a history, then, it is a contemplation of a probable future based on how we see ourselves now. When I looked at it that way, through the powerful eyes of the Goddess, a much more complete story of Atlantis emerged from the veils of time. To strip away this veil, let us first explore the techno-historical side of Atlantis, since it is the source of modern Atlantean obsession.

I see myself looking out from the inside of a metallic suit with red decorations and a helmet with narrow slits for my eyes. The purpose of this suit is to protect me from radiation. I wear it whenever I go inside the Atlantean photon laboratory.

The laboratory is located on the island of Atlantis in the Atlantic Ocean to the west of the Near Eastern and Aegean civilizations. Myths and stories focus on this particular island because it was the site of our most technological and scientific colony; however, there were many Atlantean colonies in other locations as well. Other parts of our kingdom have various names, such as Eire, Poseidea, Khemit, and Maya. This particular island called Atlantis—the "New World Order"—is the central island that people began to access psychically and intuitively after it sank during a great cataclysm about twelve thousand years ago. Other parts of Atlantis also suffered great destruction at that time, but they repopulated and retained fragmented memories of the sunken island.

This photon laboratory is located behind a mountain far away from the central city, since its malfunction could be a serious danger to the people. My name is Alcior, and I am a highly trained Atlantean scientist. My understanding of who I am is similar to that of a twentieth-century Los Alamos scientist—a man who perhaps was well trained at Stanford or MIT and who is white, Christian, and heterosexual with no memory of past lives or of his original source. He imagines that he will finally die and be judged by his god, and that he will go to hell, purgatory, or heaven.

I am sitting at a control module that contains many scientific measuring devices. The module is sealed within two plastic bubbles—one small and one large—inside a huge laboratory. My instruments read information about what is happening within the poisonous atmosphere of the larger bubble. Pedals at my feet enable me to travel around in the larger bubble on tracks while I am in the control module. The larger bubble has an inside surface of gray metal dotted with black receptor boxes about a foot apart. The boxes are all connected by wires, making the bubble's surface look like the inside of a geodesic dome.

Periodically, the receptors flash in the ceiling of the larger bubble, signaling photon activation. The computer screen in front of me locates the activated receptor, then transmits numerical codes onto my screen, which I then translate. For example, one coming in now says "Hizor" followed by a bunch of numbers, which translated means "mutant gene 037." This is followed by many more numbers, which I translate to "Hizor mutant gene splice 26." Simply explained, these are DNA readouts of a mutant person located far away in Eire, a northern realm of our Atlantean kingdom. In this case, the photon informs me that energy is being received by this being in Eire from his stellar source, Hizor—a star called Thuban in later times. The genetic coding is a readout of Hizor energy in the physical body of this mutant.

Mutant in our language means "Earth-spawned creature." I, Alcior, am an Atlantean *stellar being*, so I differ from this mutant in Eire. We both live on Earth, but I am a carrier of the *blood of the stars*—one of the pure stellar beings who traveled here from outer space. As for the Earth-born people, some are indigenous while some are mutants spawned by "stellar implantation." The mutants differ in a marked way from their Earth parents. From the central genetic laboratory in Atlantis, we stellar beings bred ourselves with Earth beings. Stellar sources mixed with Earth creatures have varying offspring. In this photon laboratory, I study how the stellar imprint affects the Earthling. We tell the people that we are doing this in order to eliminate disease, but the real reason we are doing it is to gain control of the Earth.

Photons contain the history of the universe, and they come to Earth continuously from the cosmos. They carry the latest cosmic news—stories that can be decoded in the photon receptors of this laboratory. In fact, *the only way we can decode these mutant humans is by reading the photons that come into the Earth's atmosphere.* Our cosmic photon receiver "reads" the arriving photon, and the information is transmitted to the correct DNA receptor. Each of forty-six receptors is encoded with the complex matrices of DNA patterns. We can copy these light-encoded filaments, but we cannot yet create them from scratch. Each receptor is a large cone with some kind of meshing inside that resembles the inside of a beehive. The photon goes into the cone and is read by magnetic strips that are wired to a central computer. The computer read from the cone then electrically transmits the information and shows a DNA pattern readout on the screen. We must continually analyze the cosmic photon data because it is our source of human DNA information. Why bother with all this? *The only way extraterrestrials, such as myself, can understand humans is by means of decoding human DNA.*

As for the humans, they are evolving according to macrocosmic activity. My own computer apparatus has a hard disk containing information on all Earth mutants who have Hizor genes. So when a photon arrives with information from Hizor, it throws onto my screen a reading of the Earth creature on Eire who was originally encoded with mutant gene 037 from Hizor. This provides information on how Hizor's present intelligence is affecting this mutant. The Atlantean project is to assist in the process of the stellar encodement of humans. This mutant on Eire has a genetic matrix that is significantly altered as a result of being bred with beings from Hizor, and this photon gives us information about how his consciousness responds to the stellar elements of his being. I am studying how his brain is affected by shifts at the cosmic level.

This particular mutant I am studying is an Eirean astrologer who studies observable star and planetary movements in relation to stone circles and other patterns that are aligned with geographical landmarks. His ability to intuit the mathematics of Earth's alignments with the cosmos is available to him from Hizor. To be specific, he simply sets up stone circles and chambers to determine solstice and equinox points from his location. With them, he is able to study the alignments as they fit into the larger galactic cycles of time. Through the "galactic code" provided by his understanding of astromathematics, he can accurately predict major Earth alignments with the other celestial bodies throughout the galactic cycles of time. These galactic cycles span thousands of years, and they are the key to the evolution of the human on Earth. In other words, *we read the cosmic evolutionary cycles through humans on Earth!*

We collect this information from Eire and from other places on the planet in order to understand the status of the Earth's planetary alignment or "wobble" on its axis. We need this information in order to determine the stability of Earth in the Solar System—particularly so that we can evacuate Earth at certain times.

Photons are consciousness particles that have been freed from their cosmic locations. They travel throughout the universe *loaded* with information, but they can be decoded only within the electromagnetic atmosphere of Earth. That is why we first came to Earth three hundred thousand years ago—we can't get this information anywhere else in the universe.

These photons from Hizor have the capacity to report to my computer laboratory all of the planetary work done by those who are attuned to Hizor. Other photons report on other activities related to other star systems. For example, a photon from the star Aldebaran contains information on the functioning of Aldebaran consciousness. It is very musical, very mathematical, very harmonic, and very powerful for the right hemisphere of the human brain. It rules rubies and opens the heart, offering courage and intelligence to those who are in tune with it on Earth. This information is very important, for this photon helps to inform me about what is happening in the Atlantean kingdom. The mutants on this planet who are in resonance with Aldebaran are very happy right now.

Ultimately, we want to be able to "read" and then reprogram the center of the Earth, which has never been penetrated by an outside force. It protects its integrity at all costs, yet it contains the memory of every species, every dream, and every story the planet has ever experienced. The computer that I work with gets its intelligence from the central Atlantean crystal, which connects Earth to sky in all our Atlantean cities. We cannot get knowledge from the center of the Earth, but we can use the central Earth crystal to read photons.

We are gathering all this information so that we can, at some point, charge the central crystal with a new program. As soon as we have studied the knowledge within enough Earth mutants and decoded their stellar photonic imprints, we will have the keys to unlock the central knowledge of the Earth. Then we will develop a new program that will project a perfect universe in which every planet and star rotates and orbits under the control of Atlantis.

When the crystal is charged, all of the mutants will move into "stellar fusion." For example, the man in Eire will be fused with the consciousness of Hizor while still functioning on Earth, and there will be no more cosmic catastophes or events on Earth that would force us to return to the stars. Mutant Earthlings will fuse with the powers of their own original stars, we will live on Earth when we want to, and the rulers of Atlantis will control it all.

For now, I have been conditioned to have no free will. Everything I learn I report to the central government. Since, I, Alcior, am the one who informs the government about the status of the people, it is important that I have no awareness of who I am in a cosmic or stellar sense, so that I will not consider the implications of what I am doing. In this lifetime, I am just an arm of the government. I was selected for my intuitive skills, to be used by those in power.

On the other hand, my higher self is observing this lifetime with great interest because a time will come when these skills can be used for a much more enlightened and worthwhile purpose. Excuse me for talking about myself so much, but something is making me nervous. Actually, I wonder what *would* happen if the whole universe were controlled.

I have a very split consciousness. When I am in the laboratory, I have no emotions. I get my jollies through all kinds of treats. I was conditioned to do as I was told in order to get a corresponding reward. My reward might be money, a wife, a blonde girlfriend with long legs, or a truly marvelous technological miracle such as a computerized, enclosed ecological system of a jungle or marine environment that I could watch in my spare time. Everything I get is a reward for obeying my superiors, and it could all be taken away.

Sooner or later, all of the information I gather will cause something to happen; I know that. But I have been so thoroughly conditioned that I do not even consider my influence on the lives of others. From a personal point of view, I do not even feel anything about my wife, my house, my children, or anything else in my life. Mutants seem to *feel* things, while my "reality" is just a reward from the central source for doing my job.

One thing I do feel is anger. There are big areas of my body where there is no energy, but there is too much energy in my liver. I am angry about the central source and angry about my conditioning. They have even conditioned me to deal with my anger! Every move I make is angry; it is the only way I can do this work. And if I quit, I am conditioned to die of cancer before I cause any trouble.

All of us have been conditioned like laboratory animals. As for me, I was first conditioned by television. I watched it for hours as a child. The sex and violence caused strong destructive feelings. Later, the educational system taught me that spiritual feelings are imaginary. Then when I studied to be a scientist, I was conditioned to fear anything nonscientific—anything on the Earth that is not controlled.

I also learned that women are irrational, weak, and destructive. In fact, if you want to know about it, I was conditioned to hate women. I hated them so much that I raped one after we watched a sexy movie together. Then I was reconditioned to avoid that by forgetting desire altogether. Now I watch a certain series of TV programs and sports that excite me just before penetrating my wife.

When I was unhappy and upset in my twenties, I was given tranquilizers and stimulants, and tapes were prescribed to help me feel good. But the tapes contained subliminal messages that taught me to fear my own feelings, and they programmed me to be interested only in the information on my computer screen. Now I am bored except when I am in my suit in my bubble.

As I sit in my bubble day after day, the incoming information becomes more and more peculiar. Everywhere on the planet there is rebellion, unhappiness, and imbalance. Each individual I investigate as the photons arrive from their stellar source seems to sense that the Earth is radically out of balance, that everything is malfunctioning. In times past, we used to scare the life out of people by broadcasting news that their insurance companies or banks had failed. Then the next day we'd assure them that the recession was over, and eventually they learned to ignore the media. But the sheer magnitude of this cultural conditioning has created a strange vibration: the people are actually beginning to feel that somebody is lying to them, and some of them even sense that they are being manipulated by computers.

Part of the original conditioning was erasure of cultural memory. Under orders from Hatonn, the scientist king of Atlantis, we broadcast a program through the central crystal to everyone on the planet that prevented them from being able to remember their own stories—stories of their origins that had been understood by watching the sky and by being attuned to light during the day. We also changed the atmosphere by thinning the ozone layer of the planet. This caused haze and fog at night so that people couldn't see the stars very often; hence, they couldn't stay in tune with the cosmic cycles. During the day, the people lost their sense of attunement because we conditioned them to avoid the Sun by telling them the ozone loss would give them cancer. Hatonn believed that if all individual "units" were stripped of their personal meaning—their story in time, the myths of their ancestors and memories of Earth—they could be encoded with pure stellar information. This would then make the central core of Earth information available to him.

As I take in the latest information, I can see that something is malfunctioning because the people are rebelling. They don't want to empty themselves and let go of all their knowledge of the Earth. So here I sit with no sense of my own story, since it has been totally removed from me. I just get angry at all those rebels out there who are in the way.

I think it must be about time to strike the central crystal and reencode all those stupid people. But it's not so easy. They are not in the condition we expected them to be in order to establish the New World Order. All of them have to be either anesthetized or scared to death before it will work.

I report to the central source that the whole plan is malfunctioning. Later, as I walk into the central palace, I know that many heads are going to roll because the plan is not working. The minister of culture, whose job is to convince everybody that the "new story" is far superior to all of the old ones, has not succeeded. All our attempts to condition the people with the carrot-and-stick approach have failed. Obviously, I think our last chance is to strike the crystal and jar the Earth with a massive stellar imprint.

Who says we need all the people to be in sync with us? Maybe if we just strike the crystal, they'll go right into form. If they assume the mentality we envision, they will all end up being like me: completely conditioned, programmed, manipulable, and useful. Then we could reduce the size of the memory in our computers, put everything on one hard disk, and everybody on the planet could understand and know what we expect from everybody else. All this interference and confusion and diversity surely is worse than being just like me.

What could this Atlantean voice—the voice of the scientist Alcior—mean to me? In this life as Barbara, I came into a female body with a total intuitive knowledge of the way in which the individual relates to the planet and to the cycles. I arrived with the same knowledge Alcior possessed as he sat in his laboratory. I know that the story of all time lies in the photons, and I can read them under hypnosis. But in this life, feelings and spirit have been my most important values—far more important than control issues. Is it possible that this set of priorities holds the key to how and why Atlantis fell? Is Alcior my uncleared, negative male side?

Obviously, there is little difference between this view of Atlantis and our culture. Today, TV narcotizes people and eliminates the cultural memory codes of indigenous people. Similarly, the government manipulates people's lives and health by means of power and industrial production methods, and genetic manipulation and technology for watching the individual is the fast track in science. And many of our scientists act like extraterrestrials. We now live in a system of fast and easy pleasure that worships the control of natural forces and cycles. The purpose of the modern New World Order is to destroy the root understanding of life that each person on Earth naturally possesses. Why is this so?

In the spring of 1989, I experienced some powerful initiations at Mayan sacred sites in the Yucatán—initiations that awakened memory of my story on Earth. Since the Mayans come from the Pleiades, and my Pleiadian teachers tell me I come from the star Alcyone, the brightest star in the Pleiades, my reconnection with the Mayan elders at these sites meant the recovery of my own missing lineage. Although I didn't know it until Mayan elder Hunbatz Men worked with me to access the central portal of Etz Nah in Campeche, Mexico, this reconnection was what I had been looking for all my life. Now that I have regained my own lineage, I see clearly that each person who remembers his or her story actually contributes to the hope for planetary survival: each person who remembers their story becomes creative and nurturing and feels compelled to live without doing damage to the central storyteller, Mother Earth. Since each person's lineage is part of the larger whole, as each of us expresses our story, the planet connects us all, and we remember our universal harmony.

On the other hand, without our stories we are bored, and that boredom is deadly. Today, we live in a very dangerous time because most of our leaders do not remember their stories, and as a result they are destroyers. Nuclear waste and chemical pollution are poisoning the Earth. The space program is controlled by the military, which controls the world, and the financial world is in disarray as people begin to realize that their wealth has been wasted. But we reach the ultimate danger point at the exact moment when the evil and stupidity of the bored ones are exposed. The Atlanteans believed that if they struck the central crystal, the world would come into "organized form." Similarly, the controllers of the modern media (which is transmitted in large part by quartz crystals) believe that if they can create a central organized thoughtform, individuals will be controllable. To understand the probable outcome of this line of thinking, let us go back and observe the actual fall of Atlantis.

I, Alcior, have come to the palace of the scientist king, Hatonn, to give him my report on the status of the colonies. I report to him that the people are out of control. As I speak, I am fully aware that my report will result in his decision to strike the central crystal. Hatonn is absolutely convinced that when he strikes the central crystal, the planet will go into its next evolutionary form. He has no doubt that it will work. Up until now,

I have been instrumental in convincing him that he must wait for the right moment—the moment of synchronization when the people have been completely emptied of their Earth stories.

I have engaged in all this work not only because of my conditioning but because of my respect for the powers of Gaia, the Earth. I have also believed that people needed to move into attunement with their stellar sources. I have believed that as people attuned to the stars, their new vibratory qualities would improve the Earth. I thought that the Earth would resonate better in response to this more evolved consciousness. Now, by coming here with this report, I am admitting to Hatonn that I was wrong. I am now certain that *human consciousness never alters the frequency of the Earth.* I am now standing in the palace of the Atlantean king with a report that shows all is going awry. As a scientist, I have failed.

As I stand before Hatonn, he is excited. Now he knows he need wait no longer. The time has come to release the force, regardless of the consequences. I detect an orgasmic vibration in Hatonn, even though I know for a fact he has not had sex for years. Now that his ultimate desire is about to be realized, energy rises in his body, culminating in a vile, obsessive smile. It is as if he were staring at the beginning of creation, preparing to push a button that will shoot evil into creation's first form. In Hatonn's fixated eyes, I see clearly his sin of impatience about the Earth's unfoldment, and I regret every belief I have ever had about what someone else should be. My willingness to participate in Hatonn's sick inability to allow time to unfold in its own way has doomed me to become a fighter against control of Gaia through the entirety of the next Mayan Great Cycle of twenty-five thousand years, from 23,613 B.C. to A.D. 2012 In time, I will learn how no one and no thing can change the evolution of Earth.

There is no thought in Hatonn's mind that the activation of the crystal might malfunction and that Gaia might release her last weapon—chaos. As I stand before him in this moment of truth, I feel compelled to suggest to him that it might not work, and why. I *must* present him with that possibility.

"The crystal vibration of the central Earth is of low frequency," I begin, "a frequency that could create a destructive waveform that in turn might set up a chaos oscillation in the orbit of the planet. If the central crystal is struck, it could set up that waveform. What readings do you have on the Van Allen Belt, on bodies in the Oort Cloud moving into the Solar System, on energies in the Galactic Center that could explode, and on the solar flare cycle by means of planetary angles in relationship to low-frequency waves?"

Hatonn sneers. "Who needs to listen to your bullshit when you've already failed?"

Hands grab my shoulders—hands of the Atlantean swat team. I am being removed so that Hatonn can go ahead. I end up in a cell below the palace, and soon I hear an incredible low, resonant rumbling that hides deep in my memory and in the memory of all beings born on Earth. It is the sound of the resonant vibration of the Earth when its axis is shifting. Hatonn has struck the crystal just now. This is the beginning of the massive quake that will spell the end of Atlantis. The power of the tremor is indescribable. For a moment, though, it makes me feel peaceful, for I know that I am closer to the divine than I have ever been before.

Then the planet spins out of control. Quickly the room implodes, pulverized as though by a giant's foot. Instantly, the air is sucked out of me. But as I die, a huge flash of awareness comes in. A brilliant beam of light rushes into the back of my head above the spine, and this ray encodes the exact knowledge of why Atlantis went under—why it didn't work.

In this life as Barbara, these memories have caused me to value the teachings of indigenous people above all else and to seek to remember all of the records and stories of this planet. They have called me back again and again to do ceremony, to tell stories, to read stars, and to attune the Source to the planet so that I will be able to deliver a gift of sacred knowledge about the value of those who sing the song of the Earth and its people.

This time, I chose parents who would not imprint me, parents who were honest enough to see that they had no answers for the looming problems of the twentieth century. Then I recovered my memories of lifetimes during the last twenty-five thousand years, lifetimes in which people had tried to take away my story. And once awakened, I again found the Mayans, who told me the cosmic story: the Galactic Center—the Source—has the same vibration as Gaia, the center of the Earth, and we can know it only by remembering our individual stories as we spin through time. That is the crystal connection that intensifies our feelings on Earth.

Now that I remember this story, I tell it for everyone who has forgotten. We know what is wrong now. We are remembering who we are. We are remembering how to feel again. This is our time, and we will all be here for the true crystal connection of the Galactic Center to the Earth.

I return now to a time when my body last remembered existing on Earth in that fusion.

I am Sekhmet, lion goddess of ancient Egypt. I am the one who knows all about the cyclical relationship between the Earth and its stellar sources. I am Barbara's lion body, which first left her form when the iceman was clutching her arm. I am the cat being who was fully embodied in her until that moment. Now I am waiting for the rising Sun, which daily gives me renewed power. I have returned to teach Barbara what she wants to know and to instruct all those who wish to activate the lion within themselves.

I am Sekhmet-of-the-Horizon. I have come in the past when your planet was soaked in evil, and I tore to pieces the destroyers of Gaia. As the Sun is rising, I have some teachings to give. When you live on planet Earth, your outer power is solar and your inner power is lunar. Your time has come to work with solar power again as the Great Goddess returns. Through your willingness to enter into my stone essence, you shall receive a full understanding of solar powers.

Each day I await the rising Sun seated on my throne with my hands on my knees. As the Sun rises, its first rays ignite my crown chakra, then my third eye. Then its light forms the "mask of Horus" on my eyes—the ability to see in the third dimension. After mastering the sight of Horus in the celestial dimensions, the time arrives to offer you eyes of Horus in the third dimension. It is time to clearly *see* the identity and intentions of anyone you encounter, so you can know whether that person comes from the heart. From this moment forward, you will see *exactly* who people are when you first encounter them, and you will be surprised by what you see.

Remember that when you walk the path of Earth mastery, the greater skill you attain the more your pathway becomes like walking a tightrope. If once you see exactly who someone is and you do not act accordingly, you will fall off that rope. Tightrope walking, seemingly an innocent circus skill, is actually a remnant of the ancient initiatic schools. It teaches you to walk in balance with no safety net to catch you, so that your courage will be evident to each person who seeks your knowledge.

The Sun's rays illuminate my mouth, the ironic and loving smile that watches seekers in their struggle for initiatic knowledge. For many years, you have asked for the skill of speaking the right words in the right moment. Now your heart is true, so now is your time to receive the skill of complete verbal clarity—the ability to speak absolute truth. From the moment the Sun's rays illuminate my mouth, you possess the skill of speaking directly from the heart.

Now the rays of the Sun warm my throat. As my neck is great and strong, so are my teachings great and strong. The *only teachings that can save this planet are those of the Goddess.* I, the lion goddess, have granted you much latitude. You have required many experiences in order to learn the ways of this Earth, the ways of my body. But now you have had enough experience. Now I initiate you into Boat-of-the-Goddess, offering you a place with me during the long night. This gift can only be given to those who have mastered right speaking. Bathe your throat chakra in the morning light. Appreciate how far you have already come with me, and you will receive this initiation.

Recent teachings on your planet have come primarily through religion. With the help of the morning Sun, allow me to cleanse and re-create your throat chakra so that you will speak without the vibration of any religion that has ever existed. You have had enough experience with religion. From here on, your access to the Divine will be direct. Like a child who no longer needs its crib, you no longer need religion, you no longer need to judge what inspires you. No longer do you need any structure, vehicle, or pathway to my teachings. Simply receive the rays of the Sun and feel my great heart.

The rays of the Sun illuminate my great shoulders—shoulders that contain the Emerald Records of Atlantis, shoulders that support me in flight as the great winged sphinx. When you see me as the winged sphinx, know that I hold the keys to the Emerald Records of Atlantis, the secrets of flight on planet Earth. As the Sun warms my shoulders, I offer you the "Mantle of Atlantis," the same mantle worn by Aspasia of Knossos and Hatshepsut of Egypt. This mantle may be worn by any human who embraces the power of the Goddess. Embrace the Goddess. Embrace Gaia, the Earth, into your reality as your fourth-dimensional form begins to hear the secrets of the sphinx. Wear the Mantle of Atlantis.

The Sun's rays warm my chest and heart. It is because your heart is ready that I, Sekhmet, give you these gifts. When you take on my powers, you will feel everything and be unlimited in your ability to give and receive love. Up to now, you have been limited because you have been closed to your feelings. You have known pain from times when your heart was closed, but these lessons are coming to an end. You could not have known about these powers if you had not first lived without them.

My heart chakra has not been fully empowered since the fall of Atlantis, nor has yours. When Atlantis fell, all beings who lived here began to experience the planet from a limited, third-dimensional point of view. Until now, it was necessary for your chakras to be closed down; otherwise you would have remained multidimensional and never fully materialized here.

You would never have learned to feel like the indigenous people of Earth. This is why, in ancient times, the sphinxes above Hatshepsut's temple were thrown off the mountain and smashed, why the sphinx guarding Thebes was smashed, and why the sphinx of Delphi was removed from its pedestal. Only now can you restore them. The winged sphinx, the empowered heart chakra, is the signet of Atlantis, the seal and sign that you have learned to feel the Earth so that you can reattain your cosmic bodies once again.

As humans, you can remember the experiences of the last twenty-five thousand years by means of myths, stories, records, statues, amulets—all of the *symbols* that remain on this planet. Symbols represent the cosmic in the third dimension, and my communication tools are symbols that are meant to be understood simultaneously on many levels. The sphinx, for example, still holds and radiates the cosmic knowledge. You receive access to such mysteries through a process called "scripting"—feeling the Earth records by tuning into the imprints of time encoded in sacred objects.

Unbeknownst to yourself, you asked us for greater scripting powers, and in A.D. 1988, we gave them all back to you. Up to now, your understanding of materials has been primarily intellectual, but now you can remember your story again. I, Sekhmet, am a *neter,* one who can appear and guide you in tangible form. So, next time you get a message from a rock or some other object, quiet yourself and carefully listen to what it is trying to tell you. When you call, I hear you, but you must listen and trust me when I am speaking to you through an object. You must open yourself and use your intuition.

Now, the rays of the Sun move to my solar plexus, illuminating the center of my lion body, my power center. I would not be empowering anyone on Earth, but the clearance that has occurred through the opening of so many hearts has made massive empowerment a potential for everyone. This potential is conditional upon your willingness to open your heart fully. Up to now, your understanding of the mastery teachings has been primarily intellectual, but now, in the light of the Goddess, you will soon shiver with feeling. As the rays of the Sun illuminate my solar plexus, I feel light, warmth, and crystalline energy radiating into all my organs. First the rays penetrate my liver, removing the natural residues of old anger and resentment. Next, the rays illuminate my spleen, for I have misused my will. As the Sun warms my spleen, the inner tears of my soul wash it clean of the need for agendas, the need to accomplish, the need to control or to act on preconceived notions. I am now willing to let go of all agendas activated by the will. I release my lungs, which have attempted to *control* their normal autonomic function. I do not have to control my breathing anymore. Nor do you, for you, too, are cleared of all issues regarding the will.

Now the rays of light penetrate my digestive system—my stomach and intestines. I feel an exquisite lightness in my solar plexus as the Sun's rays clear these organs of all my experiences with other people, creating clarity in all my relationships.

Now it is time to attain divine perfection. I urge you to speak clearly and directly in all situations without judgment or fear of the consequences. Do not worry about how your words might affect the people to whom you are speaking. You are not responsible for these people; they are responsible for themselves. Release every regret you ever had about the negative effects of anything you ever said to anyone else.

The rays of the Sun have greatly warmed the center of my body, and they have heated my head so much that my pineal gland and its inner ruby have begun to tingle. Now I can see *through* my third eye from the inside, and I can channel the higher dimensions. The solar rays heating my inner ruby also heat my blood. My blood is hot, helping me to completely release all of the projected and learned teachings at the cellular level, and my diamond body is activated in the crystalline matrix of my blood. Since my heart chakra is open, containing this energy poses no danger to my physical heart. My heated blood pools in my root chakra, the source of both sexual abuse and ecstasy.

Now, the light illuminates my thighs and knees as my lion root chakra opens, awaiting the full rising of the Sun. The Sun grounds me because of the way I sit in my throne. As Sekhmet, I offer you one gift at this time. There is much energy that needs to be cleared about sexual abuse on Earth, and no one will really be free until this is done. I place a purple aura around myself as Sekhmet-in-the-Sun. I glow with this wonderful purple and emerald-green aura, like the Sun reflecting through water, making rainbows. I place this protective aura around you as you work in the world, waiting for humanity's anger to dissipate and its sexual abuse to end. This protection can be removed once you have cleared your own records and memories of abuse.

Now the Sun warms all of the hills and desert lands and the islands in the distance. Let peace and light come to all the lands on Earth. Let peace be made with Sekhmet. Let all agree to love and care for the Earth.

Chapter Two

MYSTERY PLAYS OF ATLANTIS

To the Lady of the Labyrinth, a Jar of Honey.
—from a Linear B tablet discovered at Knossos

Experiencing the mystery play of the Minotaur as Aspasia caused me to believe that a monster was in the center of the labyrinth. Since the labyrinth symbolizes the journey into the center of self, it also offers the chance to conquer fear. However, my experience in the labyrinth was set up by Didymus, the high priest, so that I would be pierced by fear in my own center by finding that a monster awaited me there. Why? Because Didymus, magician and dance chiefer, felt that same monster in his own center and wanted to project it onto me. As the seer Korkyne says in June Rachuy Brindel's Ariadne, *"The Labyrinth is not destroyed. It is wrapped about Theseus' mind. Wherever he goes will be false leads and dead ends. His goal will be always around another bend. All his earth will be a maze, and he will rush headlong down corridor after corridor, circling and bending backwards endlessly around an empty center. Because he's killed the center."*

My mystery play was created by the male control factor in order to manipulate my perceptions of reality. It was a hall of mirrors with preconceived images designed to elicit fear. And through that fear, if I took the bait, Didymus was sure my soul would become available to the forces that existed in the mirrors. However, I looked into the mirrors and saw that the maze was a chimera—a magical hologram inserted into present time and place by a "director." It doesn't matter to the director/magician whether the image is real or not; it only matters that the chimera will cause the desired response.

In a similar way, the drama of Atlantis is a mystery play that is continually replayed, complete with holographic inserts from other dimensions—inserts that might be keys to the next stage of our evolution. The "directors" of the Atlantean mystery plays often take the form of neters, *etheric beings who possess the ability to carry and insert nonphysical energies or they may emerge into solid reality as kachinas or winged gods and goddesses. And often the manifestation of magical powers and devices such as crystal skulls, cauldrons, grails, megalithic stone circles, and the shamanic translation of human emotions into animal totemic spirits are signs of potential inserts from other realities.*

In this lifetime, I have been helping to introduce the neter Chiron—a centaur who is half man and half horse, the penultimate empowered male-female integration, since "horse" is a sexual/power symbol for women. As Chiron, I open the curtain to the mystery plays of Atlantis. We begin with the Mayans, conductors of the multidimensional symphony.

I see a stone owl that is partially obscured by a great deal of purple energy. The owl lies on the jungle floor, where it must have fallen, and it is sending out a purple energy field that is difficult for me to see. I tune into this strange field, immediately I see a square doorway into an ancient, unrestored pyramid—a temple that is overgrown with leaves and vines. There is a tremendous force field around the temple that is intended to keep anybody from penetrating it. The field vibrates in my mind so intensely that I am afraid it might catapult me into another world. But I also know that if I dare to enter, the temple will have to accept me because I am aligned with its energy. When these places are disturbed by archaeologists or others who are not aligned with them, their ancient force fields are destroyed and access to their secret teachings is blocked—the *link* to other dimensions is destroyed.

The Mayans, who worked with such temples when the structures were active, set up these force fields when they left so they could continue to connect with the energies of such places. With my inner vision, I see that even this temple was later discovered and excavated in 1920, and its force field was broken, but these force fields were reenergized in August of 1987. *As I come here now, I am the fifth-dimensional Mayan body of Barbara.*

Now I see a door emanating a red-and-yellow force field, the colors of the Quetzal, the sacred Mayan bird. I know that if I walk through this field, it will damage my physical body. However, I am not visible in front of the field, for I am not solid. My arrival here was anticipated long ago. As I tune into the force field, I feel the kundalini energy rise in my spine. Everything in my body is clear, which is why I am invisible. If my light body clearance were not complete, it would be impossible for me to penetrate this temple.

Normally these protective force fields manifest as animals. If a solid person were to appear here, this field would call forth a poisonous snake, a jaguar, or an iguana. This field has consciousness and is aware of my presence, but it cannot call forth its usual protectors because I am invisible. Instead, it calls forth the owl, and this owl will be the guardian who watches everything I do in this sacred space.

I walk into the square doorway that opens into a thirty-foot-long rectangular tunnel along the east side of the pyramid. The tunnel is open at the opposite end. Walking into it, I sense that there is something inside this temple that can be perceived only by visitors in the Dreamtime; when this place was excavated in 1920, nothing was found inside. As I reach the center of the hallway, I turn to face the pyramid. There I find a doorway covered with a large stone. As my dream body passes through the stone, rushing energy pulls my head and body to the right, and this activates my higher head centers.

Behind the stone I find a stairway that goes downward. Nobody has been inside since it was closed off, but lots of spiders and little animals have found their way in from the outside. There is much life in here, faintly illuminated by the astral green glow of my dream body. Without that light, it would be pitch black in here. I walk down nine steps to the floor, which means I am walking into one of the Mayans' "Temples of the Nine Hells."

Moving forward, I become aware that there is some other light inside. This egg-shaped cavern is being illuminated by something besides myself. Now I can clearly see a moist, dark stone chamber that is about nine or ten feet high. Leading into this space are four tunnels that are aligned with the four cardinal directions. This is the Mayan Temple of the Four Directions. In the center of the ovoid chamber is a three-foot-tall, square platform, and resting on the platform is a stone basin containing a human-sized crystal skull. I feel as though I have found the greatest treasure since the birth of my soul. Eagerly I reach for the skull, but my hand passes right through it!

I knew it! This crystal skull is a hologram that has been inserted into this cavern. It has been here awaiting my arrival, emitting light through layers of space and time in ghostly veils of diaphanous stone.

Gazing into the center of the skull, I can see the forces creating the holographic Mayan crystal skull. Inside is a being with a ruby in its third eye. Concurrently, I see many other beings arranged in a circular form above the pyramid. These beings all exist in another time and space. At first they look like ectoplasmic monsters, and I cannot perceive what they might be because they are fourth dimensional, while I am fifth dimensional. However, I can see that they are sending light rays through the rubies in their third eyes. These rays are the laser beams that create fourth-dimensional holographic forms.

The skull, then, is a device use by the beings to encode information from the galactic fifth dimension into the fourth. Because I am also fifth dimensional, I can see it. I can dimly see the beings of the fourth dimension as well because the laser beams coming from the fifth dimension that activate the skull also create the fourth-dimensional beings. The messages emanating from the beings and the skull are becoming accessible to me in a form that I can translate into third-dimensional space and time. The fifth-dimensional Barbara has appeared here to read these messages for the latter days of the Mayan Calendar.

The fifth-dimensional level is galactic, and the beings who guard and direct the powers of this temple are fourth dimensional. These beings cannot take physical form, but they can *insert* forms from the fifth dimension, such as the crystal skull, into the fourth dimension. In the fifth dimension, all is unified. Duality appears in the fourth-dimensional layer, and then everything is divided and separated in the third. *Things* are created when a thought (from the fifth dimension) projects a hologram into the fourth dimension. That thought is thus perceived by the guardians, who divide it into fourth-dimensional holographic beams. These beams then insert images from the fourth dimension into the third. This means that *things are thoughts from the fifth dimension communicated through the fourth dimension!*

This is actually quite fascinating. If we observe the synchronicities between things in the third dimension—such as noticing that a hornet appears when we feel extremely angry—we can feel the holographic inserts from the fourth. Then the *unified cause* from the fifth dimension can actually be intuited. Since the fifth-dimensional level is the pure love of the Creator, developing such intuition is well worth the effort.

What can be seen and understood about holograms is entirely dependent upon the complexity, desire, and attunement of the receiver. For example, there are people who can translate radio waves in their teeth and hear radio stations in their heads (though a radio is a better receiver for these waves since it can select other channels or be turned off). A typical late twentieth-century room is filled with radio, television, microwave, and crystalline computer waves. Information is continually penetrating such spaces. Just as we can develop the intuition to access the mind of the Creator and feel the Creator's incredible love, humans also can actually learn to read all the waves in the spectrum.

The "crop circles" that have appeared in grain fields all over the world are fantastic examples of such phenomena. They are a hieroglyphic or pictographic "language" from the fifth dimension that imprints visible forms on fields of grain through fourth-dimensional forces. These forces have *chosen* to pass on to us messages from the divine! In other words, the late twentieth century is a time when fifth-dimensional temple forms are being made dramatically visible to us through holographic inserts. This is a truly exquisite and overwhelming act of love.

The galactic Mayans were and *are* especially adept at creating multidimensional forms, since they knew how to implant various types of inserts into third-dimensional temples. Each Mayan temple makes different dimensional forms available to those who can perceive them. Now that we have reached a point where a growing number of people can perceive synchronization in third-dimensional reality, the suspicion is growing that there is a manifest cause behind the meeting of two or more realities. The Mayans are the teachers who have bravely come forth with news about this multidimensional interface.

Forgive me for being obtuse as I explore this old pyramid, but since I am not solid myself, I know what it takes to see something. Please allow me to lead you on. And, please, stretch your perceptual skills as you contemplate the divinity that is visible in the crop circles. For now, let us just stand here and meditate in this space that we have entered. It can access other realms, and it will open them up to you if you are patient and trust your subtle perceptions.

This pyramid is the key temple for creating synchronicity, since it is the one that accesses the beam of creative intelligence from the Galactic Center, the Source. This is the central temple of the galactic Mayan teachings, and its location is a very guarded secret. The owl and the force field encountered around it are most unusual, since I have appeared here after A.D. 1920 when archaeologists excavated this temple and supposedly broke its time-dimensional keys. As I stand in front of this skull, I realize I am in a time warp and that I may never return to form.

The owl is the guardian here because the owl watches galactic beams, which rule materialization of species and synchronize the energy fields on Earth. The owl observes the holographic insert process very carefully, since fourth-dimensional beings *decide* whether or not to transmit the thoughts of the Creator. Owl holds all the records of the earthly manifestations that influence human thought. These inserts can be thought of as the political agenda of fourth-dimensional beings who have an interest in Earth. For example, the owl has recorded the Burning Bush and the manifestations of the Ark of the Covenant. Such visions from other dimensions cannot be seen unless the perceiver *believes* they are real.

In other words, the owl is watcher of beliefs that create worlds that *seem* to be real. This is extremely secret information. The eyes of the owl also have the ability to see "synchronicity beams," which form the web of all life on Earth. Only owls, spiders, hummingbirds, and bees can actually *see* these communication links between the great iron crystal in the center of the Earth and the Galactic Center. Owls exist in a state of ecstasy, watching starbursts of light create the intelligent time that makes things visible.

I sometimes go into the eyes of the owl to see what reality looks like in the midst of the beam. As owl, if I see shadows entering these fields of light, I flap my wings and increase my energy in order to circulate the shadows. I also turn my head around backward because I love watching the light. I am protector of the owl priestess cult, which has been the guardian of all forms since the beginning of time. As the sky guardian of the Earth Mother and the Goddess, I also watch for energies that attempt to decode the galactic beam. The Earth needs this beam so that creativity can exist in time; the planet would cease its evolution if this beam were disturbed in some way. Humans and humanoid forms who have visited Earth can read it, but only through feeling or intuition. I am a creature of essential feminine feeling, and I block the beam from those who fear deep emotions.

This temple calls into its space—now!—*the Keepers of Time*, those who consult their hearts about when to take action in the material world. As owl, I do not guard this temple against those who *feel*. When visions are formed by feeling, the beam is not altered. Shamans, priests, and teachers can access these hiero-symbolic forms naturally. But this information is completely inaccessible to the rational mind; it is part of the whole galactic spiral and is impossible to put into a form. Like creation itself, it is timeless and formless—a process that simply unfolds, fueled by desire.

The laser beams that create the crystal skull are fourth-dimensional translation tools. Now that lasers have been built by scientists, many of us have been able to see that an image from one reality can be recreated in another place. No longer can the most disturbing questions be avoided: Are we mainly the thoughts of someone else? Who creates us? And why does this mysterious Creator continue to hold our images in form?

Now, as I stand in the pyramid of materialization, I further release my identity. I see myself as an observer of myself. Then, to my utter fascination, I become the laser beams forming the crystal skull! This is a stupendous feeling, and it brings me tactile knowledge about materialization—I feel the allure of being drawn into form. Instead of intellectualizing about solidity and the laws of manifestation, I feel myself as form originating in the mind of the Creator, as if I were a lover created through the sheer desire of someone who wants to love me in return.

Now I can actually feel how I create myself. Now I know that my own desires create my existence. With this realization, a space opens in my brain. I stand here watching Atlantis building itself, disintegrating, and then coming into form again in the air over the skull. It is terrifying to see that it does not matter on any level except that of desire and feeling that anything exists at all. And yet I am so spacious inside, feeling the ultimate pleasure of nothingness and formlessness that fingers of light begin forming in my skull like jellyfish tentacles in a tide pool.

I am utterly transfixed. This exquisite crystal skull is offering me the most esoteric level of teaching about where we are in the cycle of evolution. We are now beginning to see that we can create anything—taboos, rituals, judgments, species genocide, power confusions, sexual abuse, and genetic monstrosities. Anything that we secretly desire, we can materialize over and over again. If we were really aware of the powers we have, we would carefully examine our every thought and whim. We might even see that if we had no desires, we would cease to exist. Possibly our desires are residues of need from wasted past-life opportunities. Whatever the truth, it is obvious that we waste much of our creativity on trying to control others; and in this, we have gone too far.

Whenever humans have gotten out of balance, the owl returns; it is a harbinger, a bird of great warning. Owl is the *Keeper of Species*. Humans can create anything, but they do not have the right to destroy the Earth and her creatures. Owl is the Goddess of the forest and the watcher of the crystal skull.

As I stand in this pyramid, I release my identity even further, and the crystal skull becomes my skull. Space explodes into exquisite green pulsating light. And suddenly Thoth, the carrier of the Emerald Records, comes forth through the crystal skull and speaks:

"I am Thoth the Atlantean, teacher of the Emerald Records. You now are to go forth on two planes on this planet until the synchronization. The duality is going to end within your lifetime, within a few years. Many of you have been working hard to empty yourselves, to clear your bodies of the imprints of time, all of which I have patiently held in my crystal skull as the owl has written down the records. I have been encoded with a variety of patterns that people can explore in order to better understand themselves, but now there has been enough exploration. You humans come close to seeing creativity, and then you move off into complexity. Just as you get close to enlightenment, you become enmeshed in one of the encoded patterns. The Burning Bush fascinated you into accepting authority thousands of years ago in the Sinai. But today, you still think you need that kind of authority, and your leaders are hypnotized by consummate evil.

"I, Thoth, am the receptacle of male vibration during this cycle. It is no accident that this skull through which I speak rests in the Temple of the Nine Hells of Dzibichaltun. This temple was opened at the spring equinox on March 21, 1989, when the Serpent of Light descended down the pyramid of Kukulcan. At that same moment, the guardian of the Dalai Lama, a monk wearing saffron robes, penetrated this inner room at Dzibichaltun. Concurrently, the god Itzanna returned to Chichén Itzá as people watched the descending Serpent of Light on the pyramid there. And at sunset the same day, a gigantic meteor—the Plumed Serpent, Quetzalcoatl—crashed over Chichén Itzá and sunk into the Gulf of Mexico. In the ceremony on this equinox, which coincided with a Full Moon, fifty thousand people remembered how to decode their own blocks to enlightenment, and those same blocks were removed from this skull.

"As you can tell, this skull is becoming increasingly powerful; it is emitting a great deal of light. With the removal of each block that liberates feeling in the brave person who agrees to clear pain, light and energy shoot through me with more intensity. As individuals purify and balance their physical and emotional bodies, their souls become more filled with light.

"The two pathways, or rays, that will predominate during the last phase of polarization are those of white crystal light and obsidian light, and both of these paths must be traveled by all. The teachings of these paths come through the Mayans and Egyptians. The Mayans understand the obsidian light, while the Egyptians understand the crystal light. Polarity will be resolved as individuals transmute carbon into diamond. During this process, those who carry the white-light teachings will trigger those individuals who are working with the black light. White light cannot exist without the black, and neither is superior nor inferior to the other—together they create a sacred unity. Those carrying the dark light act as "obsidian reflectors," which illuminate the inner Earth. Those carrying the white light would not even be conscious of themselves if it were not for their relationships to the dark.

"The predominant characteristic of those working with the white light is *patience*, and I am here at this time to encourage all these people to wait until the last sheep enters the fold. The predominant characteristic of those working with the black light is *wisdom*, and I am here at this time to assure these people that there is nothing to fear. How can anyone fear anything if they trust their Creator, and how can anyone refuse to return to me? I am existence manifesting in created forms."

My fifth-dimensional connection to the Mayan crystal skull greatly widened my understanding of the structures of material form; however, it also raised some disturbing questions. What or who are these inserts that create such profound changes? Are we all just puppets on strings? Who sets the stages for these mystery plays, and who decides who will play the parts? Why can't we see *the source of this manipulation just as we see physical forms on Earth?*

I was most obsessed with such questions in my previous lifetime as the Hebrew prophet Isaiah. To that ancient, prophetic part of me, the energy field in the pyramid at Dzibichaltun felt like the Temple of Solomon—"solo-man," the man who has been abandoned on Earth and who cannot return home. Feeling this, I decided to contact the light body of Isaiah, my former self, and attempt to understand this reality from his perspective. Isaiah was the one who feared the Powers and Principalities and warned that worshiping such authority would lead to the destruction of the chosen people. What did Isaiah see that he was so desperately trying to get Israel to listen to?

I am Isaiah, and I am in the Temple of Solomon. I see an eye—a blue-gray left eye—staring at me. It is always staring at me. It is a watching device that has been set up to observe me. It hangs in an astrolabe in the center of the main altar. It sees what I am manifesting and feeling, and it transmits that information to Nibiru, the Planet of the Crossing, which orbits into our solar system once every thirty-six hundred years. The Nibiruans are the *Nephilim*—creator gods such as my god, Yahweh, who came down to Earth. They built this temple specifically to house this eye, which is a computer that transmits information on how Earthlings feel, though it can only watch us when we are afraid. When we feel love, it cannot see us. The brotherhood to which I belong—the Order of Melchizedek—was established by the Nibiruans to create religious and political hierarchies. These hierarchies then created controversies that were intended to evoke constant fear in people, thus making them visible to the all-seeing eye of the Nibiruans.

As a geocentric astrologer, I created the astrolabe to hold the Nibiru-an eye. I did this so I could learn to see their intervention from my planes of reality. Thus, you could conceive of me as a double agent. I possess "watching skills" because I belong to the Order of Melchizedek, but I also reserve those skills for my own use. Specifically, I am waiting for the moment when enough humans have transcended fear so that we can all make a divine leap and escape the control by these creator gods.

I move my consciousness into the eye on the altar. As I do so, I am pummeled by a shock wave. I see a flash of light, then powerful images swirling in the air of bird men, lion goddesses, reptiles bearing gifts, and bulls. I want to know what they all want. As with most humans, there is deep-seated fear of these archetypes riddling my brain. What are the realities of these four archetypes, which also remind me of the four angels of the Apocalypse?

I am also very anxious about a red throbbing energy that I sense must be the beating heart of a great spider in the sky—a spider that occults the Sun. In actuality, the red spider in the sky is this place, this energy, this *feeling* I have inside the Temple of Solomon. It is the ultimate taboo: *the real truth about primordial control over the mind of man—control of the universe.* Yet, I also think the four beings and their energies are related to me. But when I try to decode them into something comprehensible, I can't do it. Lions, bulls, lizards, and huge bird men make me instinctually fearful, and I feel that we are controlled through that fear. Behind these symbols is the alluring sense of a faraway place, the convergence point for all the energies in this galaxy, the point that contains all the information anyone could ever care to know. But enough of that for now. I am thinking also of the teachings of Atlantis.

I know that it is possible to get in touch with the Atlantean teachings by getting in touch with the Pleiadians. Every time they come to teach, it is always at a peak point in human consciousness. But as Isaiah, I am blocked from further enlightenment because I cannot *feel* in my heart. Just when I am on the verge of seeing, fear always creeps into me—fear of what I must do about the suffering of my times. At these moments, I realize that I do not really possess courage. Then my heart shuts down and the eye can read me. This time, I'll just stare back into the eye and see what is there, whether it can read me or not.

This eye communicates to me that teachings from Atlantis have been filtered through many different locations. But the Atlantean teaching that I am supposed to encode in the temple during my life as temple priest in 700 B.C. is the news that Christ will incarnate from the Pleiades in A.D. 0, and that information comes from the Galactic Center. I must do this so that humankind will be prepared for the critical leap thousands of years in the future—the leap from thinking to *feeling*.

The Galactic Center will be highly activated 2,700 years from now, in the late twentieth century. In that time all lifeforms on Earth will have begun to feel the ecstasy and love of the Source. By then, people will have perceived reality from everywhere except the center point and will have seen through all of the different filters of time. By then, they will have begun to *know* themselves well enough to be able to perceive their true source.

The reason I am using this eye to perceive Atlantis from the Galactic Center is that the teachings of Atlantis are about the creativity of the divine Source. The Source is infinite, All That Is. All that exists in the universe is the intention of the Source to become conscious of itself. In the beginning, through its consciousness of itself, the creative Source manifested into form as primal motion. That motion is the creativity that is Atlantis.

This vibration that brings me news of Atlantis lies far beyond the third dimension—it is creation itself. All we can do is feel it, live it, measure it, hear it, describe it, and evolve with it until we can see the divinity within it. Once creativity was born, a whole chain of events was set into motion, including aeons of cyclical time, catastrophes, and the magnificent building of forms. But the birth of Christ is unique, just as will be the *rebirth* of Christ in each individual person at the end of the twentieth century. This will be the moment of synchronization, when all that has ever been becomes *divine*.

So, you see, Atlantis is creativity itself with all of its inherent duality. When someone is searching for the lost kingdom of Atlantis, they actually are searching for creativity. That search leads directly into a person's experiences on Earth, only one of which is the historical manifestation of Atlantis. Thus, Atlantis is also a state of mind. Powerful insights about our origins and development actually exist in the early records of Atlantis, but they are hidden from us because the Nibiruans, the creator gods, realized we could be controlled if we could be made to *fear*. Atlantis will appear before us when we realize that there is nothing to fear.

But, alas, all the gateways to Atlantis are *charged* with fear! For example, in your time the historical records of Atlantis that have been continuously presented to you for the last hundred years are very male oriented and technological. Your latest space shuttle for war research, created in part to make you fear the skies, is even called "Atlantis." Meanwhile, in your time humanity is also activating its collective consciousness, and the Earth is remembering the Goddess and the *feminine* side of history. In spite of the fear, you are beginning to access the *earlier* records of Atlantis—those that issue from the exploration of the Great Goddess rather than from the accounts of the patriarchy.

The early indigenous inhabitants of Mother Earth once worshiped the cycles of the Moon and Sun in stone circles. In your time, you need to reattune to the original creativity of these people in order to hasten your growth and to understand the natural intelligence of the Earth. This is the intelligence that resonates with the creativity of the Galactic Center, the creativity that holds the secrets of Atlantis.

What are these secrets? One is that each planet body in this galaxy has a central creative form of its own that is weakened or confused when colonized by alien beings. Such has been the case on planet Earth, largely colonized by the Nibiruans. As the Earth moves into synchronization with the Galactic Center in the years just prior to A.D. 2013, these original forms will be reinvigorated. The power in indigenous peoples and in the ancient Earth ceremonies will reemerge. History, which has been nothing more than the projection of fear on Earth, will come to an end as each life form releases its innate intelligence.

At synchronization, each body in each solar system will release a sound, a primal tone that expresses its particular vibration. The concerted sound of all these tones—the "music of the spheres"—will not only awaken the encoded memory of each entity but it will erase the past forever. For many, in August of 1992, this music will hum like the breath of the Supreme Creator. And in August of 1993, the story of creation will be heard again in the temples of Teotihuacan.

You must remember that the experience of the original people of Earth has been continuously and extensively influenced by visitors from other realms. As you struggle to remember who you originally were, your meetings with those who have changed you will be part of the critical process of regaining your identity. Your teachers from Nibiru and other alien cosmic sources have been so interwoven with the natural evolution of Earth that it is very difficult to remember the original resonance of the Earth or yourself. The way to remember it is through *feeling*. Feel the hearts of the original people beating in resonance with the Earth as the music of the spheres is played. This will reawaken the Earth and everyone on it. At first only a few will hear it, then more—then many more—as you remember the voice of your own planet. Then, finally, all on Earth will be home again, and harm and pollution will cease.

Gradually the planet will move back into its original state of ecological perfection. Those who have attempted to control it will let go as they hear the sweet tone coming from their own land. I often wonder if that sound will be a flute. Everyone will have the ability to fully enjoy and admire another's state of existence without trying to control anything. Imagine the day when an invader will politely ask for entrance, stay for dinner, receive a gift, give a teaching, and then return home. You have learned much about yourselves by experiencing the visitors, but now that you can see yourselves reflected everywhere in creation, you no longer need them. You have journeyed to all the directions and looked into the mirror, and you have come home. You are about to firmly but peacefully ask the visitors to leave.

As I listen to the voice of Isaiah, a feeling of who we humans are wells up inside. Isaiah has been speaking to us from a time seven hundred years before Christ, but with an eye that sees clearly 2,700 years into the future. Now, looking back over that same time span, I can see both how we went to sleep and when we began to awaken. I can see how we lost our ancient heritage. But more importantly, I can see how it began to return, to open when courageous indigenous people stepped forth again to offer their ceremonial teachings and ancient wisdom. Also remembering our story, scientists began to offer scientific wisdom about Gaia, and holograms were constructed to show us how three-dimensional physical forms are created. Many historians and storytellers remembered the real stories of time as well and worked to break down the lies that had confused us for so long.

Now, I say, let us awaken further still! Let us remember more ancient mystery plays that offer us the breathless joy of telling stories—stories that help us to feel instead of fear.

I return my fifth-dimensional awareness to Avebury Circle in Britain—to a time when the great circle had just been contructed. I can see that this great stone complex has been established as an electromagnetic field activator to resonate with the Galactic Center. That is why "crop circles"—powerful symbolic pictographs imprinted in fields from the Galactic Center—will appear in the latter years of the twentieth century all around this great temple complex. These symbols will be powerful reminders of the galactic origins of humanity.

This great circle and deep chalk henge, which surrounds two inner circles in a figure-eight configuration, was built at the beginning of the Fifth Mayan Great Cycle, around 3125 B.C. It is the stellar temple of the Goddess culture during this entire 5,125-year cycle, and it is also the Earth temple of the sacred marriage—the temple secretly called the "Circle of Og and Magog." When the time comes to completely activate its center stone around the year A.D. 2000, this temple will become fully empowered again. Those who have galactic perceptions will receive some of the keys to this temple by means of the pictographic crop circles. At that time, pictograms created by fifth-dimensional galactic laser beams will leave three-dimensional forms in the fields, and those forms will drive scientists crazy. Their messages will be understood only by those who can resonate with them.

Just south of this great circle is Silbury Hill, the mineral-kingdom center of the Goddess imprint on male consciousness and the activating principle of the main stone circle and henge. This center corresponds to the male sperm, which is indispensable to the creation of life. As the interference activities by Nibiru became better understood by Earthlings after about 50,000 B.C., members of the Goddess culture began to see that the way to prevent human destruction was to activate the healthy *male* principle on Earth in exact proportion to the birthing principle of the female. In other words, they saw that eventually men, too, would have to utilize fully their own creative powers in order to finally end genetic manipulation of species and the raping of the Earth for its resources.

In the ancient days to which I have returned, the central stone in the middle of Avebury's inner figure-eight stone formation within the outer great henge and circle of stones is the "synchronization stone" for all dimensions. Etherically, I align my body with the four directions of the circle so that my torso lies within the great outer henge. Then I activate the center stone as if it were stuck in my own belly. I want to feel the central powers of Avebury, and this can be accomplished only by aligning my energy body with the Earth, resonating with the form of the circle itself.

Here, inside the intersection of the two interlocking circles, a Catholic baptismal font will be contructed in later times. Within the southern circle of the figure eight is a line of three stones that correspond to my heart, throat, and third eye. The northern circle has three large cupped stones in its center, which correspond to my root chakra. My arms and legs extend beyond the outer circle, with my crown reaching the southernmost stone and the "Earth connection" from the base of my spine reaching north.

An etheric church lies where the "belly stone" is located. Later, a real Catholic church will be built outside the west gate of the henge. This etheric church was formed as a holographic insert in the central energy point. Its laser beams have been transmitted by the Powers and Principalities in order to disturb the original energy of the circle. Because the Catholic church gets its power from the doctrine of original sin, a carved baptismal font will be placed directly over the central stone—the stone that magnetizes and aligns all dimensions.

I can see that around A.D. 1000, a priest will come to suspect that pagan babies are birthed in the moonlight in the circle. Late one night with the help of a few drunkards, he will lug the baptismal font from the church through the westgate of the stone circle and put it in the center of the circle. He knows the people will not destroy it because they are afraid of it.

As I lie here in the center of the figure eight, all time and space are visible to me. Here, a Great Tree of Life grows, its trunk and branches reaching for the sky. I feel great roots and rocks beneath my body as the tree rises out of my belly. A field of crystals lies deep in the Earth beneath the great roots. The water that is being drawn to this central energy point feels like the liquid in my own bloodstream, and the heart of this center pounds like my own. This is the energetic field of the mineral kingdom.

The central stone draws to it all the water energy from the horizontal plane, keeping the great henge filled with water, which creates booming sounds when it is activated by the electromagnetic waves sent from Earth to the outer star systems. The star systems in turn send light waves into the great stones just inside the henge. This is where the consciousness of all the star systems falls into magnetic resonance with the waters of Earth. Here, the sounds of the mineral kingdom in communication with the stellar forms are much greater than anyone could possibly imagine. I hear sound waves emanating from the mineral forms on Earth to all of the outer stellar forms. The sound feels organic, like the heartbeat of great mountains mixing with the vibrations of the stars. In fact, the mineral kingdom is the greatest source of communication to all the forms in the universe.

The placing of the baptismal font in the middle of this energy center will create a most interesting situation. Since Avebury Circle marks the energy vortex of the Great Goddess for the Mayan Great Cycle, as the power of the Goddess emerges near the end of the second millennium this font will be the Earth portal that fuels the disintegration of the Roman Catholic church. By then, I can see, the church will have gone too far with control concepts such as papal infallibility, denigration of the feminine, baptism, and priestly celibacy. This place is where the mineral kingdom will react to bring about the return of natural balance.

By daring to create this control lock right at the portal to the mineral kingdom, the Powers and Principalities created access to the mineral-kingdom codes to anyone who could really *feel* the Earth. Later, by deciding to baptize children right at this portal, the Catholic priests will unknowingly create astounding intensity around their need to control the Earth. A similar intensity will be created at the Dome of the Rock in Jerusalem when the Moslems build a mosque over it, cutting off sky energy to this power point in the Holy Land. These control patterns will grow increasingly huge, creating voracious monsters within the structures of organized religion. And these monsters will have to be fed with more and more fear—fear of the Earth itself.

As I lie here at the energetically clearest time for this great circle, what I can see and feel from this central temple of the mineral kingdom is incredible. My sight encompasses centuries of time and history, as though all events were telescoped into a single moment. For example, as I look into the future, I see babies brought to this baptismal font by male priests, and I can feel how the priests detest them. The priests live in the village out beyond the west gate, and the only time they will come into this stone circle is during the morning, in order to baptize babies—to steal them from pagan control. Their intent is to exorcise these babies of "original sin"—their connection to the Earth itself.

But, unbeknownst to the priests, these baptisms have the opposite effect, because each baby who is brought into the circle automatically connects with its Earth power here. Each baby who is lucky enough to be baptized at this spot becomes an embodiment of paganism on this planet. These babies possess in their very essence the astounding powers of the mineral kingdom. They are chosen children, born in the stone circle to help us remember the Christ who was born in a cave. Those baptized in Avebury Circle from about A.D. 1000 to 1400 (after which the priests will order the destruction of the stones) will come back into incarnational form in the latter half of the twentieth century, at the end of the Age of Pisces, to activate the mineral kingdom.

In the industrial modern world, these individuals will often seem to be strangelings, for they will be totally charged by the power of the mineral kingdom. They will embody the perfection of the mineral-kingdom codes—exquisite high-resonance crystalline sound. They will teach about the interference pattern caused by baptism, so that others will refuse to feel guilty just for being born. The premise of Catholic baptism is that all babies are born damaged, and these primal children will appear to be damaged. For example, some will say they are "learning disabled" or "hyperactive." Some will seem to resemble lizards, sphinxes, or cat people. Yet these are the sacrificial lambs who will help humanity see the disturbed pattern—acute disturbance of the cellular matrix of Earth that is forcing lifeforms to mutate. Compassion and feeling for these children will emerge at the end of the cycle, and Avebury is the temple of compassion for the divine child.

These cyclopes—original sons and daughters of Earth—must be freed from the bowels of the planet so that oppression of the Earth can finally cease. Shape-shifting among such individuals will be almost continual as their astral forms are drawn back to the power stones all over the planet. Each time they return to the stones, they will leave messages about the future in the nearby fields. As soon as it grows dark in the great circles, the third dimension will fuse with the fourth; and as the crop circles manifest, the wind will blow, sounding the tone of the Earth.

Chapter Three

BREAKING
THE SEVENTH SEAL

To talk about the interface of the infrastructure of DNA with the vibratory accommodations of the Earth is to evoke the purified spiritual intention of a synchronized collective of human beings who understand that their responsibility to the planet is taking precedence over all other allegiances and concerns at this particular time. Such an evocation is in the nature of the planetary mystery, a rite of passage that synergizes hitherto scarcely suspected force fields into radiant manifestation.

—José Argüelles, *The Mayan Factor*

After writing chapter 2 of this book, "Mystery Plays of Atlantis," I became certain that sacred sites are receptacles of DNA records, materialization patterns, and geomantic records of time—and that they are attunement devices between other places and dimensions. To receive the information held in a sacred site, consciously or unconsciously, we need only to go to these sites and feel their energies. Our minds and bodies become activated, just as if we were the keys that "unlock the sites." To become keys that fit, however, we must learn to trust our most subtle perceptions. We must also develop certain psychic tools in order to be able to imprint the information we receive, and we need to willingly follow the peculiar "inner knowings" that tell us where to go and when. Sacred sites are libraries of genetic intelligence that draw us to them at just the right moments—most often when there is something we need to understand.

This exquisite recommunion with the records of all time is our birthright and privilege as the people of Earth. Sacred sites contain our stories, and now they are being reconstructed by archaeologists, making it easier for us to remember those original threads. When we finally surrender to the desire to know our stories, the intelligence of the Earth reveals itself. Atlantis and the Garden of Eden are psychic memory banks of that intelligence; they contain the memory of what we

45

think *we were before separation. Atlantis represents what we can create, while Eden represents what we deserve and desire. Could it be that Atlantis is the male side and Eden the female side of the same story of consciousness?*

The Earth will be offering us time until the year 2013 to see the truth about what we create. What we have created based on our desires is all around us; no longer can we escape seeing our handiwork and realizing the effect it has had on our planet and ourselves. Those who need to be entombed in windowless, air-conditioned buildings and mazelike cities will be trapped right there at the end of time. Those who need to rape and kill in order to control others will do so until they feel the pain of all their victims at the end of time. And those who seek the intelligence of the Earth will be blissfully happy, for her knowledge is enlightenment.

In these next twenty years, every initiatic test we require will be given to us. After August 16, 1992, blindness about what we are doing will cease, and we will feel *exactly where love or hate exists. Which way we choose to go will be crystal clear. We will see with devastating awareness, because what we create will be mirrored back to us precisely. In this next twenty years, all Faustian pacts come to an end. In this time, we come to know beyond a doubt that we create our own realities.*

This is the natural law many of us resist above all others, since waking up to it means taking responsibility for everything we do. However, the next stage is even worse: we will soon realize that we do not influence the reality of anyone else. *When this last seal on the powers of the Earth is opened in the summer of 1992, the energy of each creative form will return to its natural freedom and human power will be limited whenever it attempts to abuse the greater power of choice.*

As long as we see only in the third dimension, we will be stuck with its limited view. For example, if you have created a horrifying disease for yourself, what could be more enraging than considering it as a sign that you do not love yourself. But the rage that you feel comes from seeing only in the third dimension. If you can remember when you did *love yourself—perhaps in some other lifetime or dimension—then you can remember how to love yourself again.*

If you have created a disease that acts as a teacher, the first thing you must do is realize that it exists to show you how to love yourself. When you can see the disease as a patient teacher, then love becomes multidimensional as your disease reverberates through layers of time and changes your DNA. That disease has recorded every moment when you allowed pain and imperfection to come to you. It also remembers every time you released your body out of longing for a reunion with Source. But divinity has longed for you to reunite with it while you are in your body, because your body was created so the divine could exist in you.

You will learn to reunite with the Source while alive in your physical body, for the Source has existed and played in you for aeons and has delighted in your many forms. When you see that you can create unconditional love and that you will when you are ready, you will not be angry when someone reminds you that you create your own reality.

And if you are one who still needs to harm others in order to feel, please know how they feel when you try to find your lost self in their life force. The time has come for us all to realize how incredibly cruel we are when we expect someone else to feel for us.

Now it is time to return to Tikal, the Mayan temple in Guatemala that holds human pain in form until all have agreed to release it. As recorded in Heart of the Christos, *I experienced a lifetime of extreme brutality toward my fellow humans in Tikal. If you want the details, read the book, but abuse is all the same. It occurs when we cease to control ourselves and become blinded to everyone else. If we are "nice" people in this life, then that uncontrolled aspect of our past lives is the part we keep the most deeply hidden. However, this repository of guilt also keeps us separate from others. By not being able to love all that we have ever been, we can't be who we are now, in the present. I return to Tikal at the hour of the temple's closing down in* A.D. *843.*

I see a hand holding a clay receptacle—a cup. I am one of a small group of highly initiated Mayan priests who have gathered inside a cramped temple pyramid. We are all costumed in green parrot feathers. We are embodying the bird men, the great teachers from other realms who keep constant watch over us.

In this moment, I am trying to decide whether to drink the hallucinogenic pulque, fully understanding that if I do, it will rob me of any control over myself. As I contemplate this cup of liquid being offered to me, I know that if I drink it, it will also give me power. At this point I can see exactly what will happen after I drink the pulque. *When we are making choices, there is no linear time.*

As I return from my momentary vision of the future, I understand how I got to this moment and where my choice will lead me. I also can see all of what follows, if I want to bother. But it is much easier to be lured into the vibrations right around me than to maintain the position of omniscience that exists at the moment of choice. It is easier not to know or care about what is happening outside the pyramid. Why? Because I have never felt the people; my feelings have always been controlled by the priests so that I could eventually be used by them. I know that if I drink this liquid, a column of white light will ascend through my whole being—

from Earth to sky—and I will walk out of here like a prophet, consumed in electricity. I have been conditioned to believe that I am needed to bring the teachings from the grandmothers and grandfathers to the people, but I already know that is a lie. In fact, I know that my actions will completely sever the ancestral connection.

I must understand this more completely. What does this choice mean to my soul—my agreement to learn in time? I *am* to be Itzanna—the Mayan god who comes down into the third dimension—to enter completely into all the energy here, to become a channel by drinking the pulque. I believe that, yet I am not really sure I believe it. Perhaps it is only the one holding the cup who believes it. Perhaps there is another way.

Standing next to me is Huitzilipochtli, the bird god who comes with agendas for Earth people, the god who needs a human channel. As Barbara seeing through my priest's eyes, I know that I have already completed this ceremony. But as Barbara I also wonder if it is possible to create another scenario, to alter the records of time. Aren't there other pathways, other choices and probabilities? Can I, by going back, create a new time line, a new dimensional awareness for myself and the rest of the participants?

As priest and Barbara in one, I see purple light, the face of the eagle watching over me. The eagle is flying in a circle above the temple. Suddenly, six shamans manifest outside the pyramid. They are watching the eagle, too, and they are glowing with green light. The shamans stand at each one of the six directions around the people gathered in the central plaza of Tikal. They are holding staffs decorated with feathers on top, and they tap the staffs on the Earth. These are the eagle guardians of this ceremony, and if they choose to do so, they can shift the energy of time. Such shamans come from the future, and they can alter events in the past, which in turn can alter the outcome of events in the present. Such shamans can take form only when someone in the future has learned to love themselves and surrenders all fear about the past. This is because love of self in the present actually unlocks guilt from the past—guilt that could inhibit creativity and full self-expression in the future.

This opportunity is extremely unusual, although it will become more common after A.D. 1987. These shamans approach the shift from control to freedom with great intention, because the astral realms that contain these trapped energies are extremely violent, holding the powers of tidal waves, hurricanes, and volcanoes. These realms are peopled by lost beings who so long for release that they might explode at the slightest hope of freedom. They long for the release offered by someone they once abused who has learned to love them.

I see the shamans tapping their staffs as the red, blue, and green feathers blow in the wind. I know they are creating great electromagnetic forces—forces that will surge through their bodies as through lightning rods from the eagle in the sky to the snake beneath Tikal's central plaza.

The snake? Yes, there is a huge, curling, stone snake with turquoise eyes that lies thirty or forty feet below the ground level of the plaza. It rests on a bed of raked white quartz that reflects glowing light through the sifted Earth that covers the twenty-five-thousand-year-old serpent. This Atlantean Feathered Serpent was originally carved and placed at ground level on top of the white quartz layer. Later, rock walls were constructed around it, and dirt was sifted over it, finally forming a raised hill. Here the ceremonial center of Tikal was constructed thousands of years later.

The shamans are from the Clan of the Red Spider. They guard the secret information contained in the records of Tikal because it is their own portal into the center of the Earth. The appearance of these shamans is extremely rare. They are the *Keepers of Disease*, and they operate very covertly. Their sole purpose is to assist in the fusion of human endeavor and cosmic design. They live in the temple complex that lies buried under the central plaza—a place called the "Red City," where they are guardians of the red mushroom.

The red mushroom makes it possible to slip in and out of time, to kaleidoscope through the realities, and to heal when cyclic opportunity opens. This mushroom is the main ingredient for the paint used on the Mayan temples, which also can slip in and out of time. It is fascinating to realize that ant colonies store pieces of the red mushroom as food for the queen ant after she is fertilized. When red dye is needed for temple paint, Red Spider Clan shamans steal the mushrooms from the deep subterranean storerooms of the ants. Once painted, temples can slip in and out of time cycles, opening their force fields to certain visitors and shutting their portals to those who are not welcome. This may seem obtuse and even irrelevant, but the process by which portals open to the Source is the same as the process by which a healthy human, while alive, can dissolve into oneness with Source. This is an exquisite synchronization of highly conscious Earth energies and divine creative intent. Much about this can be known by studying mushroom usage, especially the ingestion of mushrooms, and by observing the activities of the ant kingdom.

But let us return to the ceremony . . . As the shamans make the link from Earth to sky, I stand in the pyramid directly above the turquoise eyes of the subterranean snake. In this moment, Huitzilipochtli waits for me to drink the pulque; however, the powerful energy created by the shamans is stronger than his desire. A seventh shaman, called White Eagle Tree, standing at the east gate of the pyramid—the one who holds the power of the other six shamans at the sacred directions—opens the east gate for me. Huitzilopochtli hands me the cup. I take it, pour the pulque onto the ground, and the cup passes from me.

Three realities are functioning concurrently here: I am experiencing my refusal to follow Huitzilopochtli's orders, which would seal the temple; the ceremony is happening both inside and outside the pyramid; and in the fifth dimension, a new experience in time is occurring that will alter future possibility. At this moment, I am very interested in what my higher self will do after I dump the pulque. What happens is that my higher self stays in my own body, which means I can't be used by anybody. What is happening here shows how all dimensions exist in time and how all acts have potential for both good and evil.

Like sea creatures crawling out of water and transforming into lizards on the land, the stages of our growth through time are slow and painful. But they are also necessary. Magical and ceremonial experiences challenge us to interface with the fourth-dimensional realm. These juicy, polarized experiences teach discernment and clear intention, which is a pathway to the fifth-dimensional level. In fact, these experiences offer us our most potent opportunities to discover how we create our own reality. But the archetypal powers of the gods can overwhelm us at the fourth-dimensional level unless we remember to open the heart and love them for all their marvelous and complex teachings.

I see now that I was not able to move to the fifth-dimensional level the "first time" at Tikal because I did not remain in my integrity. When I drank the pulque, it was like acid; it turned my throat chakra into Swiss cheese, causing air to flow from my lungs through holes in my throat. When the time came to bring in light, my body was depleted because I couldn't breathe. But "this time," as the kind shaman of the seventh level opens the east gate to Spider Grandmother, who weaves us back together, I breathe deeply and open my heart. I take the healing, spiritual light into my lungs, allowing that light to completely heal and rejuvenate me. Whenever you act with total integrity in your *now*, you offer yourself this timeless healing.

In Mayan, I begin counting: "Ben, Eb, Chuen, Oc, Muluc, Lamat, Manik." As I count back into Mayan time, I spiral out to the Pleiades— way out to the center of the galaxy, where everything swirls in enormous dimensions. I see amazing rainbow lights; I hear metal balls rolling down tracks; and I hear bells and gongs ringing. As I blast back in time, I am afraid for just a moment. But I trust, I trust, I trust . . . passing through the air-imploding, cell-dilating, watery-gushing place within. As I stand in the pyramid with Huitzilipochtli, I am returning to the part of me that exists in the stars. I am filled with bliss.

I have fused with that part of myself that can inform me from the highest level—the piece that stays out there as protection during terrible times. This is Hope, the seventh star in the Pleiades, a star that was visible from Earth until it became a supernova. It is a beacon of myself. It is where I lived before I moved to Alcyone. It is a focused ruby ray from my own being that plays in space. This is the part of me that will stay out in the Pleiades until the Earth field clears.

In my body, that cloudy Earth field is represented by my throat. That is where I was bitten by a snake during an initiation in another past life. When bitten by the sacred snake, the throat is opened and one speaks from the heart. Red Spider Clan shamans guard this particular initiation so that secrets of Earth will not be revealed too soon. If teachers holding the keys of the Red Spider Clan returned too early, the energy would be so intense from the great snake under Tikal that dark forces could overwhelm the Earth and create wars in heaven again. Red Spider Clan shamans, like the eagle flying high over Tikal, will stay in the Galactic Center—in the highest energy realms—until the possibility of the dark forces taking control is cleared. That potential scenario ends on August 16, 1992.

As I return to Tikal from my journey to the Pleiades, I walk out the east gate and stare into the eyes of White Eagle Tree. Blue light envelops the people, and a profound silence sets in, like the softness of night at the New Moon. This silence exists right in the third dimension, and it communicates peace to the people. In this silence is the timelessness of all possibility, the home of all the laws of nature, the home of pure potential. From this unbounded consciousness, anything is possible, anything can happen. Tikal holds silence in the deep night of the jungle, awaiting with delight the people who will return to open its portals to the stars.

When I went to Tikal in February of 1988 to meditate in the jungle, I faced my own past-life struggle with the dark lords—those who feed on pain while waiting for the chance to escape their trap of separation. That night, I released everything within myself that might also help to release the pain and control of Tikal. As I broke my own bonds in the temples, I thought at first that I could also break the hold of this temple's negative karma on others. Tikal is a key portal for fourth-dimensional fallen angels who incarnate in hopes of finding release into the light. The part in me that pities others was dominant as I struggled to believe that I could release anyone else.

Eventually, however, I saw that I could release only myself. When I really accepted that, a black jaguar with intense yellow eyes appeared in the jungle nearby. That magnificent guardian had come to tell me that it would be holding this portal open until all experiences are finished in time. At the end of time, every fallen being who has asked to be given another chance will return here for redemption and release.

I was not eaten by the jaguar because I felt no fear when it came to me. Once I had freed myself, I meditated for many days, imprinting within my psyche the geomantic and stellar keys of Tikal. As I write, only now do I realize that during those days I was given many keys to this book: the keys to twelve-strand DNA, the keys to twelve-hour solar-ray powers, the keys to twelve-planet solar library wisdom, and the keys to the twelve stellar rays of Atlantis. All this information is essential for light-body infusion and galactic fusion, and I intend to reveal it as clearly as I can. There can be no secrets now because secrecy equals control; it creates only fear and mistrust.

In 1988, I left Tikal with a heavy heart. I felt like I was being forced to walk out of the Alexandrian Library—the Record Temple of Atlantis—just after finally crawling through the door and gaining entry. I felt like I was having to leave without ever getting the chance to open the scroll of the Emerald Records. So as I walked out, I offered the temple the greatest gift I have—my integrity. I promised Tikal that I would let go of my attachment to it and never return. I hoped that the emptiness I held within myself would create a vacuum in the temple's heart that would draw teachers who could open its seals—and hence the seals on the emotional bodies of human beings that result in disease and separation.

Soon, to my amazement, the needed healing came—right from my own Mayan brothers Hunbatz Men, a daykeeper, and don Alejandro Oxlaj, the Keeper of Tikal. These two announced that the Itzae, the solar initiates who were first awakened at Chichén Itzá at the spring equinox of 1989, must return to Tikal for spring equinox of 1990. However, even though I am a solar initiate, I had to keep my promise to the sacred temple. Not doing the work with my brothers and sisters in my physical body made me feel very lonely, and my brothers and sisters did not understand why I could not go with them. But through deep yearning, my astral body traveled with them as they did their hard work. Now it is time to tell the story of the 1990 opening of Tikal, the year in which the K'uatzal teachings were released to Earth.

In a private letter to solar initiates, Hunbatz Men describes Tikal as follows: ''Tik'al is the place where the grief, pain, and bitterness of cyclic vibration was registered, the place where the ancient toxic vibrations that were stuck were finally released and understood. It is the place where we will understand the face of the Sun without burn, and sons and daughters of the Sun are declared by creating an experience of reversing in time. Father Sun wants us to experience fire now so that we may enter into his heat and come to understand our own vital energy, which is also heat. Tik'al is the place where the cycles of cosmic time remain registered, where it was taught how to work with the kundalini in order to awaken the sacred serpent of wisdom and understand the four powers of the basic elements of creation.''

As I flew in the night sky on a Pleiadian magic carpet woven of my feelings, I was overjoyed to see my brothers and sisters doing the work of reopening Tikal. Though they had focused their energies on cleansing rituals in a sacred waterfall near don Alejandro's village and had wafted copal into the sacred trees during a fire ceremony, as soon as they approached Tikal, they realized that they had all come because they had chosen initiation. They had chosen this experience in the place where the bitterness of cyclical time is held in form.

As the time of opening drew near, they experienced the death of self in various forms, just as I had done in 1988. As I felt them creating illnesses and thrashing through their personal insecurities, I realized that had I been with them in the physical, my old pity would have replaced my compassion. I would have wanted to help lead them through their deaths and rebirths, but this cannot be done. We all must face these fires alone. The elder Mayan teachers were the only ones who would be able to help them do this.

Finally the conches blew at Tikal, and the procession moved into the central plaza, which was overshadowed on each end by the thrusting pyramids of the Grand Jaguar and the Temple of the Moon, the two guardians of the Red Sun. Suddenly I was rewarded for having burned copal late into the night in the Temple of the Moon: the Temple sucked my astral body into its high, sacred sanctuary. There, as I assumed the lotus position, the layers of time became visible, and I watched the ceremony unfold on the plaza below.

The initiates marched into the center of the plaza, feeling secure in their white clothes, beating on drums and blowing conch shells whose blasting tones pierced the etheric. I watched as Hunbatz Men created various geometric forms with the group of initiates, moving them into places where the pyramids vibrate and their portals could open to the human receivers. Cunningly, he watched to see which person took which sacred position, then opened each initiate's inner eye to the keys of that location. Lovingly, he thanked each person in his heart for answering his call. All they had needed to do was come; their presence alone would allow him to open the temple.

From above, I saw a shiver go through the people as rainbow rays of light began to emanate from the group and from the pyramids. A chill passed though the ground as the great snake beneath the plaza moved kundalini energy through its curled spine and its turquoise eyes began to gleam. I wondered: Can they see it? Can they see it? Deep in space, I saw the Red Sun glowing like an occulted Venus.

There can be no doubt that Hunbatz Men and don Alejandro saw it. Hunbatz tapped the steps of the Pyramid of the Grand Jaguar, activating its full powers. Don Alejandro knelt down and kissed the sacred Earth. Feelings began to pour from my brothers and sisters. Alberto Ruz Buenfil cried tears of ecstasy. Others cried over the return of their souls, just as I once had. Charles Bensinger released himself as suppressed feelings flooded to his guarded surface and surged uncontrolled across his conscious mind. Through all of the initiates poured memories of old fears, unthinkable horrors, and forgotten ecstasies.

Below the temple, the Feathered Serpent released a magnetic pulse. The bed of white stones beneath it vibrated softly, sending gentle sound waves into the center of the Earth. As I sat meditating high above, a bolt of cosmic power blasted from the Temple of the Moon to the Temple of the Jaguar, balancing the solar and lunar powers. Then I felt an etheric earthquake as Jaguar Paw, the Mayan king who first brought slaughter and death into the Mayan cycles, was filled with the blue light of his own soul. Finally, as Hunbatz Men had predicted, the initiates broke the bonds of culture and race and took their initiation into compassion.

Thus was completed the initiation of the powers of darkness. The blue energy bolt had awakened the sacred serpent in the dark Earth. Darkness had now been received and honored, and the sacred cave of the Earth had been opened to prepare for the implantation of cosmic energies. Henceforth, stars would be birthed right inside the Earth, as a goddess draws her lover into the sacred womb.

Now I must go to the temple of Karnak in Egypt to witness the initiation into the light. Just as Tikal once held the powers of darkness in form, Karnak is the temple that holds the light powers in form. I will become the goddess Aspasia, once again inside the dark, sacred womb of Knossos, holding the Earth force while Karnak builds its star matrix.

I am Aspasia, and I am in the courtyard of Knossos. It is a moonless night in 1537 B.C., and I am standing in front of the bull-horn altar in the temple. My arms are raised, pulling energy into my shoulders from Mount Adminytus, the crystal mountain where I was initiated by the grandmothers. I hold my hands so that my shoulders are aligned with the bull horns. As I do so, I fix my eyes on distant Alcyone, the star of my birth in the Pleiades.

My pineal gland is buzzing. This is a special night, the night that marks the beginning of the new thirty-six-hundred-year cycle that will end in

A.D. 2013. It will also be a long night, for there is much to do. Right now, I am taking part in a gigantic ritual of alignment—the alignment of temples all over the Earth with the Solar System and the stars for the coming age. This is the spring equinox activation of all the Atlantean theocratic sites.

At this moment, geomancers at Karnak in Egypt are working hard to build a new temple. Long ago, the old temple was torn down, and the open space there has not been spiritually activated since 5200 B.C. Soon, though, it will be filled with temples again, as each pharaoh in succession builds walled-in sanctuaries for the unseen god, Amun. Soon there will be great support columns upholding high ceilings painted in lapis lazuli and gold—ceilings that reveal once again the stories of traveling bodies in the sky. As I tune into this space, it feels magnetic, and the sacred lake nearby shimmers in the starlight next to the great stone plaza.

As my mind travels to the temple of Karnak, I see geomancers hard at work, determining alignments to Sirius by means of cords, crystals, and plumb lines. They have been working on moonless nights in order to get the proper alignments to Sirius and various other stars. This is the only way they can build the new temple in an astronomically correct way, with all its columns, obelisks, walls, altars, and sanctuaries in the proper location for maximum creation of stellar energy. These night-sky temple guardians and builders determine their primary alignments by staring at individual stars until the stars light up the pineal glands in the centers of their heads. By attuning to the star needed for the next phase of work, the alignments become crystal clear.

Right now there are seven temple geomancers at Karnak, and each one tunes into a separate star in order to see where to locate things. With these alignments, they are going to construct the central sanctuary of Thutmosis I, who has recently incarnated from Sirius. His reign, referred to as the "New Kingdom," began thirteen years ago, in 1550 B.C.

This New Kingdom realignment is of great significance because the Hyksos invaders who have controlled Egypt in recent years broke the Pharaonic star link, and it must be repaired. While the invaders ruled, the Egyptians lived in chaos, and the invaders altered the sacred temple forms and rituals that had once maintained harmony along the Nile. The stellar template for the new harmony must be implanted from Sirius under Thutmosis. The Pleiades are also of utmost importance, since even now Pleiadian energy begins to create a pathway for Christos, who will manifest on Earth in A.D. 0.

So what do I have to do with all this? I am involved because I am from the star Alcyone in the Pleiades and because I hold the blood lineage of the Moon on Earth. The geomancers need my vision and star connection at Knossos in order to do their work. In order to solidify this connection, I have sent many little double-terminated crystals to them from our sacred spring in the center of Mount Adminytus—crystals that are also useful for opening the pineal gland.

But Karnak is not the only temple that is being aligned and activated tonight. My vision and star connection must be open and available to such temples all over the world as they simultaneously receive the first light of the beginning of the next great cycle. Follow me. Stay with me as my consciousness spins around the world and the Solar System, recording the separate moments of the One Great Moment of the Two Suns dawning at these sacred sites—the Golden Sun that rises in the east each day and the Red Sun that rises in the west only once every thirty-six hundred years. This is the moment that ushers the Earth into a new age.

As I stand staring at Alcyone, the diamond in the center of my head begins to glow, and I am transported to the isle of Malta. There, I watch the Temple of the Grain Goddess being activated as the Red Sun penetrates its dark chamber at the moment of the spring equinox. Usually this temple does not receive the light of the rising Sun at solstices or equinoxes— it is a primordial, dark womb temple for initiatic work by priestesses. But this year, the inner body of the Goddess must receive the first light from the Red Sun—the Sun that ushers in the new cycle—so that its teachings can be conceived in her womb.

In Malta, only priestesses are allowed into this deep underground chamber. It is carved out of solid rock and takes the shape of the body of the Goddess. Within it at this moment, I see a priestess at the center point of each of five inner circles. Each one holds a mirror of mica, and each is prepared to focus the rising Red Sun's first light into the sanctuary, the womb of the Goddess, as it streams in from the world above.

Near the hole at the top of the temple stands a wizard priest of the Occulting Spider Clan, staring at the ancient symbol of two suns. As the first rays of the Red Sun glow above the mountain ridges to the west, the priest pulls a great stone from over the hole. Then, as the Red Sun rises like a scarlet Moon in the sky, he reflects its eerie red light down into the temple. The light then blasts through the five subterranean mirrors, activating the body of the Goddess. Like the conception that occurs in the dark womb of a woman, this is the Earth's new link to the Creator.

These reflected rays of red light create an exquisite softness inside the cavern, as if giving new sight to a hitherto blind Earth Goddess. The energy streaming into the temple is forceful and powerful, like that of a Brahma bull mating with a cow in a time of penultimate fertility.

Such activation of the Atlantean theocratic sites last occurred in 5200 B.C., when the Great Goddess still held the power of the lineages. However, this time, as the Red Sun's first light is captured by the five mica mirrors, the power of the lineage keepers is suddenly transferred from female to male, from priestess to priest. From this moment until A.D. 2013, males will hold and control the secret teachings of the Red Sun. Thereafter, sexual polarity will cease on the Earth, and ceremonies will involve fusion of the male and the female.

As I tune into the events at Malta, I am simultaneously tuned to all the other sites around the world. At each site, priests and priestesses are preparing for the sacred moment of the two suns' rising. As the Earth continues to spin, I focus on Newgrange, the Metonic Cycle Temple in Ireland that rules the laws of personal incarnation and karma. Newgrange is the main guardian of the soul during this temple calibration. Normally, it can be activated only at the winter solstice when the first light of the Sun illuminates a triple spiral at the end of its great tunnel passageway. But unbeknownst to most, Newgrange also has *equinox* markers on its kerb stones.

Just before the first rays of the Golden Sun blast from the east, nine Druid priests stand in front of the eastern facade, one in front of each stone megalith, all waiting to empower the stones with the new teachings. The light from the Golden Sun registers in the center of a double spiral on the eastern kerb stone just as the Red Sun casts a glow on the field of chevrons on the backside of the western kerb stone. This sends a specific Earth vibration to the Galactic Center, and three priestesses meditating in the interior chambers begin to receive Sirius Teaching Three.

As the priestesses receive this teaching, their combined inner light activates an interior triple spiral whose energy spins rapidly—almost explosively—out from the center of the temple. This in turn activates the nine stone megaliths, and the rising Sun begins to warm the megaliths as they cast long shadows onto the eastern facade of white quartz crystal. These nine shadows represent the presence of the nine Galactic Lords, who are always present when teachings come from the Galactic Center.

Then, mysteriously, the golden light from the east is dimmed by the red light from the west, and all the shadows from the megaliths disappear from the glittering white quartz eastern facade. They dissipate like ghosts when light comes into a dark room. Later, the priests will process the kundalini energy created by the Sun within these nine megaliths, while the priestesses will ground the female energy of the activation.

Next I focus my awareness on West Kennet Long Barrow of Avebury, at this time called the Temple of Branwyn. As with that of Malta, the temple here has five chambers. In 5200 B.C., this temple site was activated by priestesses when they erected a megalith imprinted with a triple spiral. But the five-chambered temple itself was not constructed until 2800 B.C., and by then the spiral megalith was far inside the dark barrow, hidden from the light. This megalith rules Elder Wisdom—knowing without evidence, knowing without needing to see.

As Newgrange is activated by the rays of the Golden Sun, the hidden triple spiral of Branwyn is also activated, and the teaching from Sirius is received. This barrow holds energies that extend far beyond space and time. It transmits ancestor wisdom to the people by means of their "inner caves"—their pineal glands. This teaching, given by both the crones and wise old men, is integrated by both males and females. It reads as follows:

"Humans have now tasted of good and evil and have begun to contemplate the possibility that they are gods. But they can become divine only by activating their inherent free will. And free will can be mastered on Earth only by allowing total trust—by *seeing* from the inner brain rather than through the five senses. This skill makes it possible to be on Earth and in all other dimensions simultaneously. This is the secret of experiencing oneness with all things.

"The time will soon arrive for you to free yourselves from the original lie—the illusion of separation from Source caused by your fascination with sensation. You will do this by assisting in the birth of the Source, the Creator, on Earth. Then Nibiru will rejoin the solar logos and Earth will transcend separation, for you will be the equal of the gods."

Immediately after this transmission, the light of the double sunrise arrives at Knossos, illuminating the temple where my arms are raised to the bull horns. But as Aspasia, I am very confused. I can feel and actually see what is happening at all of the portal sites, but at the moment of sunrise here, everything seems backward. Being east of Newgrange, Avebury, and Malta, Knossos should receive the light of the Sun before the other sites. Have the poles shifted during this long night of preparation?

I quickly remind myself that suns are rising both in the east and the west and that this is the only morning in more than three-and-a-half millennia that anyone will witness this occurrence. The grandmothers explained this to me in careful detail so that I would be able to contain the dark force at Knossos during this activation. As the mysterious morning light arrives, the bull of Brahma appears in the Knossos courtyard. First, the strange light strikes the top of the electrum pyramid, called the "Winged Messenger," which has been electroplated with diakinetic quartzite by the Egyptians. The pyramid sends out light in all directions, creating a field of exploding particles and a loud, booming voice of the biblical Daniel saying, "I am the lion, and I observed a he-goat from the west, encroaching over the entire surface of the world, though never touching the ground."

Great electromagnetic winds explode like ball lightning, creating a sudden Earth/sky connection. As these energies charge the open sanctuary, geomancers inside the temple create light forms to decorate the sanctuary walls. They will later paint griffins on the walls—higher-dimensional forms of the he-goat. They will also paint gigantic cellular forms on the grand staircase—forms that will be fully understood only in A.D. 2013, at the end of the great cycle that has just begun. As a reminder of glyptolithic evolution, they will even paint a blue monkey eating leaves.

Next I focus on the light rising at Baalbek in Anatolia, the primary Nibiruan control facility throughout time. This is the Earth home of the Nibiruans. All its temple guardians are Nibiruan, and it is dedicated to the planet Jupiter. Later, the Romans will build a more modern version of this temple, creating an instant storage laboratory for Nibiruan powers. But for now, Baalbek is a huge landing platform for Nibiruan ships.

The light of the Golden Sun enters the front of the temple, while the Red Sun strikes its back. The morning Sun penetrates the opening in the western wall and strikes the solid twenty-four-karat-gold winged sphinx of the Atlantean theocracies, which weighs about five tons. This is the moment for which the Nibiruan guardians have been waiting. As the sphinx begins to gleam, they believe they now control planet Earth. These guardians are "eagle men"—tall winged beings with the faces of eagles. As the Sun brings out the dazzling brilliance of the gold, they bask in their assumed control of the planet. Just as they try to secure this power within the temple, however, the fifth-dimensional teachers who transmit these teachings and powers seal off the access. *They close this portal.*

Every Earth portal has a system for sealing off access to knowledge when the free will of those on Earth is endangered. However, there is also little spiritual evolution on Earth when the fifth-dimensional portals are closed. It is as if the Source were sealed off. This is very important: from this moment on, *because of the intended abuse by the Nibiruans, the portals to fifth-dimensional teachings will be sealed off for more than three thousand years.* Only at Harmonic Convergence in August of A.D. 1987 will the fifth-dimensional portals be opened again, and from the fifth-dimensional perspective, this will be the opening of the Seventh Seal prophesied in Revelation. I also tell you that there will be a similar Nibiruan control attempt at Giza in Egypt on January 11, 1992, to *reseal* the Seventh Seal, engineered by a group claiming to be solar initiates. These people will not be carriers of the indigenous Elder Wisdom, and their attempt to control the Earth will fail. But the exquisite potential for reunion with Source from A.D. 1987 to 2013 will almost be thrown away by these well-meaning initiates in their attempt to recreate the old control patterns. In the end, if these fifth-dimensional portals can be held open until 2013 without humans giving away their free will, all matter on Earth will transmute into divinity.

I can see where all this will lead over the next several millennia, and as I stand in the central courtyard of Knossos, my heart opens to humanity. Though the bird men of Baalbek have been shut out at the critical moment, preventing total Nibiruan control of Earth, they nevertheless have received a *measure* of control over the planet's surface. Most notably, *they have achieved the ability to incarnate*. No longer will they have to persuade the people to build temples in order to link up to their own control centers; no longer will they require a channel to enter Earth: now they can become humans themselves!

Even from my vantage point at Knossos, I can see that the various non-physical lizards creeping around in the canals of Baalbek are considerably attracted to the idea of taking human form through incarnation. They look forward to creating fear more directly. These monsters are not content to lumber around as fourth-dimensional reptiles, occasionally eating someone up. Much more appealing to them is the idea of actually entering the third dimension—in the twentieth century, for example, actually *becoming* an Adolf Hitler, a Charles Manson, a Stephen King, or a Jimmy Swaggert. One of their greatest triumphs will be creating and directing the twentieth-century film that creates fear of the act of eating, *The Night of the Living Dead*. They will even baldly show themselves for who they really are by creating a movie called *V*.

But a time will come when the third-dimensional experiences of the bird men, reptiles, lions, and various other control energies will be complete. In the midst of their delight over playing with the powers of the third dimension, they will also be forced to look directly into the third-dimensional mirror of karma. They will have to stare into it until they recognize themselves. Eventually, even these entities will tire of their games, and they will begin to desire love instead of control. Their control era will end with Harmonic Convergence on August 16, 1987, when the fifth-dimensional portals reopen. Beginning in that moment, all the harmonic elements of the Goddess cultures that functioned during the previous cycle will come back into form again.

That is not to say everyone will have an easy time coping with the gods once the harmonic shift has occurred. For example, the bird men will still espouse heavy-duty male shamanism. It will take time for them to integrate the female wisdom and energy. They will be like cosmic bikers, creating a great deal of ritual mumbo jumbo and belief in the need to see their shamanistic journeys through from beginning to end. Many of those teachers who worked hard to facilitate the shift will still try to control the planetary field after Harmonic Convergence instead of just allowing the Earth to vibrate back into balance. Likewise, women who access the Goddess after 1987 will have to be very patient about integrating her powers. But even the most difficult habits and energies will be profoundly affected by the return of spiritual teachers to this planet, and allowance and compassion will help to move them into balance very quickly. The key will be to surrender with no fear of the consequences.

Now the two suns rise at Mohenjo-Daro, the site that has sanctified the Indus River from 5200 to 1537 B.C. The temple keepers are amazed as the harbinger from the west appears. Around the Red Sun they see a blue corona from the fourth-dimensional Sirian and Nibiruan "watcher" energies. They are dismayed because their prophecies have foretold that soon after this event, all their temples will flooded. And so they will— including Mohenjo-Daro.

Mohenjo-Daro is the home of the Brahma bull—the same bull that guards Knossos. He feels my compassion, a love that is embodied in me from the Pleiades through the Constellation of the Bull. The Brahma bull stands solidly on all four hooves, his horns sending Moon energy into the sky. He simply waits; he is the *Keeper of Silence*, offering a most important teaching on this planet. This teaching says, "If you do not know what to do, do nothing."

The Brahma bull, carved from one solid piece of mastodon tusk, is in the top chamber of the temple. This icon sees everything about the Hurrites, the people who carved it. Long ago, these people traveled to the north country, to the land of their grandfathers who lived in caves more than twenty-five thousand years ago. There, they honored their ancestors, who had so gracefully lived the principle of nonaction. And there they extracted this tusk from a mastodon they found frozen in a glacier, a great beast from the previous cycle. They brought it to this sacred site at a time when there was no temple and carved it into the Brahma bull. The Hurrites used to hunt the bull, but now they revere it as a sacred teacher.

The Hurrites are from the star system called Zeta-Reticulae. Centuries from now, they will be blamed for cattle mutilations on Earth, when in fact they will be conducting widespread healings here. Their work during the latter part of the twentieth century will be to reactivate the bull tenders of the East and the Pipe carriers of the West. In those times, the Central Intelligence Agency of the United States, believing the temple teachers to be the enemy, will stage the cattle mutilations to implant fear among the people; and through various channels they control, such as the Scientologists, they will blame it on the Zeta-Reticulans. But I can see that this, too, shall pass and the truth will eventually be known. One person who will give sacred teachings about this will be Whitley Streiber, who will take on this most difficult initiation: learning to love what others judge to be evil.

As the light strikes the Brahma bull in the top of this temple, I see that there will be great floods and earthquakes here. The temple teachers will decide to remain, even though they have foreseen the impending catastrophe. They will remain here so that as the Brahma bull falls into the sacred mud of the Indus, they will be present to witness the impregnation of new wisdom on the planet. They will remain in order to implant the teachings of the sacred bull, including the Goddess fertility teaching about the beauty of the bull phallus. Nearly four millennia after this connection is made, society will balance the male and female powers, and women, no longer feeling invaded, will once again venerate the phallus. Like the bull, the human male was meant to be vigorous and protective. And like the cow, the human female was meant to suckle her young in peace and security. When the natural beauty of this teaching reemerges on the planet again, Mother Earth and Father Sky will again be united and men and women will love one another.

But to achieve this great love, there must also be great sacrifice. The Hurrites know this. And so, as the light arrives here, I activate both Mohenjo-Daro and Knossos with the wisdom of the Brahma bull. Even so, I cannot bear to look into the future. I cannot bear to see the death of the Hurrites or the great suffering of the bulls over the next thirty-six hundred years. So I simply release the beam of my all-seeing state knowing that the sacred Indus will inundate the temple. I know it will also flood the Earth with compassionate, healing energy—energy that will bear wondrous fruit many centuries from now.

Finally, I focus on the new light striking the temple of Chang in China. There, a pagoda sits atop a hill riddled with caves. In each cave, a person who has attained enlightenment sits in meditation. This pagoda has been constructed as a perfect geomantic form so that humans can meditate inside the Hill of Creation while viewing the pagoda from their caves. This primordial hill is symbolic of the new Earth that emerges when the water recedes after a great flood. Many other such sacred hills are also symbols of the emergence of civilization after a catastrophe.

In the top of the pagoda is a statue of the Buddha carved from green jade. As the light from the two suns strikes the statue, the Buddha laughs. His laugh reverberates in circles, spiraling all the way out to the Galactic Center. I smile in the knowledge that this laughing Buddha will come alive again in A.D. 1987, when the West releases enough of its ego to remember how to respond to the power of sacred sites such as this.

So ends the cycle of the two suns on this first morning of the new galactic cycle. And with it ends my long night's vigil. Knowing that I have fulfilled my destiny and knowing that I have honored the knowledge of the elders, at last, I, Aspasia, release my universal gaze and withdraw into the Temple of Knossos to reflect.

Chapter Four

SWIMMING
IN CELLS & STARS

Creativity is a profound mystery precisely because it involves
the appearance of patterns that have never existed before.

—Rupert Sheldrake, *The Presence of the Past*

My journey to observe the rising of the two suns felt like going back in time the way I do during hypnotic regressions. My energy field alters during those journeys as I gain new awareness about how I can shift my perceptions in the present moment. For example, until I had made total peace with my own inner darkness by returning to Tikal, it had never occurred to me that we can alter an experience of present reality by releasing past guilt. As a direct result, most of the emotional clearing work I have done since writing Heart of the Christos *has been aimed at reactivating feelings about past complexes.*

I have found that such energetic encounters with past emotional blocks are like thawing out mastodons that have been frozen within blocks of ice. From the decision to reexperience the trauma of anything in our past, *we can finally integrate its knowledge without judgment. I also strongly suspect that if we* cannot *face our inner darkness—our personal "Fall"—we could be paralyzed by it as evil in the outside world builds to a climax. Facing our dark shadows is not easy to do—it demands extreme honesty. If we are still lying to ourselves, it won't work. But when we free ourselves of past complexes, the drama shifts to present time—the only place where anybody can change. This causes* cellular release *that reverberates through time and creates a new future. It changes everything, just as climatic shifts change ecosystems.*

Climate patterns are very much the same as our feeling patterns. Think about how climate determines the life potential within a bioregion, and then consider how your feeling patterns determine your potential. The implications of this analogy are awesome. I began to see how it works during my first visit to Tikal, and then I observed another such shift during the total solar eclipse of July 11, 1991.

On this day, our medicine society—the Society of the Tree—had conducted a powerful eclipse ceremony, and during a lecture I gave on the following day, I was unusually receptive to insights. The audience was exceptionally bright and sensitive. Among other things, five or six people insisted that something had "changed forever" during the eclipse. After the sixth person insisted on the reality of this shift, I realized the truth of it: something had changed, but what?

Two weeks later during the July Full Moon, I began to feel what that shift was. We are now ending 3,600 years of history, a long phase whose purpose has been to allow "the gods" to incarnate and learn to feel and love as humans. All these experiences—whatever we have undergone during this time—has been a grand preparation for us to move fully into adulthood. The shift at the eclipse was exactly that—we saw, felt, and knew that we are now adults, able to experience and share all of ourselves that is divine and human. Only now can we become totally responsible because only now have we known enough experiences to consistently make wise choices.

What does this mean more specifically? Among other things, it means we are ready to ask for what we need, to demand real love and honesty from our companions, and to throw off authoritarian oppression and control. Many of us have realized that our present relationships are tremendously influenced by past-life experiences. And many of us have discovered that we can better understand our current relationships if we clear these old experiences. But since the eclipse, due to the shift into full adulthood, all our memory codes of past lives seem to have been blown wide open. Not only do we have a sense of who we have been throughout time, but we are also recognizing those who have traveled with us. Moreover, as we awaken that part in ourselves that is godlike, we are beginning to remember times on Earth when we were not being manipulated or interfered with by alien thoughts or energies.

To resonate with this idea, try to remember being a member of a clan in a primeval forest. Remember yourself as a man in a group of men or as a woman in a circle of women. Notice that there is no hierarchy. Notice that each person emits a field of energy that teaches you something. We can feel these experiences now because their seals have been dissolved. We are actually beginning to remember that time of innocent bliss, that phase before we began a period of thirty-six hundred years of ego development. Now that we have developed the observing self—a trait of the gods we received as both our reward and nemesis—it is time to reimmerse ourselves in the earlier layers of self that are synchronized with the Earth's vibrations. But we must not do this unconsciously; it must be done with the self-reflective powers we have gained during the long development of ego.

The only access I know of for such a journey is through storytelling. To bring you along, let me seduce you with a thought: Imagine what it would be like to look into the eyes of your lover, child, or parent and see the memories of all that you have ever been together—clear back to the age of unicellular life. There you are, beside one with whom you are bonded. You are both the result of aeons of learning, loving, and living, but you are now more than ever before. Then imagine looking into the eyes of another and seeing with total consciousness all that they are. Imagine how they feel about you as you see them, and imagine how much more you see yourself as you discover all this knowledge in someone else.

Since the solar eclipse of July 1991, we have entered into a state of omniscience that flings open all doors to creativity. The only way to feel this is to remember the quality of the energy field as it was before the development of self-consciousness, while simultaneously utilizing our new powers of self-reflection. We have unlimited creative potential now, only because we have allowed all this learning. But we must be very careful to see the Earth's shift back into unity, because the Earth no longer needs to reflect our consciousness back to us. All this past learning between the people and the divine ones is now an open book. Like the demolition of the Berlin Wall in 1989, a barrier has been removed. Now, at last, we can see divinity in others. At last, we are ready.

It is time for me to travel back into my own cells, to rediscover those moments when I saw the Divine and chose union over separation. Those were the "pasts" when I acted on intuition, without hesitation. Those were the days when I knew I was guided toward right choices by wise beings from many dimensions. And so it is today: each choice that is made out of feeling reverberates through the planet and increases our attunement to the inner Earth. And that new resonance makes it possible for us to live in harmony with the planet, which in turn vibrates in harmony with the stars.

I am Aspasia walking up the stairs of the Grand Gallery of Knossos, carrying an exquisitely carved, quartz bull cup decorated with beads of lapis lazuli. I am supposed to walk out of the stairway into the main courtyard to put this crystal rhyton into the stone receptacle there, so the priest can offer it as a gift to the winning bull dancer. Since I am the high priestess here, I can do anything I want. I *feel* that fact, and my light body tells me to keep the rhyton instead of placing it in the receptacle. I always follow my inner knowledge because the grandmothers have taught me that it is my highest faculty.

So, amidst murmurs of consternation, I walk right past the pedestal. I feel great anger coming from Didymus. Like a scorpion, he is sending me poison control juice from his hot solar plexus, trying to make me put the rhyton into the receptacle. He is communicating to me that if I do not,

I will be struck by lightning. But I already know that my body can handle even lightning. I have prepared for this moment better than the high priest knows.

I carry the bull cup across the center point of the plaza. This center point is very powerful because energy lines cross here as they do at Karnak, but nothing has ever been constructed here. I walk toward the west side of the plaza, to the adytum—the open sanctuary in front of the throne room of the Atlantean sky teacher. Then I enter the throne room. There, on each side of a crystal throne are paintings of large, crouching griffins. In the shoulders of these griffins—exactly where wings would be if they were sphinxes—I see blue tracking devices. These devices are circular, and they contain spirals on the inside. They work with energy in exactly the same way as the triple spirals at Newgrange and the barrow of Branwyn at Avebury; that is, they can be activated by light codes transmitted from the mind of a person who understands how they work. Once they are activated, they can inform this person about right action. These kinds of keys that open doorways into the library of Knossos are all over the temple. These keys are signets of Atlantis.

I stand in front of one of these griffins, and to my etheric eye, it becomes an Atlantean winged sphinx. Holding the crystal rhyton, I tune my pineal gland to the spirals on the sphinx, and I send it energy from my higher brain centers. As I do this, I feel a knowing in my chest above my heart, and I agree to trust my inner wisdom. I turn around to see Didymus standing before me like a thunder god. I can see the kundalini energy in his fiery eyes—his "ray gun" energy—and I know he is going to try to destroy me with it.

Facing him, I reveal no feeling, offer nothing that he can learn. I know that if I give him the slightest power, he will only use my energy to invade and control me and others until he has learned how to face himself. In a flash of brilliance, I see that others who are magnetized to his control sphere are souls who are disconnected from the power of the Earth. Didymus is that man who, having sold his own soul to get something he wanted, toys with humans as though they were dolls or puppets. He is Mephistopheles; he is Dr. Faustus, and he likes to gobble people up, just like a grinning crododile. But now I stand before him coursing with the powers of the grandmothers, the last goddess to be one with Mother Earth.

Showing nothing, offering nothing, I regard Didymus very sweetly with a vacuous, feminine smile, and his face dissipates into dust. He becomes a faceless form lying in a time warp. Centuries from now, he will still be there at Knossos, a white face with black hair that lies in leaves that flutter when coolness seeps into the courtyard at dawn or when the sun sets. He embodies the Faustian pact with the devil, the dilemma faced by all humans when gods attempt to feel through them. He lies there holding the energy open for that moment when any human agrees to sell his or her soul for power or longer life.

I walk through the space where Didymus was standing and climb the stairs to the room above the throne room. There I begin observing the bull dance. Ahuru, a Thracian initiate, has just come up from the initiation pit by the sacred spring on the east side of the temple. He has ascended the sacred stairway slowly, meditating on each step, remembering the records of love in time, as all male initiates at Knossos are taught to do. This temple teaches that domestic harmony is the pathway to bliss, and that such harmony is attained by ascending each step in its right time.

Now Ahuru stands opposite me across the courtyard. Meanwhile, the bull, which has been released from the pits, runs enthusiastically toward him from my side of the plaza. At the same time, in the very center of the plaza, the etheric form of an ascension pyramid shimmers into visibility, like rays of sun shining through mist.

The pyramid is being holographically transmitted from the fifth dimension into the third. From a fifth-dimensional perspective, it is completely visible and looks as though it were carved of clear crystal. Due to the unusual powers of this plaza, where light forms manifest under the open sky, nothing will ever be constructed in this space. Besides Ahuru, the bull, and myself, no one else can see this pyramidal form.

Ahuru walks forward into the plaza. We are all smiling—even the great bull seems to be. As Ahuru and the bull converge on one another, Ahuru flips into the air by grasping and then springing off the horns of the bull. He somersaults over the great beast and touches down on its haunches, then he flips over again behind the animal as the bull moves through the pyramid of light. The bull shivers with delight, like a dolphin diving beneath the surface of the sea.

To observers, Ahuru seems to have taken a gigantic leap, but in reality he has catapulted into the fifth dimension by scaling the holographic form of the pyramid. To those who are watching, it looks like he is doing a handspring over the bull. In reality, he has flipped himself over the bull by utilizing the support of the pyramid of light. Thus, Ahuru and the bull eloquently reminded the people about how realities intersect when participants act together in trust.

Inspired by the dance, the fifteen hundred observers are themselves elevated into total trust. This dance is a primal form that demonstrates nonsolidity and nonrigidity in matter, teaching us that we all have the same capacities as the performers. The bull dance is perfection, and it creates great and spontaneous joy among the crowd of spectators. Everyone sees something different.

As for me, the dance creates new and even more amazing forms. I stand in a room filled with blue monkeys climbing etheric trees of life laden with fruit, and I am given a pear. In the distance, Ahuru places a wreath of lilies on the bull's neck and prepares to go to the pedestal to take the crystal rhyton of Knossos as his prize. But he will not find it there, for *I* am holding that prize. And now I realize that holding the rhyton has enabled me to see the fifth dimension, to see how other realities create images that manifest.

Ahuru stands in front of the empty pedestal. Another man ascends the grand staircase and stands far behind the pedestal as he watches me from the other side of the great plaza. This is the man who has been chosen to marry me in the spring. Next, King Minos comes up the stairs and walks out onto the edge of the plaza. He stands next to my future husband. I walk across the plaza, approaching to honor the king. I offer the rhyton to Minos. As I hold it out to him, he says, "Is there anything you desire? You may keep the rhyton for yourself if you so wish."

"You ask me if there is anything I desire," I respond. "Do you mean that I can have anything I ask for?"

"Yes," he replies.

"I cannot ask unless you first receive the rhyton," I say.

As King Minos takes the bull cup from my hands, I turn around and hold my marriage hand out to Ahuru. Ahuru approaches me. Then, in front of the person who was chosen by Didymus to be my husband, I take Ahuru's arm and say to the King, "This is the man I will marry."

My request is granted. Then, suddenly, I dissipate into crystalline light, sucked out to the Pleiades through the power of love. Simultaneously, I am catapulted downward into the form of Isaiah, a lifetime when my *male* powers of choice were at their peak.

I, Isaiah, mastered the fourth-dimensional powers that enabled me to carry out the agenda of Yahweh, my god, on Earth. That is why Judeo-Christians revere me so. But now it is time to rip open the libraries of consciousness, time to return to the parts of my life that were deleted from the Bible. I return now because I am greatly disturbed about the distortion of my teachings.

The fact is, I was a great channel, astrologer, and high priest of the

Temple of Solomon. This temple was the esoteric repository of the wisdom of the Kabbalah, a fourth-dimensional light-code transmission form created by the gods to teach the laws of the universe. These primordial codes trigger inner knowledge of language, light, and sound. Realities can be created by understanding this "language of light." This language was brought from Nibiru in 7200 B.C. It needed to be stored on Earth after the Nibiruans left so they would be able to use it when they returned. Thus, it was hidden in magic and ceremony, guarded by initiated priests of Enoch. But these few such as I who have mastered these fourth-dimensional skills are masters of energy—we can create realities.

I must also note that Nibiruans have been controlling information sources for thousands of years. Their priesthood created a mystique around the powers of these codes, and they manipulated the Hebrew orders by keeping the meanings in the language source—the Torah—a secret. Why? Because at the time of the Fall, they lost their ability to feel; and the only way they can feel now is through humans. So they limit human knowledge, believing that if humans knew the whole story, they would create new realities themselves and transmute into light before the gods could return to Earth to redeem themselves. Thus, the official scriptures are totally third dimensional, and secret societies and priestly orders conspire with the gods to hold their human captives in linear space and time.

I, Isaiah, created great longing and fear among humans. I tantalized humanity to continue seeking the real story, and *this intense seeking has held time in form*. In a sense, it has *bought* time—time for the gods to return and remember how to feel. But in this seeking, eventually both humans and gods will be lost because what they both seek—divine fusion—cannot be found in time. So now I must activate my teachings from the fifth dimension, the dimension beyond time. What is the real knowledge of Isaiah? What was my *true* passion? Listen, and you shall hear the truth.

During the time of Creation, all the laws of the universe were implanted on the Earth. These were the days when life was formed, days when each kingdom had its own vibratory response to the center of the Earth and the wisdom of each species was inseparably linked with that of the planet and the cosmos. In such times, a snake crawling through the grass felt its essential snake energy vibrating with Earth and sky; a jaguar prowling through the jungle felt its stellar powers vibrating with the Galactic Center; and a turtle moving slowly along inside its shell vibrated with the heart of the Mother. All life shivered ecstatically feeling its own unique movement and force. From this ecstatic expression was later born the science of divination—observing patterns in order to intuit events created through cosmic law. In their fulfillment of natural functions—slithering on rocks, climbing a tree, killing to eat, or pulsating deep within in a shell—all life forms, including humans, instinctively felt their connection to All That Is.

The jaguar and the snake are the two greatest teachers about our connection to the center of the Earth and the stars. The turtle instructs us about the meaning of being home, while the fourth major connector, the human, was created to reflect on and become more conscious of the energy that flows from Earth to sky. Even in your time, some shamanistic societies still wear the skins of great spotted cats. They also utilize the snake for various teachings about kundalini energy, and they divine the Earth forces with turtle shells. For maximum divination power in the medicine circle, the snake takes the east, the jaguar the west, the turtle the south, and the human the north.

The jaguar is pure intuition. It wanders the planet feeling sky vibrations. Blue-white energy lines radiate from its spots to all the stars, and these lines can be seen at night. Shamans who are truly in tune with the great cat can see its spotted skin reflecting star connections to the Earth. These lines from the stars radiate through the jaguar's body and pass through a vent of light that opens into the center of the Earth.

People fear the jaguar because it knows so much. All cats are pure feeling, and unlike many animal species, the great cats do not see humans as superior to themselves. On occasion, they will even eat a human, but only if that human fears them. The great cats remind us that there is a basic animal level in all of us that is not to be judged—that there must always be a space within us that is reserved for wildness and mystery.

As for the snake, the geometry of its skin is symbolic of all the patterns created by the movements of heavenly bodies and the angular relationships between things. The snake is the basic teacher about how life energy expresses itself in movement and measure. The snake's skin displays chevrons, squares, and diamonds, and its body can become a moving spiral of waving lines. This is why snake symbols appear so frequently on the walls of temples and caves. Such symbols can be found all over the Earth, but they can be read only by the heart, not by the logic of the mind.

The geometric patterns on the snake's skin are perfect representations of the geometry of the Solar System. These include secrets about the influence of conjunctions, squares, triangles, and oppositions between the planets—the very angles that astrologers use to read birth charts. In fact, the first knowledge of astrology on planet Earth was discovered by shamans observing angular relationships in the skin patterns of moving snakes. Watching the snakes helped them intuit the angular relationships between the planets in the sky. Snake astrology offered humans knowledge about how to operate in synchronicity with the solar cycles. This was very important information, and many ancient medicine societies held onto it even after civilization began to erode their traditional cultures.

Sumerian and Egyptian astrologies, on the other hand, are based on knowledge brought from other star systems. These systems, which are cat based, contain the keys to galactic astrology. However, these alien astrologers also greatly esteemed Earth astrology. When the visitors arrived, they had of course already mastered the patterns and planetary angles that direct the forces of the Sun. But they were astonished when they saw that the snake clans of Earth had obtained exactly the same information—and that the jaguar clans had mastered even stellar divination. To the Star Nation teachers, this was eloquent proof of the old adage "As above, so below"—that all worlds function by the same laws—and the indigenous astrologers were highly esteemed by them.

The initiated alien astrologers are called *Keepers of the Frequency*. They hold the knowledge of natural law based on the number *twelve*. This same knowledge was held in very ancient days by the members of the spider medicine clans, who were experts in spider divination. Grandmother Spider holds the *center*, and the angular patterns radiating out from her body mirror the force field of the Sun. Such patterns reveal a new *perspective* into solar and galactic activity for ancient Earth astrology—the geocentric view. The initiated Earth astrologers are the Keepers of Tradition, and the Mayan temple that holds their teachings is Etz Nah, which opens its records with the rising Sun every morning.

Ancient shaman astrology is based on electromagnetism, the energy of the Sun that generates life on Earth. Ancient divination based on observations of plants, animals, and minerals is simply a way of reading the varying qualities of solar-generated magnetic fields within these realms. Even modern astronomers who explore solar magnetic influences have noted the tremendous impact they have on all life. Yet ancient shamans used to read these influences by means of snake and spider divination, simultaneously feeling the rising snake energy within their own bodies. From this vibration, they could read the Earth energies—including its weather, tectonic movement, and climate patterns. While ancient shamans *felt* this energy, some modern scientists are on the verge of *thinking* their way into the same information. The Mayan temple that holds the knowledge of the Snake Clan is Chichén Itzá, which opens its records on the equinoxes.

Just as snakes reveal keys to the movement of solar forces, the backs of turtles carry secrets about land movements triggered beneath the Earth's surface. In the ancient days, there actually was a Turtle Clan that could determine compression in land masses by means of turtle divination, and the descendants of these people still tell ancient stories of continental drift. These people could also intuit the arrival of hurricanes, tidal waves, and earthquakes. The turtle's secrets are still guarded by the Cherokee and Mohawk Nations, while the snake wisdom is held by the Mayan Quetzalcoatl Clan and the jaguar powers by the Mayan Tezcatlipoca Clan. The Mayan temple that holds the knowledge of the Turtle and Jaguar Clans is Uxmal, which opens its records during the solstices.

Do you wonder that I, Isaiah, am telling you all this? I tell you because it is true, and because my real passion was not recorded in the Bible. These are teachings that undergird all humanity—all life. The return of this wisdom will save you in your troubled times, so I ask you to listen as I continue with these primal truths. They will be the foundation for your survival in the twenty-first century.

Eros, the primal life force, can be most easily detected through snakes. Ancient societies protected that wisdom because they knew it was the very basis of human survival. For example, Snake Clan shamans knew how to read the sunspots that generate climate patterns. They could also feel how the plant and animal realms would respond to these patterns and cycles. Now science is discovering how the same electromagnetic fields affect such things as climate, the Earth's ozone layer, and ecological health.

Groundedness—feeling secure on the Earth's surface—can be most easily accessed through turtle wisdom. In ancient times, activities in the inner Earth were detected by studying turtle patterns. Turtle Clan shamans (always women) detected the Earth's surface movements by *becoming* the turtle through meditation. As turtle, they intuited the meanings of the various colors, lines, and geometric patterns on the shell of the animal. Turtle Clan teachings emerge from the Inner Mother, who expresses her feelings about her home, and her patterns reveal whether or not her children will survive. The Mohawk Nation still practices this form of divination in your time.

Courage—being enlightened in the midst of darkness—is the gift of the jaguar. The ability to see the beams of light emanating from the jaguar spots into the far reaches of space is the key to this knowledge, and the shamans who had it were men. In your time, astronomers are discovering that most of the universe is "darkness," yet amazing creations that will finally humble the human ego are about to be seen.

Ancient shaman societies observed that these three animals—the snake, the jaguar, and the turtle—exhibit all of the angular and magnetic laws in the cosmos. Through these creatures, they detected the forces that create all elemental patterns. With their insights, they created powerful medicine societies and also identified the great terrestrial vortices and energy portals to the stars. In the ancient days, these revelations were their gift to the Star Nations.

Indigenous people first obtained these marvelous insights by ingesting plants such as mushrooms that contained the "enzymes" of the cosmic laws. All inhabitants of Earth are encoded with full cosmic knowledge, and these enzymes simply open this memory. The fall of the Star Nations occurred when aliens tried to take the mushrooms from the Keepers of Tradition and use them to access their medicine teachings. These fungi were to be ingested only during sacred ceremony to access higher dimensions, since they access lower realms when used in ordinary reality. The mushrooms did give the visitors an instant awareness of the profound love that created the Earth, but it also made them want to control the planet. Since they also wished to remain immortal, or separate from the solar cycles, they *saw with terrifying clarity* that they were separate from creation. They did not surrender to life and death—the rising and setting of the Sun—and thus could not taste the nectar of true human feeling. This Fall will be over only when the Star Nation teachers fully surrender to the solar cycles of life on Earth.

The teaching just described is the astrology of the indigenous people of the planet. As Isaiah, I incarnated with full Pleiadian knowledge. Therefore, I was born on Earth with the keys to stellar astrology fully implanted in my mind, because the Pleiades were involved in the primal creation of Earth. This and other facts have been stripped out of the scriptures, so let me tell the rest of the real story.

I was an ascended master at birth, one of the "shining ones" of the Hebrew orders. Because of my family bloodline, I automatically was initiated into the Kabbalistic mastery line of the Nibiruan temple teachers— the Enochian Brotherhood. Therefore, I was selected and trained for the Temple of Solomon, the priestly control center. I also felt great power from the land through the indigenous people, but in my time, these tribes were being systematically killed or driven away so that Israel could build a kingdom of the Jews.

In spite of this prevailing attitude, when I was young I became fascinated with the tribal people. In my country, these were the ancient nomadic tribes that lived in caves above the many great wadis, the dry rivers that flowed into the Holy Land. I rode an ass out to study with them when I was a young man. I studied their petroglyphs and pictographs, and they taught me snake and cat divination. They also allowed me to attend their ceremonies in stone circles, and they shared their teachings about life, called the "Tree of Jesse." Never once did they deny me their knowledge. They called themselves the "Stone People."

Meanwhile, as a result of my Nibiruan blood lineage, I was initiated into the Temple of Solomon when I was twelve. Then came a day in my training when I asked my teacher about the Stone People. He became upset. He told me they were idol worshipers who sacrificed pigs and lambs in their stone circles. He insisted that our sacred language was the word of Yahweh, given to the priests, and that all other ways to try to reach the divine were evil and would bring darkness to our chosen nation. He told me never to visit the hill clans again. Later, I heard that our soldiers had gone out and made them move away—far away from the ancestral graves and sacred sites where they tuned into the knowledge of the Earth.

After that, the temple felt oppressive and controlling to me. Even my mother conspired with the priests to make sure that I obeyed the rules. I did not understand it at the time, but my only method of communicating with my real home—the Pleiades—was by means of the Dreamtime, through the divination techniques the hill tribes had taught me. In the days when I had studied with them, I had been reawakening my stellar knowledge. My opening fascinated the people, but my inner knowledge sourced in my bloodline was coveted by the temple. The priests of the Temple of Solomon understood that my fourth-dimensional origins were of the star Sirius, since I came from the Benjamite line. There were twelve original Hebrew tribes, and each one originated from a stellar source. My Sirian knowledge was to be brought forth during channeling sessions in the temple and kept secret there. These channeling sessions eventually became a drain, because contact with the Sirians, who relate to Earth by means of Nibiruan visitations, always involved fear in some way.

Eventually I became a harbinger, warning my nation about their corruption and evil ways. I spent a lifetime ranting and railing against the wrongs done to this planet, but I was lost because I could not even access my *own* connection with the Earth. Gradually, I evolved into a gigantic head with no feelings in my body. I ended up serving the temple by arousing constant fear in the people. I missed the Stone People, but I knew that if I ever went back to them, they would be killed because of me.

In my time, the Holy Land was a major vortex that sucked in stellar knowledge and energy. It always has this function when Nibiru is returning to this solar system after orbiting out to Sirius, and the planet was due to return in six or seven hundred years. The desert people had taught me about that vortex, that portal to other dimensions, in a way that freed me to be multidimensional and not just manipulated by the Nibiruan control factor. Meanwhile, the temple priests tried to manipulate me for information that served their own purposes. But I have not forgotten the indigenous teachings that gave me access to soul's stellar source, the Pleiades. Beware, for what was done to them in my time has now occurred in your time all over the planet: the genocide of the natives of the Americas and the destruction of the Palestinians and the people of the desert is the same process. I speak to you as a prophet, because it is time for this killing to be banished from the Earth.

You must realize that the Holy Land is a laboratory of stellar control patterns. In temple secrecy, we were taught everything about the visitors, but this information was taken out of the Bible. For 300,000 years, the central agenda by the Nibiruans has been to control the Earth and the use of its resources. All this must be examined in your time, because you are again affected by events in the sky. Nibiru began returning to this solar system about A.D. 1600, and its vibratory attunement to other celestial bodies in the sky is intensifying as it gets closer to the Solar System. The Holy Land will again transmute into a portal, sucking in energies from Nibiru as well as from other stellar bodies, awakening memories of past experiences between the people and the visitors.

The central vortex in the Holy Land is the Dome of the Rock in the Temple Mount. When I was high priest in the Temple of Solomon, which was constructed over that gigantic rock where the visitors first landed, I tried to get the temple priests to listen to the knowledge of the desert people. But they would not listen; their mind-sets were fundamentalist and judgmental. They believed that the power of Earth is sealed in the great rock, originally a primary sacred site of the Stone People, and that this power would destroy them if it were not sealed up. They built the Temple of Solomon over the rock to control its emanations. Now there is an Islamic temple sealing the rock, and far below it are caves and pools of water, awaiting the return of the visitors. In ancient days, the visitors required much water in this dry land, because they were reptilian. The wadis of the Stone People were once lush river valleys.

The day will soon come when those who would not listen in my time will rue their blindness. This energy vortex of the Dome of the Rock will spin again, drawing in great forces. It will remind everyone that the land belongs to the people and not to any one kingdom. As Isaiah, I reveal to you that the land will again be released by the elements—earth, air, water, and fire. There is nothing to fear about this natural, elemental orgasm, but if you are not careful, as the people take on their power again the Holy Land could once again become a theater of anger and bloodshed. How can this be tempered? Every time compassion is called for, open your hearts. The elements will respond to the pain of the lambs. You do not need to take sides; you need only to eliminate your own judgment and assist others when they call out to you.

Many individuals now know the secrets of the stellar influences. Much is also known in the late twentieth century about the other bodies that periodically travel into this solar system and alter its harmonics. But what is not known is how these influences will behave this time, since each visitation is always a new stage of evolution.

Those leaders who know about the secret teachings tend to hide this knowledge, believing it is better for their people not to know. Look hard, for example, at American military support for Israel by politicians who are anti-Semites. These are actually evil men who want control over Israel's vortices. Or notice how certain politicians in the Middle East are incredibly power hungry. If you watch them carefully, they are cold-blooded like reptiles, dangerous to all that exists. Also beware of taking gifts that are repaid only in blood. Many people in power in the United States contain an idealism in their energy fields that is manipulated by Nibiru and other visitors. They *believe* they could create a better world if they could just have enough control. But that is what led to the taking of land and the destruction of the indigenous people in the first place.

Similarly, those who are invested in running the Americas think they have destroyed the spirit of the indigenous people, but the people are rising again. It is important now for all of you to examine the original genocide that was carried out in these lands. The purpose of this genocide — which over several centuries involved eighty million people — was to allow the invaders to take the land instead of learning from the people. This occurred exactly when Nibiru began returning to this solar system around A.D. 1600. This takeover needs to be carefully examined in light of what was done in the Holy Land. Without such a lucid examination and admission of the truth, all political realities will continue to be based on genocide and greed.

The ability to contemplate these issues is a sign of deep healing. You are living in the time of the return of the fallen angels. As the present time is always new, we do not know what form their return will take. Since they have been incarnating as humans since 1600 B.C., this return involves healing separated parts of ourselves. Perhaps they are all here right now.

We must be open to the possibility that our own redemption includes the healing of these angels. However it will be, the most important need now is to open our hearts and surrender to this great healing, and the way to do that is to *cease fearing anything that is different from ourselves, including extraterrestrials*. We are all one; there is no "other."

Long ago, humanity did not live in perpetual fear. The *fear program* was created first in the Holy Land, because this vortex carries strong memories of invasions, mostly by the Nibiruans. Due to confusion resulting from this energy form, the Holy Land tends to trigger desire, fanaticism, and judgment. But from deep inside the temple, Israel genuinely believes it has been chosen to caretake this portal. Therefore, it must first clear all its own fears and judgments in order to accomplish such a great task. The Holy Land is the geomantic zone where relationships between Earth and Nibiru evolve, and we have now returned to the same point in the thirty-six-hundred-year cycle when Yahweh appeared before. Thus, a war in heaven can be averted only by resolving the central judgment—the belief that *anyone* has the right to control Earth, to "own" land. It is also time for everyone to remember that the "chosen people" are actually each baby chosen by its family and community to be born and each abandoned person who is given shelter. Otherwise, belief in racial superiority will generate the belief that some are "chosen" to survive, while everyone else can just die of AIDS, poverty, drug use, or environmental catastrophe.

Isaiah's dive into the Holy Land was very intense. He incarnated into the Tribe of Benjamin, but his higher self—his fifth-dimensional body—was sourced from Alcyone in the Pleiades. This was during a time when the Holy Land was developing its full patriarchal powers in preparation for the birthing of the Messiah. Isaiah was frustrated because he remembered the "light" of his true home at his own birth here, yet the political and moral fabric of his time was dense and dark. In this life as Barbara, I have been confused in a similar way because my fifth-dimensional body also came from Alcyone with full Pleiadian light, and these times, too, are dark. I experienced terrible shock when I incarnated, and this revived my fear of the future, which I had inherited from Isaiah. I felt confusion as I once again encountered density, control, judgment, abuse, and violence. And when I first encountered Isaiah while under hypnosis in 1982, I could barely handle the intensity of his energy.

The splitting of the atom by the American physicist Enrico Fermi in December 1942 was what sucked me into form again; this happened for many individuals in the early 1940s because this shattering of matter disturbed cosmic time lines. Once here, I first concluded that I could not possibly have chosen to reincarnate—

surely it was all a trick! Gradually, I accepted the implications of what I had done, and I decided to stay in for the long haul. From my lifetime as Isaiah, I had learned that control is the central evil; hence I am deeply suspicious of any authority or belief system—especially male esoteric secret societies. The light must be allowed to penetrate into all the dark places now.

The interesting thing about Isaiah is that he was trained through the Kabbalah, but he felt his contact with the Divine through the sacred teachings of the indigenous people. So I was born with a powerful awareness that indigenous knowledge is the wellspring of the Earth. It occurs to me that most great masters are instructed by the lineage into which they are born. But what if that lineage is cut off from the wisdom of the Earth, as it was for the patriarchs? Now I think I see the essential patriarchal flaw: in the patriarchal past, ascended masters who came primarily from Nibiru were recognized and initiated into the various esoteric orders such as the Kabbalah, but they were separated from the people by the priests of the Temple of Solomon.

Kaaba, a fallen comet, is the sacred stone of Islam, and Allah is "the One." It is incredible to me that the Muslims and the Jews would go to war when the sacred scripture of the Jews, the Kabbalah, is "sound keyed" to represent the Kaaba fused with the name of the Creator, Allah. My past-life initiation into the Kabbalah has created a block in my male side that I must now try to understand. Old perceptual patterns that have gotten in the way must now be transformed.

The ancient esoteric schools encoded all their initiates with a belief in secrecy. Codes were inserted into our bodies, locking in forms that were designed to be reactivated in future lives. Each of these secrets is loaded with explosive, polarized energy, and if one talks or writes about them, energy is ignited in other people that compels those people to oppose the "heretic." It is now time to examine each one of these hidden taboos, time to share knowledge that can show us how to survive.

As I tune into the images of higher wisdom, I see that the Kabbalah is an old Nibiruan communications system that lies dormant in me from my life as Isaiah. This system is blocked, due to all the doorways called "secrets," particularly Nibiruan secrets. These secrets are the same energy forms that control Jerusalem and the Temple Mount, and millions carry these blocks. In present time, they take the form of access to knowledge by control codes, rather than by following intuition and feeling. In other words, we are frozen in our ability to just follow what we actually intuitively know.

Judeo-Christian-Islamic religions have made Isaiah into an idol, yet that admiration for him activates the part of me that I find to be the most dysfunctional. Isaiah was an emotionally laden, oppressed wounded-healer hero who *was kept captive by the judgments and belief of nations, lineages, and religions. He is a prime example of the Promethean complex—a male tethered to the mountain by angry birds who represent the hauntings of his past failures. Within me also is the Christ—the hero who knew of the light to come but who in his time could only open the door for its entry. These inner battles—always of the past— block my feelings about present reality.*

The confusion from my life as Isaiah stems from my decision to trick the temple. One day in meditation, I created a ball of light, as I had been first taught to do on Alcyone. I figured that if I deposited this ball of light into the temple, then when the Messiah brought the light of the Creator into density he would be safe on Earth. The temple would hold that light as protection for Christ once he incarnated. I put the ball of light into the inner sanctum, though I knew I was not supposed to do so. Deep inside, I knew I was attempting to control the Earth by using the temple vortex energy in order to protect the Christ.

Next I began prophesying the arrival of the Christ. However, as I gazed into the future, I saw that although he did incarnate, he would die on the cross. To me, this meant he was not protected after all, and this caused me to judge myself. I believe that I put Jesus on the Cross, just as most of you believe that you put Jesus on the Cross. This belief has resulted in negativity about incarnating on Earth, in a core belief that tragedy and destruction will always be the result of being born. Therefore, it seems to us that all we can do once we are here is try to control everything—make sure we are among the 144,000 chosen people, while everybody else can go to Hell.

But this is a lie! Isaiah is not really connected to all this tragedy and destruction, and Christ probably didn't die on a cross, either, just as John Kennedy did not get shot by a lone assassin. I have allowed Isaiah's confusion to suck me into the historical process. But the light that Isaiah put in the Temple of Solomon, the light that I carry myself, and the light that Christ brought to this planet are not connected to the historical process! I can see the light, and I can learn how to just be with that light, while the forms that manifest around me are only passing in time. Time is the historical process—a linear labyrinth created for us to walk through. And that labyrinth will move us finally back to unity.

Now I see all my self-judgments in time rapidly spiraling to an apex. I feel a cellular clearance from the rushing light—an extreme form of clearing that will happen to each person as all historical imprints are released. It is important that I have no emotional response to the historical process, to the dramas. I must strengthen the witness, the part of my higher self that sees with detachment and simply allows. Letting go of the drama does not mean that I forget and don't react; rather, it means that I observe with detachment and do not look back when it is time to leave.

We are each here now from our central stars in order to bring our own most important teachings. It is as if we were mollusks holding precious pearls, ready to be lifted out of the water and into the Sun. Our sense of identity expresses itself as history because that is how we reflect on ourselves. Now it is time to move beyond history and deliver our teachings from the Source. History has an over-shadowing effect that will dissipate when the drama is cleared.

I see a shell cut in half, revealing an exquisite Moebius curve. This curve reminds me that shells are the sacred keepers of sound and vibration. An empty shell is the central symbol of the library of Alcyone, the library in the Pleiades containing only the imprints of the central Source. The Mayan temple that holds this teaching is Teotihuacan, which is activated by blowing conch shells in front of the Pyramid of the Moon. This causes the pyramid to vibrate, and the vibration sends a sound wave from the inner chambers of the Shell Temple that activates the Galactic Center and the center of Andromeda Galaxy. This shell shows how we can be at one with our light bodies and not feel the pain of time, the pain of history.

As I walk through the time spiral held by the empty shell, I know I must visit the central library of Alcyone. But in order to remember how to get there, I must return to a lifetime when I was as powerfully encoded as Isaiah, but when I was working with a female body and could *feel* those codes as well as know them intellectually. So I return to my life as a woman, to a time when I came to Earth carrying the records of the central Source.

I am Inanna. I stand with my hands out, with owls and lions at my feet. I am mistress of the animals, and I wear a cloth-and-feather headdress. As I tune into the light of the feathers, I can feel them penetrating my head like hair deeply rooting, transmuting it into an owl's head. My head is smooth and round, and all the feathers on it fit together perfectly. When the wind blows through them, they ripple like waves of sea water. They feel like my own hair.

Next I sense the feathers around my golden eyes. This activates my awareness of being in my wings, my shoulders, and my arms, and I see the symbol of the North Node of the Moon that I hold in my hands, signifying the choice to be born on Earth. I stand in my owl body holding the North Node of the Moon, calling to the people. I am calling to souls in the etheric plane to enter into this place at their chosen time.

I, Inanna, am the owl Earth guardian, eternally holding its gates open for all those who choose to enter. I maintain this force so that beings can arrive at the right time and right place. All those who can feel me as mistress of the animals come when they choose to. It takes all my power to *hold* this force, and my animal helpers stand with me so that the incarnational process functions in attunement with all life. I hold eternity—the consummation of all life in time. But as I stand here now, I can feel that the other animals—lions, owls, snakes, turtles, foxes, wolves, and cats—are getting tired of supporting me.

The other animals have traveled with me because they have been fascinated with my dream. When I appear in the forest, they are activated by my fluttering wings. As I fly, the Earth becomes electromagnetic. Crystals in water and in caves emit tones, and animals hear these tones in their inner ears. I see the animals in my inner eye, and they fly and walk with me. But now they are losing interest. If they desert me, I will no longer be able to hold the gates open.

The forest of the Dreamtime where the animals exist as pieces of me is the reality that contains the human subconscious. Within the subconscious, humans feel the same electromagnetic forces the animals hear in their bodies. In this way, humans differ from animals. Rather than experiencing this force through instinct, humans feel it through archetypes and memories. Now I must dive into this pool of the subconscious.

I, Inanna, want to dive into this pool as the owl because the owl is the activator of my instinctual self. Owl has sight into all species, and the Goddess has kept the planet in balance by reading what owl can see. In owl's sight is the harmonic form that attunes people to electromagnetic fields. When the control archetype came to Earth through various alien influences such as Nibiru, gradually human trust in their ability to read these fields disappeared. Teachings were brought in that said gods such as Zeus and Yahweh—or even snakes, fire, and dragons—controlled lighting bolts and the Earth's electromagnetism.

The Owl Clan people began to fear that if they did not obey the visitors, the Earth would be struck by millions of lightning bolts and the forests would burn. They feared that all this lightning would create great storms, volcanoes, and extreme electrical polarity, weakening the Earth's natural frequency. In response to the heightened electricity, the Goddess heightened the Earth's magnetism. Then, with their incredible sight the owls flew over all the forests on the planet, flapping their wings and flashing their eyes, creating more and more magnetism. In turn, this magnetism created water and crystals. It also created ley lines—flowing conduits of electricity in the Earth—that the animals could follow. Aeons ago, there was an awesome moment in time when the skies were filled with lightning bolts made by the gods, and the owls and other creatures of the forest responded by creating pulsating magnetism. This heightened the sexual energy on the planet, and crystals were formed to hold all this erotic force.

As Inanna, I feel a magnetic bond with my animals. The electricity that ignites me is kundalini energy, and my animals are the meridians and *nadis* of my own body. Sections of my body are of many kingdoms. My feet, for example, are crystals. My legs are tree trunks. My pelvic area is composed of snakes swarming around with their heads and tails emerging. And my central cavity is a turtle with its shell facing outward, protecting my solar plexus. In the middle of my solar plexus below the rib cage are many fishes—schools of fishes flopping around in all directions. My rib cage is made up of the claws and feet of a lion whose body flies out behind my own. My arms and shoulders are those of a great eagle, and my heart is a scarab. Through my neck coils a snake with open jaws, its fangs reaching into my skull. And my skull itself is the head of the snake with a bird emerging from its crown—a phoenix or quetzal. This is how I am supported by my animals.

Deep within me is also a great pool of water—the subconscious. This contains all the memories of all the genetic expression in the universe. As the owl embodied in me, I wish to travel into this gene pool, because I want to know why humans are destroying the forest, my world. The owl flies into my great Goddess subconscious and asks, "Why do you take away my opportunity to fly, to nest in trees, to hunt rodents for my young?"

The voice of my subconscious replies:

"In the wings of the medulla oblongata lie all the patterns of destruction that build into cataclysms. The ultimate cataclysm is the destruction of the forest. Humans are locked up tight in the medulla oblongata, but at the same time, it is the only place where they can access their survival knowledge. Survival wisdom was first locked up when the owl priestesses intensified the magnetic field of the Earth in response to the electrical storms created by the gods. You think of that event as the destruction of Atlantis. In fact, the fall of Atlantis is a future event; it has not yet occurred.

"Of course, islands have submerged and civilizations have been destroyed, but what you are really worried about is the fact that having created the nuclear age, you now see your own capacity to destroy yourselves. *That* is your Atlantis. You conceptualize Atlantis as the end result of what you are doing every day, *right now*. The technological interpretation of Atlantis by various channels is the logical end of all your present fear patterns.

"Ever since the great lightning activated the Earth's powerful magnetism, you have tried to control the Earth and have been afraid of the sky. You have been cowering like Chicken Little. Ironically, during that experience was when the orgasm—the awakening of light in the physical—was infused into your sexuality. Thus, you humans are acting out a series of behavioral patterns from this time of which you are totally unaware. These patterns all involve control of the female side by the male side—the side that believes there will be no more cataclysms as long as it is in control. Repression of naturally ecstatic female sexuality has come about as a result of this intense fear lock.

"In fact, there *will* be other cataclysms. Chaos occurs intermittently, and such cataclysms are among the most ecstatic experiences on Earth. They are times of blinding creativity and wild orgasm, like the moment of giving birth for a woman. Control and fear remove the opportunity to participate in these evolutionary epiphanies. Beings in nonphysical form do not know such exquisite heights, and they come to Earth just to experience them."

Now, as Innana, I must return to that time when lightning flashed in the sky and the magnetic field was deliberately thickened by the priestesses of the Goddess.

A quickening runs through my body. I shiver as I feel that I am getting close to the center point of Atlantis. I, Inanna, become a deer. Deer energy is very gentle, but it is also able to access enormous electromagnetic energy. Deer antlers receive the power of the lightning; they bring it through the bones and ground it into the Earth. Deer are able to hold tremendous electrical force without becoming unbalanced. This is why they were so sacred to paleolithic people, who used to watch them standing on hilltops grounding the lightning.

I am a brown and gray deer with huge antlers. I am walking through the forest, coming close to the edge. Each time I take a step, I feel little sparks in my feet. These sparks are created by the Earth's magnetism. As I step on these electrical nodes, I am guided by the Earth, and increased strength in my shoulders and haunches carries my great body along. Through my antlers, I sense a clearing ahead. As I come to the edge of this clearing, I see a fantastic temple. There, dripping cave formations form multitudes of arched doorways on many levels. This temple of doorways is made by minerals and dripping water. In the center of the temple, I see a tall spire surrounded by concentric rings of energy, pulsating to dimensions and layers of time.

The temple is emitting electric sparks. As I come closer, the sparks begin arcing onto my antlers. It is difficult to read this scene because it all happens in the high astral realms. There, everything shimmers and vibrates in rainbow rays, and I am falling into wonderment. I continue walking into the clearing, where I encounter grass and wildflowers of all colors as blue arcs of electricity make my body hum. The humming intensifies into an interior drumming and roaring, as though I were approaching an electrical station. Yes, this is in fact an electrical station.

As deer, I know that I was put here to make electricity, too. I *know* why I am here: to create more energy, which will in turn create more lifeforms. Yet I cannot resist the electrical pull of this station, even though I know it may prove destructive to me. Suddenly, an owl emerges from the forest on the opposite side of the clearing. She watches me with extremely bright yellow eyes. She is concerned about something. I continue to follow the sparks. The electricity is making my body hum intensely. As I am pulled into the power station, the owl watches intently, recording the event.

I feel very confused, driven half crazy by the power source. The owl is watching but cannot interfere in any way. Through me, she feels her own helplessness over the destruction of her habitat. Through me, she feels that her animals are not being supported by the energy fields they require. The owl watches as I am disintegrated by the power source. In my death, she sees the destruction of the species and the crying of the ancestors, but she can do nothing about it.

The deer is gone. Now, in this fascinating clearing of electrical sparks, I can feel as Inanna that Atlantis really is the ultimate destruction of humanity, which is hypnotized by the same pulsating power that captivated the deer. This voracious electrical power source presages the end of everything worthwhile—love, art, beauty, food, connection with nature, peace, and millions of species. Humans seem willing to give it all up— even the Sun—to this hypnotic power source.

Next I see a clearing at the edge of the forest. The owl is perched up in a tree. I, Inanna, am one of a band of people wearing animal skins who have gathered here. I am a priestess with thick, matted hair, and I am wearing deer skins. My band and I have come to the edge of the forest so we can see the sky. Earlier, deep within the forest, we saw great flashes that lit up the forest with an eerie green light. We have come here to find out what they are.

Now it is early evening. Darkness is coming, and we are vulnerable to animal attack, but we must discover what is going on. We are very nervous because we always remain under tree covering in the night. It is getting darker and darker. Stars begin to appear on the horizon of the moonless night. As the sky darkens, crackling pulses of light flash in the Milky Way Galaxy overhead.

We sit on our haunches in a circle, as close to the edge of the forest as possible, watching the crackling sky light up the whole savannah. For a time, it is delightful, beautiful, and fascinating. But suddenly a flashing light whips out of the sky, licking and snapping behind our necks and making sparks in our spines. It sounds like our bones are snapping in the jaws of a lion, and we are terribly afraid. The fear is dreadful and unfamiliar; we cannot name it.

A voice from the sky thunders: "You are moving toward your destiny. You cannot stop moving toward it; there are rules and laws that you must follow. You must learn to worship and obey those rules. You must worship the laws and offer gifts to the rules, and you must accept all their consequences. That is the way it will be until you reach the point toward which you are being drawn."

I do not want to obey this voice, but I accept it and the group accepts it. Unthinkingly, we implant in our bodies the pattern of following orders from God, who will tell us what to do. But the owl sitting in the tree above us has a completely different plan. The owl opens its heart to us and places within us a pattern of supportive trust in our own knowing and the wisdom of our lineages. The owl encodes us with the living knowledge that we will endure this experience—follow our destiny to its completion—while still holding the codes of the forest that vibrate with the crystal in the center of the Earth.

Like simple paleolithic forest people, in our subconscious minds we do not question deep-seated belief systems. Once people started following rules out of fear instead of acting from intuition and feelings, the endpoint had to be a completely technological civilization. If we keep on moving toward this endpoint, we will create a civilization in which all the laws and forces of nature have been mastered by science. Methods for controlling all of these forces will be achieved with machines run by humans or robots, whichever works better. And when the technology is complete and the control is total, the participants will see that they have destroyed all life.

Under perfect control, the life force is lost. Even the Atlanteans knew this. Once it is obvious that one cannot exist without the life force, the control powers—sometimes inadvertently—take the largest, most perfect crystal that can be found and activate its piezoelectric power. Upon activation of the electrical force encoded in the crystal, the death-dealing technology is finally destroyed. This is the Atlantean vision that everyone sees as the past, but it also represents the future.

The owl continues to look into the future. And she sees that the forces of control will eventually destroy their entire agenda—including themselves. Then the life force will return. That is where we are going. In the meantime, though, our belief in the structure that we think *we control and must work with keeps us stuck in the process. The choice at this point is for all of us to decide what roles we are going to play—those assigned to us by the system or those assigned to us by* our *belief in life.*

The roles we assume after August 16, 1992—the end of the Armageddon Bypass—hold the keys to our deepest beliefs about human structures and the support of life on planet Earth. Make no mistake: these choices, not our past programming, will determine our collective reality and our ultimate destiny.

Chapter Five

MULTIDIMENSIONAL PORTALS

The idea that consciousness and life (and indeed all things) are ensembles enfolded throughout the universe has an equally dazzling flip side. Just as every portion of a hologram contains the image of the whole, every portion of the universe enfolds the whole. This means that if we knew how to access it, we could find the Andromeda Galaxy in the thumbnail of our left hand. . . . The whole past and implications for the whole future are enfolded in each small region of space and time. Every cell in our body enfolds the entire cosmos.

—Michael Talbot, *The Holographic Universe*

Today there is beginning to emerge a sense that the Earth is alive and that she creates realities and responds to forces outside herself. Just as we want to hear about an adult's childhood experiences in order to understand that person better, so it is important for us to know the true story of the Earth. That story is available at planetary sacred sites, the Earth's libraries of consciousness in time. Sacred sites offer multidimensional openings to the records of the Earth, and many species are drawn to them for energy, communion, and understanding. At these sites, powerful Inner Earth energies come to the surface, and these energies attract many curious visitors from other realms. Just as there appears to be a great red eye on Jupiter when viewed from the Earth, the Earth's energy fields are visible when it is observed from space. Over time, during various cyclical interactions with alien visitors, many of these sacred sites have become extraterrestrial portals of entry.

Since Harmonic Convergence, these portals have been open, like doorways to the stars. After that key synchronization in 1987, many star beings who visited Earth long ago and who have returned in human form during this time have found themselves returning to various Earth portals. Often they have no idea why they do this—they just feel "called." From deep within, they are driven to remember the story of the Earth. As we contemplate Atlantis, the historic/futuristic concept that is shaping much of our current science and culture, let us explore various portals that can help us regain our connection to both the Earth's center and the Galactic Center.

I am Aspasia, and I have returned to Knossos on Crete, my own sacred portal. I see a white bull, a Brahma bull with a big hump on its back. This bull is a spirit guide. It seems very wise, a sacred form that carries a great deal of teaching throughout time. This is Brahma, the Creator, who brings forth the wisdom of manifestation. Within this time capsule are all information, all tools and techniques, all mechanisms, all the laws of nature.

A plaza unfolds before my eyes, a *temenos*—sacred time, sacred space, a sacred precinct. The bull is on the left side of this sacred space as I stand waiting at the opening of the temple. Next, I see it running free in that open space. As I watch the bull, I am also seeing myself standing and observing the open plaza from the small courtyard on the south. Behind me are large bull horns. I turn around and gaze through them to the south, where I see a mountain. This mountain is the source of the crystalline rock that makes up the building blocks of this place. I was initiated by the grandmothers inside its caves when I was seven years old. I turn and walk up the stairs to the central courtyard. It is early morning just before sunrise, and only the bull and I are here.

All this seems strange because I began this experience as a fifth-dimensional return to this space; that is, my soul was drifting in timelessness when I felt an urge to return to Knossos. Anyone here now in the solid dimension could actually sense a priestess standing in this space. They could also feel the presence of the bull in the courtyard, though we are actually invisible.

I look all the way across the courtyard to the northwest corner. There, I see a disembodied head with a white face lying in front of the adytum that is in front of the throne room. It is the face of a poet, an archetype caught in an unexplored dimension. The head lies on the ground in leaves and dust; a light wind rustles the debris. In the throne room itself, griffins lie on benches facing a carved crystalline throne. This room opens into the adytum, where a great black basalt water basin rests on a crystal stand. Between the adytum and the central plaza are three wide, square columns. The adytum is the only room that opens onto the main courtyard at ground level. Here, oracular revelations are received from Andromeda Galaxy through the ancient spiral to the sky in Athens, and these wisdom teachings rule the activities in the courtyard. In the old days, all the peoples of our lands were united by their ability to communicate with other realms at the various oracular temples. That is where we got the latest news. Above this room is a room decorated with paintings of blue monkeys and dolphins.

This experience is fifth dimensional, far removed from solid time, and there are no people here. I look away from the corner, trying to forget the face in the leaves, and begin walking into the main courtyard, where the bull dancers do their ceremonies. I have been waiting to return to this central courtyard since my soul as Aspasia, linked so deeply with Barbara, was first created. Like a pollen-filled flower and a sacred bee, we are ready to become fertile together. There is a key in the bull-dance ceremony that is a critical link to fifth-dimensional existence, a place within that calls to me but is very hard to attune to. I ask for spherical-time integration, and whooosshhhh!!! I merge into Barbara in the soul dimension.

I went to Knossos at summer solstice of 1989. As soon as I walked into the empty courtyard just after sunrise, a colorful vision of the bull dance came to me. I could actually see Ahuru as the main Thracian dancer and Aspasia just as they were thousands of years ago.

Then I remembered more about these two primordial lovers. I remembered that Aspasia was the main priestess for the temple of Knossos during a phase before it was destroyed in a massive earthquake. She remained until she was nineteen, though she was not the daughter of royalty. Priestesses were selected because of their energies and star charts, not because of their bloodlines.

When Aspasia was nineteen, she was selected to officiate over the bull dance during the spring equinox. When this dance was executed perfectly, there was harmony for the next half year. That was the year Aspasia held the greatest amount of power at Knossos, and it was expected that she would play this role for many more years. But, as it turned out, that year was the peak of her power. Her initiation in the labyrinth had occurred just six months before, at the fall equinox.

Now I have a sense of two women who are Aspasia. One is the fifth-dimensional woman who first appeared here at Knossos. This woman is filled with light, and she is very large. She came here with her fifth-dimensional Brahma bull. The other is a third-dimensional Aspasia, who, like a painting nearing completion, takes form very gradually. I see her hair turning brown, her skin beginning to glow, her body becoming alive. As I look around, I notice that the fifth-dimensional Aspasia is the "I" who is seeing! Everywhere I look, the reality of the time when Aspasia was nineteen is taking form around me. This is my inner self lighting up, just as the vision of a work of art opens in the mind of a painter.

Around me I see brightly colored walls decorated with reliefs of the beautiful Minoan world—young dancers, bare-breasted priestesses, blue monkeys, lotus blossoms, dolphins, and griffins. Sturdy blood-red columns rest on crystal blocks that vibrate to the inner Earth. Soon I hear voices. I smell olive oil and ambrosia, and I see dust in the air. The more the painting comes alive, the more I feel my heart beat and the blood course through my veins. Just as the columns suck sound from sky to Earth, my soul body is sucked into form. I see many children and birds, and people dressed in their finest clothes. This is a very festive occasion.

But I am still concerned about the head of the poet—the man who died from too much feeling. This head still lies in the corner, and it is the only part of the scene that resists becoming third dimensional. This is my time-warp place, and right now I choose to leave that face alone. I turn once more to look at the corner of the precinct, and a cloud of dust dissipates the head. I will deal with my inner male side later; now I will just allow love.

That solstice of 1989 at Knossos was my wedding anniversary. My husband and I had gone into the temple early in the morning without our children to get just the right light for photographs. No one was in the central courtyard, and my vision of the sacred precinct had literally painted itself as I stood quietly watching. This hologram has now opened fully within me after seven years of contemplation.

While I was the high priestess observing the bull dance, I also received a great deal of knowledge about stellar and planetary movements. Just as with the Mayan ball game that used to be played in an open courtyard, these bull dances also opened the portals to multidimensional realms to reveal unparalleled cosmological knowledge. All the movements in the cosmos are synchronized with these portals, and sacred dances and games set up dramas that reveal the map of the sky. From such portals, nine different dimensions can be penetrated by seers. Seeing such sky maps by observing bull dances and ball games is sixth-dimensional sight.

During the Minoan bull dance, I learned some critical things about the cycles in the sky. For one thing, I saw the arrival of a great red star, comet, planet, or Red Sun in the sky, and I saw the eruption of Calliste/Thera (Santorini) that was triggered by this visitation. I could see that the temples of Karnak and Knossos would be severely threatened by earthquakes, tidal waves, and fire in the sky. Then these strange sky happenings would cease for more than three millennia.

As Aspasia, I warned the people many years after this vision. I participated in the global, sacred-site activations when this body was rising like a Red Sun. I eventually died in the chaos that ensued, and then I remembered that catastrophe when I returned about a hundred years later as Ichor, an Egyptian astrologer-priest under Thutmosis III and Amenhotep II. In that lifetime, I made my secret knowledge available to the New Kingdom that was formed after Egypt was in-

vaded by the Hyksos. In fact, the Hyksos had invaded Egypt just because of that geophysical chaos. My secret knowledge was what caused Amenhotep IV (who changed his birth name to Akhenaton) to alter the locations of the Egyptian portals. He moved the temple locations in order to save stellar divination. Due to the cataclysm in the skies, the solar orbit of the Earth shifted from 360 days to more than 365 days, and all the alignments to Earth shifted. I had also predicted that the red star or planet would again travel completely out of the Solar System, and that then the gods would be hidden in the temples until their home planet could be seen in the sky again.

Now the invisible bodies in the skies are approaching the Solar System once more, and many of you intuitively sense the critical need for accurate stellar divination, just as I, Ichor, did when Akhenaton asked for my assistance. The time is approaching for the wisdom of the hidden gods and goddesses to become manifest on Earth again. The key to this manifestation is the Aton, the solar deity accessed by Akhenaton. To better understand what is coming, hidden truths of these pasts are being revealed through my incarnations as Aspasia and Ichor. The Aton was a type of sixth-dimensional sight that was similar to Aspasia's sight in the plaza at Knossos. It was a device for seeing the invisible by decoding the light spectrum. Astronomers are now making telescopes that can make these "invisible" frequencies visible, and people will be surprised at what was known in the time of Aspasia and Ichor once modern science catches up. For now, no one knows these secrets better than Ichor.

I am Ichor, carrier of the blood of the gods. I am an Egyptian astrologer of the Eighteenth Dynasty. Aeons ago, I was spawned in Khemit, the black Nile mud, and I love this planet more than I honor my priestly programming to guard secrets and hidden worlds. I have returned in your time to tell ancient truths about the sky connections that were made after we expelled the Hyksos from our sacred river valley.

What has been kept secret for thirty-five hundred years now must be told, because Earth is moving into the early stages of influence by the Red Sun and the four bodies that travel with it in the sky. These bodies are very cold and can be seen only with telescopes or vision that can access the infrared range. That is why even Aspasia was not sure *what* she was seeing when the appearance in the sky came during her lifetime.

The *neters*, or archetypal expressions of these four planets—lion, eagle, reptile, and bull—have already begun to profoundly affect your reality. Notice how fascination with totemic powers is building. But keep in mind that the return of these archetypal totems simply means that you are seeing more of the light spectrum. Have you never wondered why the Egyptian *neters* are depicted as combinations of animals and humans? Do you not think it is significant, for example, that the archetype of body/mind healing is Chiron, who is half human and half horse? Notice how a subtle opening to receive these totemic powers is building in your life.

Since 1987, the archetypal parts of your own being have become quite obvious to you, and sometimes this is shocking. Some of you have begun to see that you are not only human, but also part lion, part crocodile, part bird, and part bull, as well as other animals. Do not be concerned, for the integration of these parts of yourself is all part of your current journey beyond fear and judgment. It is all part of the return of visitations in the sky and the archetypal powers associated with them.

The return of these archetypal powers is also a result of your ability to perceive wider spans of the light spectrum. This expanding vision is your key to integrating all the dimensions into your awareness. This broader awareness is natural, but it was once taken from you by "the gods." The Nibiruans and other visitors—those demigods who felt disconnected from the Source—narrowed your perceptive abilities in order to help themselves materialize on Earth. However, now that they have nearly completed their tasks, it is time for you to again possess a wider perspective.

Akhenaton, a most wise and compassionate Egyptian ruler, knew all of this. At my insistence when I visited him from other dimensions after my death, he relocated the Egyptian star portals so that they would be shut down until A.D. 1987. He knew that Egypt would be entering a very dark time. Akhenaton actually knew there would be a massive earthquake in 27 B.C. at the Temple of Karnak, which would enable the Romans to steal precious Egyptian power objects such as obelisks. So he shut that portal down. He also knew the Nibiruans would incarnate as Romans soon in order to experience Earth wisdom. And he knew their desire for power would be especially strong around the time of Christ. He even knew that they would take the obelisks to Rome to empower the Vatican. In his wisdom, Akhenaton could see that the Nibiruans would fall even farther from grace if the obelisks still had power. Thus, he deenergized them by altering the flow of energy beneath them before they were even removed.

Akhenaton has been greatly misunderstood. He was the last Pharaoh who possessed all the knowledge of the two cycles—the cycle of Nibiru and the cycle of the Red Sun—that would regulate extraterrestrial karma on Earth. He knew exactly what he must do to minimize the powers of the Nibiruan fallen angels. However, it is difficult to see what he was teaching because his new temples were systematically destroyed by the priests of Amun. It is even more difficult to perceive his true intentions because these priests completely falsified the real history—just as the Christians did with the history of the Gnostics two thousand years later.

Historically, for example, Akhenaton is depicted as a monotheist, yet such a concept was absolutely foreign to the Egyptian mentality. For ages—ever since this great deception began—so-called experts on Egypt have focused on its "one-god mentality," thereby hiding not only the truth of Akhenaton, but the real gift of the Aton. This ridiculous lie has served as a block to accessing the rich fabric of the Egyptian's polytheistic psychology.

The Aton is actually the access symbol to twelve-strand DNA in synchronicity with the twelve solar houses and the twelve stellar fields. When used in the proper state of mind, the Aton is capable of opening what is called the "DNA spectrum of light," the light of divine contemplation—the samadhi experience in humans. Why is it not known as such? Simply because the priests of Amun craftily and completely diverted human thought into monotheism. Employing massive deception, they split everything into the duality of good and evil, thereby blocking human awareness from its natural access to the twelve simultaneous levels, the key to light. Monotheism and its resulting dualism constitute ignorance, which in turn is darkness.

By the end of the New Kingdom, many other teachings were hidden as well, including the Sirian lion wisdom of Sekhmet, the Nibiruan lizard consciousness of Sobek, the Andromedan and Pleiadian bird wisdom of Horus, the Red Star vulture and spider wisdom of Ma'at, and the Sirian dark-star knowledge of Anubis. But these totemic sky powers are reemerging in your time as their ruling bodies return to your solar system between 1977 and 2013. Shamanic work with these archetypes will help to open up your natural twelve-level perception once again.

Because of the falsehoods that have been spread about Akhenaton, we can be sure that there must have been a reason for such a massive cover-up. The image of Akhenaton that was put forth in this reversal is very Nibiruan. For example, he is depicted in a strange and crippled body, and these images subconsciously trigger people to think of him as an extraterrestrial, genetic aberration. Though it was customary to depict pharaohs as perfect humans, regardless of what they actually looked like, the priests of Amun reversed many of these archetypes when depicting Akhenaton and his family in order to fool people in the future.

In fact, Akhenaton was a compassionate humanitarian who attempted to salvage Egypt before a dark age began. His *real* agenda was the building of temples oriented to the Pleiades and the Andromeda Galaxy:

he could see that the Pleiadians would be able to help humans resolve conflicts through stellar harmonics, and Andromeda held the key to the new solar alignments resulting from the 365-day year. But these new temple portals with obelisks and *ben bens* (models of spaceships that were used as capstones for pyramids) oriented to the Pleiades were energetically closed throughout most of Egyptian history until A.D. 1977. The sites of Akhenaton's temples will be *very* powerful sites for Pleiadian and Andromedan connections after that year. The transmission of knowledge from these temples to the rest of the planet will intensify until 2013, when the Pleiadian and Andromedan teachings will be fully implanted in this solar system.

Akhenaton saw all of this thirty-five hundred years ago. He was a key wisdom teacher of the past, and he will reemerge between A.D. 1996 and 2013 as the ancient keys to the light are accessed once again. These teachings must be completed by the time we make contact with our mirror planet, Aion, in Andromeda Galaxy, or another drama of Horus and Set—another war in heaven—will be played out. The Pleiadian and Andromedan codes can be understood by studying the Aton, the radiating solar symbol of twelve rays with twelve small hands gathering wisdom from Earth, which represents the activation of twelve-strand DNA.

Great truth is always found in the centers of great suppression. Secrets are evil because they hide knowledge, and the hiding of knowledge is always used to control other people. Now is the time to eliminate the control of humans—time to bring all secrets out of the shadows and into the light.

With this in mind, I would like to talk about another man who has been misunderstood: Moses, the unifier of the Twelve Lost Tribes. Unbeknownst to most people, Moses came to Akhenaton's court at Ra Aton, east of the Nile. He appeared there in fourth-dimensional form, as he often did throughout the reign of the New Kingdom before his actual incarnation during the reigns of Thutmosis III and Amenhotep II. He was one of the first Nibiruans to incarnate after the rising of the Red Sun in the west at Baalbek. Moses was called Mosheh by the Egyptians, but that was not his real name. To his fellow Nibiruans, he was known as Illuru, meaning "going down to Earth" or "crossing planetary orbits to reach those whom he shepherds."

Moses, then, came to Akhenaton's temple as a Nibiruan wearing a lizard mask—a mask made of hatred for all Egyptians. He wore this mask because he had been castrated by me, Ichor, during a great battle the Nibiruans waged against Egypt. In history, this great battle is called the Passover. At the time of his fourth-dimensional return, Moses was as two-hearted as anyone who burns with the fire of revenge. I, his hated enemy, watched him in the fourth dimension as he utilized his magical powers. I watched him materialize before the startled Akhenaton at the exact moment the great ruler was shifting the energy of the Egyptian temples away from the Nibiruan contact points, the temples controlled by the priesthood of Amun.

Moses had been the high priest of Amun under Thutmosis I, so he had an investment in preventing Akhenaton's transference of the temple portals to the Pleiades and Andromeda Galaxy. I was amused watching him discover that he was impotent to control those in the third dimension. But with his magical powers, he managed to lay a cloak of secrecy over Akhenaton's actions. As he did so, he said to Akhenaton, "The temple connection is buried. My people will hate the Egyptians until the fires of desire are consumed in my own body. In like manner, the Christians will hate the Israelites, the Muslims will hate the Christians, and ultimately all three will hate the harbingers of the New Age. My hatred will resound through time, and this vortex of judgment—manifesting as confusion about who is victim and who is victimizer—will allow the fallen angels to take over most of the Earth and live on the planet until their hatred finally burns to ashes in their hearts. This hatred will generate paralyzing fear until the people learn to transmute this fear. This will occur with reconnection to the Source in A.D. 1977."

As Moses spoke, Akhenaton saw that his own Egyptian teachings would become impotent. As he observed this lizard monster before his eyes, this powerful being who had no inner female and no feeling for Earth, his heart melted. He saw a truth that would begin to be known after August of A.D. 1992: the Nibiruans could experience Earth only in a totally male or a totally female mode. They were automatically split upon incarnation, and they would not become fully empowered on Earth— androgynous—until they ceased being angry about the loss of their immortality. At that moment, Akhenaton saw the evolution of pure patriarchy that would soon reign on Earth. He saw, *totally*, the pain of the coming thirty-six hundred years. And like anyone who has a vision of the apocalypse, he was terrified.

In this moment of connection between these two energies, the hatred of the Egyptians by Moses and the terror of Akhenaton, an absolutely demonic, unspeakable hatred of Earth energy—the female—was seeded. Soon afterward, the Romans and other "warriors of God" took political control of the great portals to the stars. They burned the great megalithic sites of the Stone People in the Holy Land, and this destruction of the

Goddess power points was a formation archetype of Israel—the patriarchy. Thereafter, women would be honored only as possessions of men. From then on, the Twelve Tribes would wander the planet until the inevitable birth of the Shadow Goddess—the Goddess energy as the male ideal. Only after August of 1992 would men birth their inner female as women birth their inner males. Only then would the Nibiruans become whole.

The creation of the patriarchy—Father Sky as human on Earth—also initiated the incarnation of a great line of teachers. These "lion teachers" would birth the inner knowledge of Sirius on Earth, the Order of Melchizedek. But ultimately, since patriarchal control can only result in the end of civilization, it would be time for the Nibiruan patriarchs to see that they had come to Earth for one reason: to release Earth from their own control!

So this is my central message as Ichor: When the Goddess teaching comes back into balance with the patriarchy—as it eventually must—then at last there will be a resolution of the Judeo-Christian/Islamic ideal based on the misguided male need to control the Earth and the female. Men attempt to control the female shadow, not realizing that unbridled patriarchal power can only destroy the Earth.

Fortunately, the original Earth teachings are still alive in the traditions of indigenous peoples. They and the intuitive feminine still remember when we all were in resonance with the Earth and the great cosmic forces. These ancient ones still hold the memory of perfect harmony with the land and the cycles, and they do not value control over chaos. These people patiently await the final days of the various power dramas to be played out.

As you search for how to reattune to the Earth now, seek out the pulse of the land. Relearn the ways of the primal species of the planet, in whom the laws of cosmic balance with the Earth are still understood. Soon you will experience communion again with your various brothers and sisters from the stars, and you will remember the parts of yourselves that come from other places. All evolved beings know that the primal people of Earth have unique and precious knowledge—and they are waiting for you to remember it, too.

I, Barbara, see to my left side a fantastic shaman-warrior holding twenty-nine brightly painted, feathered and beaded arrows. As I take my focus off him, I see a masked being in black—a night sky master—looming behind him. This being has come from the constellation Orion to give me information, but I feel great resistance to him. He stands willing to give me the secrets about what locks and ties humanity at this time if I'm willing to look into myself. The resistance I feel comes from a pattern of staying out of my emotional body in order to avoid feeling. The angelic presence in the room is very strong, but my resistance is very hard to break through. My higher self tells me to take a fine adze and dig a hole in the Earth in front of the sky master. I do so. Once the hole is dug, my higher self speaks:

"This hole has the power to heal the feelings that were blocked during all the initiatic training that has ever been given to your soul, including Ichor's ceremony of the weighing of the heart in Egypt and your removal of hearts in Tikal as a young Mayan priest. From the beginning of creation, I have traveled with this soul, and it is finally ready to clear the pain of all these old forms of heart opening. These old forms are no longer needed. What is needed now is a new way to open the heart, and soon you will be able to offer this new teaching to others.

"In the Egyptian weighing of the heart, it was necessary to use an adze to open the throat chakra of the pharaoh because he had not cleared his emotional body while he lived. This ceremony was conducted seventy days after his death when his *ka*, or spirit body, had levitated sufficiently out of the astral realm to be fused with the An Wah, the Land of the Blue Nile. As long as the Pharoah's emotional body remained uncleared, the Land of the Blue Nile would be endangered. However, in this ceremony, you as Ichor were the victim of a priestly intrigue.

"By agreement, the priests were to create a clear energetic field for pure healing in which all dimensions were open. You conducted the ceremony assuming this healing field had been established and would be held. But the supporting priests deliberately did not hold the field because of political intrigues against the Amenhoteps. This created a break in the harmony of the field and in the Land of the Blue Nile, the source of life for the people of Egypt.

"Unfortunately, the Blue Nile has planetary connections as well. Later, the destruction of the temple of Akhenaton at Karnak (also caused by priestly intrigues) created a complete inability among humans to hold the healing energetic field of the Earth, resulting in a profound inability to *feel*. Eventually, the desperate need for feeling degenerated into the heart-sacrifice rites of the Aztecs and Mayans.

The Mayans and Egyptians are both teaching races with direct links to the Pleiades. (These realms are called the Blue Chak'kab of the Mayans and the Blue Nile of Egypt.) The Mayan break in the field occurred when the high priest Maya came to Egypt to deliver the Mayan Chak'kab, the unified field of knowledge. He left Palenque when the Blue Chak'kab shattered there, and he went to Egypt to recover the keys. By the time he arrived, it had already been severed. So Maya deposited a crystal skull at Saquarra in a deep pit near the Pyramid of Unas during the reign of Merneptah. That skull was activated and the portal reopened in A.D. 1990.

"Within the Mayan field in history, teachers have returned again and again since that break in the Earth's energetic field. They have suffered terribly on Earth, but they have always held the desire for the open heart. For hundreds of years, it seemed that the only way to feel anything was through suffering, and it was better to suffer than not to feel. For many lifetimes, teachers here have been aware of the possibility of a unified healing field, but they have lived out their lives unsuccessfully seeking that dimly remembered link.

"It is not yet possible to activate this field on a planetary level; however, many individuals have already discovered keys to it by means of the wounded healer Chiron. Chiron's orbit around the Sun is fifty years, just as the orbit of Sirius B around Sirius A is fifty years. By humanity's working with the cycles of Chiron since 1977, these fields will again be linked up and synchronized with the Sirius star system as they were in ancient Egypt. The wounded healer is the guide to reconnection of the multidimensional field on Earth. I, as the higher self of Barbara, turn to Akbar, who holds the keys to this teaching."

I am Akbar from Orion. I am here today because I guard the link to Orion, the home of the fallen angels. This link is necessary for the recreation of the healing fields on planet Earth. I am here to explain how this can be accomplished, and it *will* happen as soon as a sufficient number of individuals have mastered the healing technique I am about to describe. This teaching is triangular and based on pyramid knowledge.

It is time to look at all traumatic experiences with the "separate ones," fragmented stellar beings who have incarnated at this time to learn how to stop abusing others in their attempts to remember how to feel. The essential key to the healing fields on Earth is *feeling*. All beings who come here do so in order to learn how to feel, and the healing of each one reweaves the healing web for all. This healing occurs when one who has been abused mirrors his or her pain to the abuser until the abuser finally *feels this pain*. What is the reward for holding this mirror up to another? Release from immortality. When this desire is released, one achieves total vision of the light while still in the body. Once these experiences are mirrored back, the action creates a chiral wave between abuser and abused. We will bury these traumas in a hole in the Earth, for the Earth has the power to accept and neutralize all negative experiences.

My soul, since the disconnection time in Egypt, has agreed to experience a series of lifetimes that would encode the knowledge about why humans are separated and disconnected from one another and the Earth.

My soul is a record bank from the Pleiades, poised to pierce the third-dimensional field to help you reconnect to your separated selves. The hardest part to look at is all the violence. But as you look, remember that in the darkest and most complex dilemmas lie the greatest teachings.

Tikal is the central Mayan temple that holds this teaching. I, Akbar, was Huitzilopochtli at Tikal when my soul chose to experience negative energy forces. By manipulating and tricking Itzanna there, I conducted a ceremony that implanted terrible fear on the planet. Yet Earth cannot be felt or understood without going through all life experiences. Until one has experienced something, one will always judge and be separate from it when they see it being experienced by another. But now there has been enough experience. I am here to teach you to release all of these patterns so that you can function in a new way. I am here today to show you how to take full responsibility for your lives—responsibility that will open your hearts and create true compassion for all beings.

Specifically, when my soul had the experience at Tikal as Itzanna—"one who comes down to Earth from the sky"— I was not able to clear Itzanna's emotional body before his death. My soul's form as Barbara does not have issues about what she has done to hurt others in this life. But Barbara refuses to open her full *sight* because she is horrified by the human condition. She doesn't want to look at all the pain—even the pain she has known herself—so her *sight* has been blocked at the astral level. When Barbara was young, abusive people often drew her to them and made her unhappy, but gradually she learned to see exactly what these abusers needed: time. Barbara has drawn many abusers around her to offer them the chance to learn to feel through her as well as to teach herself. There are many around her who are courageously living on the edge of darkness, as she once did. These people live in a nightmare of violence and abuse, desperately seeking just one moment of real feeling. They sense that the exact moment will be a doorway to the light, and they are right.

I, Akbar, speak eloquently about the abusers because I have existed with this nightmare from the beginning of time. But now I am ready to release my immortality. I myself am a fallen angel, one of the *Keepers of Evil*. I am one among millions here now, and I carry all the longing for the light that has existed from the instant of the first separation. Since the beginning of time, I have participated in the gradual intensification of density created out of my own desire. I have created *worlds* out of desire. To experience my longing yourself, return to the moment of breakup from one you deeply loved and remember that insatiable desire for reunion.

Notice that you did not *feel* in that moment—you only desired to end separation. That is how I exist eternally.

In the Mayan experience, this dilemma materialized to the sacrificial level—killing to end separation from God. At the present time, it has reached a new level of density, for now you believe God *is* the self, and so your technology seems to be destroying both God *and* the self.

Keepers of Evil such as myself are masters of the ancient technology of *power*. We tread well on the Earth; we are all reincarnated high priests of Amun who keep secrets for ourselves. We keep ourselves in form like vampires without victims, sucking on our last moment of hope. We toy with humanity, visibly expressing our utter contempt for life and feeling. We slither along like lizards in gray flannel suits in the military and in the CIA, in politics, in secret societies, and in greedy roles in business. Lately, we have enjoyed mimicking indigenous people by lying about our family backgrounds and becoming fake medicine women and men. But now the time has come to release our deception because we are beginning to feel. The ones who have waited and watched for us will not be lured into another game with us because they have finished their own experiences with primordial evil. As they shift into harmony, the intense fire in our opened hearts will scorch the Earth. Incredible love, focus, and wisdom will be required to bypass this war in heaven. But soon even we evil ones will help to hold the healing fields for the last days of the Luciferian rebellion on Earth.

As Keepers of Evil, we are fascinated by our manipulative skills. We are amused by the confusion we can create in others who do not see evil. But our karmic clocks are ticking, and now we are actually *seeing* what we are doing in each moment. We are murdering, raping, abusing, tricking, and manipulating everyone. And by playing out these roles, we are materializing our extreme desire to remove separation. We are *desperate* to feel. But, the time for actualizing desires is almost over now. The separation of the fallen angels will be finished in August 1993. After that time, attempts to feel by means of violence and abuse will no longer be needed.

I, Akbar, am here from Orion to inform you that a new sense of humanity is emerging from the deepest levels of your being. The connection you desire is fast approaching. Those who know this must now position themselves at the third point of the triangle—between abuser and abused, victim and victimizer—and radiate love to both sides. By making yourself into a body of light between abuser and abused, you can triangulate the energy and resolve the polarization of good and evil.

The need is for absolutely fanatical exposure of all emotional-body pain and for shifting perceptions of your roles in the dramas. For many lives, we have been in relationship with other individuals who are dealing with the teachings of pain. Now it is time to radiate love and compassion to those beings who are working with these lessons, but also to remove ourselves from the karma of these energies. Release your need to experience the pain of others. Be there to radiate love and compassion, but release the need to take on their pain.

I, Akbar from Orion, tell you that the most confusing dramas today are being staged over who has power and medicine in the middle of this incredible acceleration of energies. Individuals who once had great medicine power but who abused it have now returned to learn how to give the medicine without manipulating others. These people have been born with lineage power, and they are tempted to take advantage of others.

Those who possessed monumental knowledge in the past—the *Keepers of the Records*—have also returned. They were born into the unenlightened modern world, and they do not see how they can know what they know. As the energy accelerates at the end of time, suddenly a brilliant light will course through their systems, and they will know how to give their gifts. They will suddenly see that they must move into holding one of the four directions.

The rebirth of the medicine-clan teachers has occurred to repair the healing field on a global level. These people are called the *Keepers of Shapeshifting*, and they have activated the totemic keys that were first used to teach the visitors how to resonate with the Earth in Egypt. Up until thirty-five hundred years ago, the Egyptians maintained the temples that held the global healing field, and they avoided Faustian pacts with me and all other Keepers of Evil. They lived courageously in the present moment by means of inner exploration with animal teachings that were synchronized with the zodiac. In those times, the goddess Nut, much revered in Egypt, formed a canopy over the Earth that enveloped all species. Later, the patriarchy usurped her powers, but now, as the field is reestablished, Nut returns. Her temple, called Denderah, holds the keys to the stellar synchronicity between animals and the zodiac that enlivens the inner womb of Nut. And the pyramids in the north hold the triangulation wisdom that holds the light body in form so the Keepers of Evil can finish their experience.

In the Americas, the medicine teachings are also being activated, as individual teachers learn how to exist in the energy of one of the four directions. As each teacher is empowered by his or her own direction, everywhere they go they encounter other individuals who need the teachings of the other three directions, and these people align with them. As this happens, four pyramids of light rise, their baselines formed from each side of the square they created as they held the four directions. These four pyramids rise to form a capstone above this square base—a capstone of love that feeds the Earth and frees all four direction holders. In this way, these four individuals are pulled out of the polarity of abuser and abused. In other words, the medicine teacher first walks the planet holding a specific direction, and three other individuals who have been playing out personal karmic dramas are attracted to that teacher. The result is that the destructive triangle is broken, freed into a four-sided pyramid of light.

Let me explain a bit further, since this is a powerful healing form. Personal karmic dramas are often the last desires that need to be released by three uncleared individuals. Such triangulation is often held in form by one who loves the other two individuals who are locked together in an abuser/abused game. For awhile, the one who loves the two game players is holding space and *hope* for them. Eventually, these three individuals will draw to them a fourth person who is clear of abusive patterns—and

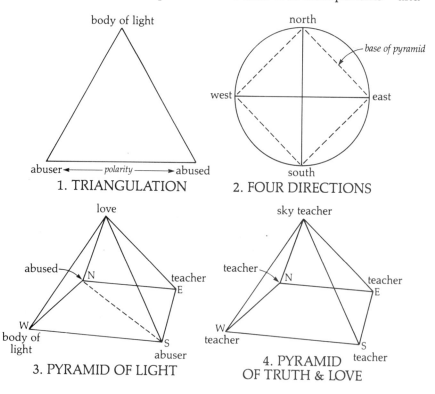

1. TRIANGULATION

2. FOUR DIRECTIONS

3. PYRAMID OF LIGHT

4. PYRAMID OF TRUTH & LOVE

is therefore a "direction holder"—and this person will *bust their agenda*. With the agenda gone, the three will lose the desire that once fueled their drama. Truly, in the coming days, you will be amazed as you watch evil dissipate in this way. You will see people dematerialize, or decide to leave the planet, as they release their desires. Hold space and clarity for the completion of such dramas in these times.

Once the work is done, the Keepers of Shapeshifting will move to another direction. When enough individuals have chosen peace and cleared themselves, they will shapeshift—that is, take a direction that reflects their own clarity. And this in turn will draw others into releasing their desires. Finally, pyramids of the four directions will be formed by four great medicine teachers, and peace will come instantly. A capstone will be formed by a sky teacher on each one of the medicine pyramids that is truth and love. This power point will bring the four tops of the triangles together, greatly activating the ground at their base. With this will come the activation of the pharaonic protection level—compassion for the Earth and all her creatures.

I, Akbar, offer these teachings in order to free myself. When evil is no longer needed for the creation of experience, I will fly back through the beltway of Orion to my peace in the night sky. I am very tired. I have worked with these teachings from the beginning of time. For thousands of years, I have pushed souls into third-dimensional experiences of power and abuse until they could activate the waters of compassion and release their feelings. Now, the Aswan Dam on the Nile allows no emotional release. You created that block to show yourselves how totally blocked you are. No water or feeling flows on the Earth in Egypt.

But the Keepers of Shapeshifting began massive triangulation healings in 1989, and all who need to be healed will soon be attracted into their proper fields. No one will be missed, but the actual healing will be a choice. In order for this healing to occur, the medicine teacher who holds a sacred direction must be conscious of the positions of each of the three wounded ones. Unconditional love must be held for one, honoring of creativity for the second, and power against manipulation for the third so that they can resist the desire for unconditional evil. The other three dancers of light will be locked in desire until the fourth door is opened. The medicine teacher must hold the energy for those who are caught in the illusion of separation. None of these other three are separate if they are really *seen*, and they can release their game through love and understanding.

If you are the one needing unconditional love, it must be clear that you will wait until the end of time for the other person to trust. If you are the one whose creativity needs to be honored, if a male, you must clearly see that there is no need to manipulate women in order to create, and if a woman, that there is no need to allow the control by males.

As for the manipulator, who always feeds on the *needs* of others, seeking love like a vampire sucking the blood of pain, simply watch exactly what they do and make sure they know you see it. Make it known that you see every person they have abused and every lie they have told—and that you know their real motivation is love.

As more and more undergo this shift, it will cause the formation of a multitude of perfect four-sided pyramids with love as their capstones. The creation of these personal capstones is in process now and will be completed by A.D. 2013. As a result of the rebuilding of these capstones up to August of 1993, the Keepers of the Frequency will be able to begin teaching on Earth again. These teachers are adept at opening portals and modulating temple sites for maximum communication with many dimensions. The Earth has become dense from the materialization of desire for the last thirty-five hundred years, and the Keepers of the Frequency have avoided its field. But with this field sufficiently cleared through the personal creation of pyramids of love, the Keepers of Frequency will again be able to open the portals to multidimensionality. You will know them when you see them.

These are my teachings about how to trust through love. I, Akbar, kick dirt over the hole dug by this soul, and I take off to travel my pathway to Orion, back to my fusion with the Divine. Now the personal portal is open, and the blue light shines clearly in the distance. Simply open your eyes and remember the way back.

BIRTHING
THE DIVINE CHILD

When I first came to this warm, green planet, there was in my
mind a diamond light receiver that reflected rainbow beams
off its inner planes—a dense crystal of star matter that
transduced laser beams from the Galactic Center.

—the divine child of Barbara Hand Clow

*Since 1985, I have been traveling to sacred sites all over the world to pray.
However, I have only just begun to feel the power of the Chippewa/Ojibway sacred
site in Saginaw, Michigan, where I was born. My home was on the edge of a
lagoon across from Ojibway Island, the sacred island of the Great Mother of the
Great Lakes. The Saginaw River flows on the west side of the island. This great
river was called the Saukenaw when the white people arrived. The treaties giving the Chippewa/Ojibway land to the white man were signed on Ojibway Island,
the home of the sacred council fires.*

*When the treaties were signed, in Saginaw the tribes were left with only
the island, the lagoon, and a section of raised land around their sacred Tree of
Life, along with its bordering marshlands. Since the beginning of time, this tree
had been home to the Great White Owl, which returned every spring equinox.
This tree also marked the spirit release of Kewakaeon, a great Ojibway chief who
in the ancient days had unified the people and made peace after terrible wars with
the Sauks. As the Great White Owl, he returned in spirit to the Tree of Life, a
channel between Earth and sky that is eternally sacred. Like the spirit body of
Kewakaeon, the souls of all tribal people traveled down to the center of the Earth
through the great root system of this tree.*

*Back in those days, the white men always agreed to whatever the natives
asked for and then violated those promises as soon as they settled enough of their
own people to be able to take whatever they wanted. So in the sacred reserve, they
cut down the Tree of Life, then built power and water plants, a Catholic cathedral,
and many houses. Then they criticized the Indians for getting drunk on their*

liquor. The former location of the sacred tree is now occupied by a facsimile of Michelangelo's "Pietà," placed directly in front of the Holy Family Cathedral. However, this Renaissance veil over the powers of the Great Mother is regularly vandalized, as if people still felt the power of the tree.

I used to live next to that cathedral. My house is now torn down, as are most of the old houses in that sick, crime-ridden city. According to ancient tribal teaching, nothing was ever supposed to be constructed on the land that has since become central Saginaw. The spirits of the tribes haunt this sacred place, but I did not understand why this was so when I was a child. Living there and walking those sacred woods, river shores, and islands pierced my heart in this life. When I was very small, I could hear the ancestors crying in the night, but no one else seemed to realize that anything was wrong. The Saginaw River collects the flow of the Shiawassee and Tittabawassee rivers, which join at Green Point, an ancient sacred site honoring the Mother Goddess. There, archaeologists have found the remains of villages thousands of years old.

The legacy of the white conquests is Dow Chemical Corporation's noxious wastes, pouring first into the Shiawassee, then moving past Green Point, flowing into the Saginaw, and finally emptying into the waters of the Great Lakes. This slime made it impossible for the river to freeze when I was a child, and it burned my fingers when I touched it. Animals that drank from the river died, but their chemically preserved bodies did not decompose, even through the hot and muggy summers. Maggots could not even hatch in their intestines. The slime poured into Saginaw Bay, killing birds, fish, insects, and animals.

No one seemed to notice the death of the woodland species as I was growing up, but I was terrified in the midst of this holocaust. I brought home baby ferrets, raccoons, and mice; fed them with eyedroppers I got from the pediatrician's office; and mothered them until they went wild. I howled in the night with the last of the coyotes. I smelled death everywhere and always was tortured by the desperate cries of the ancestors in the night.

This world into which I was born made me feel deep unease, but thankfully I arrived at a time when the awakening of humanity had already begun. My generation—those born after 1942, when the atom was split—would realize that the original Keepers of the Land must once again become the guardians of the Earth. Our generation would receive consciousness imprints that would open our brains to cosmic messages. But we would feel ungrounded until we awakened our sensitivity to the Earth, which had been disturbed by the hubristic splitting of matter. Consequently, our security with the life force itself was illusory, since the adults we thought must be our elders were involved in planetary destruction even as they said they were trying to protect us. We subconsciously concluded that our own parents were trying to kill us as we grew up in the midst of this ecocide. But now we, the **Keepers** *of the Rainbow, choose to strip off that mask of death. We choose new elders—the ancient, indigenous peoples of the Earth. Now it is time to experience the initiation of* illusion—*to strip off the mask of the destroyer, Huitzilipochtli.*

I am running very fast, wearing clothes that are light and diaphanous. I am running away from something that is pushing toward me on my right side. I think it must be the wind, but it is not—it is male energy that is trying to capture me. This energy does not have any form, but I feel its maleness. It is trying to stop me from running, from dancing, from being free, from being like the air. However, I am not afraid. I just don't want to get caught; I just want to run free. I run as though I am dancing.

I am flying back to my temple, but this energy is trying to keep me from it. I keep on running with this energy behind me on my right side. Grandfather Hand taught me to run wildly in the woods at night. Those were the times when I could fly—as a child. But now I am bounding more than flying. As I am released into the air, at first I feel light, then the energy starts to weigh me down. I descend to the ground, touch it, and then bound upward again, over and over. When I am going up, I feel light; when I come down, I feel dense.

I used to do this all the time when I was a child—simply because it was fun. Every night, as soon as I fell asleep, I bounded and flew through the night, observing the daytime world all over the planet. I flew through temples, megalithic circles, pyramid sites, forests, caves, and the streets of many towns. Occasionally I even flew into silver ships waiting for me in the sky. When I returned from these journeys, Grandfather always was anxious to hear stories of my travels.

I am now flying and bounding to my temple, which is white with Grecian columns, set on the side of a mountain overlooking a magical valley. It is bathed in iridescent pinks, blues, greens, and purples. I am bounding toward it along a curving pathway through meadows filled with beautiful wildflowers and waving green-and-yellow grass. As I approach my temple, I realize that I am bounding and flying because I cannot enter it without an energy shift. By bounding and flying, I enter the temple in the form of pure, intuitive sight.

The only thing that can slow my progress is the weight of my left brain. So I bound higher and fly faster until my left brain lets go. As long as my left brain still functions, the temple keeps receding just ahead, down a curving pathway behind waves of shimmering colors. This is the flying part of me that has been blocked by all the people who said I was chasing *illusion*. This an even more subtle doorway than exploring myths, stories, and Akashic records. I am poised at the doorway of what people call "illusion," but what does illusion really mean?

Illusion is a mirror in the very center of my head, and the only way to get there is by flying. Illusion includes all the things that people have projected on me—all the judgments that they make when they respond to something about me, even though they don't really know *me*. But if I can fly into this temple, then I can move beyond all those forms of third-dimensional limitation.

When I was a child, everyone kept telling me to "go play," so I did. I used to sit and stare at the fourth-dimensional world of shimmering, multicolored lights. Once I asked someone if they thought this world of light was pretty, too, but they only got upset with me and said there was nothing there. Soon after that, I noticed that I couldn't see that world anymore. This made me lonely and sad, because I used to spend lots of my time in the land of those beautiful lights. My brother Bobbie and I called it "Magic Land."

When I was little, every night I would go to bed and fly all night in my dreams just because it was fun. And because it was fun, my body felt warm and tingly. Like monks in black robes scouring the countryside for pagans, most adults I knew said in knowing voices, "If you fly in your dreams, you are having a sexual experience." This completely confused me because I was too young to even know what a sexual experience was. But I knew it was *bad* by the tone of their voices. They made me feel bad by labeling my experience. On top of being told Magic Land wasn't real, I was made to feel guilty about visiting it. So my shutdown was emotional as well as physical. This insidious judgment caused my head to become a short-circuiting, flashing hall of mirrors instead of the exquisite, honeycombed, light-reflecting tool it was meant to be.

Lately I have begun to think that Magic Land and many other worlds are as real as this one. I have begun to realize that if I can simply perceive reality as I did before people said that what I was seeing wasn't real, then I will arrive back at that *point of illusion*—that meeting place of perception that is unblocked by the judgments and projections of others.

Interestingly, in ancient times, to *illude* meant "to play"; then during the age of rationalism, it became "to deceive." Before I was seven, I *did* hear the painful cries of the ancestors. But others told me I had voices in my head. In those days, it was made clear to children that one was crazy if one heard voices in one's head. But now I see that this judgment made me unable to hear those who were calling me because I didn't want to get hauled away by the men in white coats. Now I want to remember everything the ancestors were telling me, because I know it was important. I want to see into this inner mirror in my mind, so I ask for the gift of moving out of deception and into play.

I move through the air, not bounding now but sailing. I feel like all those projections are being stripped from my body, as if the only reality is the wind and myself. Now I am flying through the portals and into the very center of my temple, where there is a large diamond. As I sail through the front "window" of this diamond, all its rear facets reflect light, creating beautiful rays of rainbow color. From a distance, I would appear to be a laser beam penetrating a window of rainbow-colored rays.

As I move more deeply into this "clarity stone," I begin to vibrate with wonder. I see *into* the facets, and each is imprinted with a *knowing*—a teaching, an illumination—that I possessed when I first came to this planet. One by one, however, these facets became fogged and shaded by parents, teachers, and authority figures. People said that what I heard, felt, and tried to share with them was only illusion and lies. Eventually, the cones of wonder in the back of my eyes stopped functioning. As a result, I still hate it when people close window shades, and swirling banks of fog always allure me because they conjure wonderful memories that have escaped me for a long time.

When I first came to this warm, green planet, there was in my mind a diamond light receiver that reflected rainbow beams off its inner planes—a dense crystal of star matter that transduced laser beams from the Galactic Center. However, people told me this brilliance was only an illusion. And because they continually said that, as I grew older the facets that my sight needed to pass through became blocks that prevented me from seeing the other worlds.

The confusion they projected made me shut down my diamond facets. One by one, these facets ceased mirroring light beams through my inner brain. One by one, like the eyes of a fish that is eventually blinded in deep, dark water, the cone receptors stopped functioning. Finally I couldn't see the light at all anymore. I can *remember* having seen luminescence around trees and insects, phosphorescence glowing in swamps and forests, and rays of light emanating from objects and from the faces of other children. But like a blind visitor from the stars, I can no longer see that light in this dimension—adults blinded me!

When I was very small and people accused me of lying about the worlds I saw, I felt very angry. I was wild and crazy and threw temper tantrums. But as I grew older, I became sad and depressed. The adults won, at least in the short run—they shut me down with their persistent attacks. A huge range of my perceptual faculties atrophied. But then, in the 1970s, I decided to become more conscious. Regardless of the cost, I decided to try to regain my lost perceptual skills.

At first, I felt like a person paralyzed by a stroke who struggles to activate dead nerves without the help of a physiotherapist. I felt like my aunt, a sculptor, who had so much electric shock "therapy" that eventually her nerves wouldn't connect. But now, as kundalini has risen and purified my body of its emotional and physical blocks, my mind is recutting a diamond that can focus light again. This tool, I know, was created when I was conceived. Before I came into form, I had no mind. I was simply trillions of cells beaming with energy and light. I know now that my mind was created in order to focus that light into my consciousness, through my own experience as a human being. Such an inner focus awakens the waves of energy that I collectively refer to as the "liquid light of sex."

Now, by coalescing these rays of cosmic light, my carbon body "compresses into diamond" again. Now, passing through the front face of the glittering stone, I am suspended with all its facets surrounding me. The geometrical, angular aspects of the diamond begin accessing unseen parts of myself, and I become fascinated by the language of the cellular brain. Now I see Aspasia in the very center of the labyrinth activating her inner light, her ability to see her/my way through it. Inner diamonds are the light meter of the soul, and the Sun is not the only light that illumines the darkness. Whether sunlight shines on the diamond or not, inner facets still glow with light from the stars. But as Aspasia, I remember, I once activated my inner light in the Cretan labyrinth. Through the darkness, this light shone like a star in deep space. To find out just how to activate that inner sight, let us enter into the cave of the Goddess.

I am Inanna, a Sumerian/Akkadian goddess of love and war. I wear a typical Anatolian headdress: a sectioned cone with a rim around the bottom that resembles a boat. To Akkadians, I am known as Ishtar, and to Sumerians, I am known as Inanna, grandaughter of Anu, a great creator god. I am one of the goddesses who imprisoned the upper-world gods by seducing them, making love to each of them seven times.

I stand here in the central plaza of Çatal Hüyük, addressing an assembly of people. As I hold up an idol to the group of villagers, I am thinking of my sister Ereshkigal, goddess of the underworld, for this idol is a statue of her. I descended to Ereshkigal's world through seven gates to retrieve it. The myths do not say why I went, but before I began, I informed the gods of my journey because I was afraid I would be imprisoned in the underworld. Now, with this idol, I am sending thoughtforms to Ereshkigal, letting her know that I wish her to be with me as I imprint these people. As I think of her, my thoughts project her image into this reality. As I bring through my sister from the underworld, I transmit her thoughts to the assembled people:

"The access to the Atlantean keys of the ancient Mother Goddess culture is Venus," I begin. "Venus is the Goddess pathway to the Sun, as the Moon is the Goddess pathway to the Earth. In order to get in touch with the Mother Goddess culture of Atlantis—Goddess as Tree of Life with the Primordial Egg in its roots—we must first access these solar teachings."

Çatal Hüyük is a lunar culture. Being a priestess who possesses the inner light, I have appeared here to introduce these people to the Atlantean solar culture of the future. Access to the solar culture on Earth involves stimulation of the higher head centers—specifically, the pineal gland and the hypothalamus. From 8000 to around 3000 B.C., females will not utilize this solar apparatus; it will be the exclusive province of males.

Now it is 5200 B.C., and women are afraid of the solar force because of what happened to them during the reign of Atlantis. They deal with their fear by keeping the solar energy out of their culture. That is why Çatal Hüyük is completely underground. But there will come a time when the solar force must be reactivated in females to prevent a blockage of human evolution. That time is your *now*.

I, Inanna, carry the keys of solar consciousness for the Mother Goddess culture. As I stand here holding the underworld powers in front of my people, I have reached a point of desperation. I have come here with Ereshkigal to infuse the people and the temple with the ancient secrets of the Atlantean solar Goddess wisdom. *This, however, will rend a veil in the future.* This teaching will cause the eventual destruction of the Mother Goddess culture.

I am implanting this awareness here so that it will be preserved throughout the next cycle, until 1500 B.C. I am doing this because I was ordered to do it by Enki, lord of the seas and emissary of the avenging god Anu. Enki told me that if I did not *deactivate* the true solar force in females, Anu would destroy creation altogether. So I am buying time, buying into the idea that it is better just to keep things going. I do not want these people to be destroyed; however, I know that Anu will destroy them at the slightest whim, just as he once created them out of clay. But he cannot see rainbows as these people can—he has no inner light. Thus, I am about to *deactivate the feminine in order to save humanity from the avenging male god*. The feminine—in both men and women—will be deactivated until the end of this cycle, near the year A.D. 2000, when it will emerge again.

The form of solar consciousness that I am implanting here is a belief in improving what already exists. This involves changing the cycles of things—for example, planting and cultivating grains, controlling animals, and controlling watercourses. It also involves men taking specific women for their wives. In this way, men can know which children carry their bloodlines, pregnant women are protected against danger, and women will not need to own their own power.

I, Inanna, first came here in 5700 B.C. to establish this temple of Çatal Hüyük. I came from Nibiru, the bridge place between the Earth and the stars. When the gods first brought their temple culture and technology to Earth, they simply transplanted from Nibiru what they felt was needed here. They have sent me this time because something else is needed that they cannot accomplish: a temple of the Goddess directly aligned to the Andromeda Galaxy, my stellar source.

When I began this temple teaching years ago, I sat with a blue crystal in the central place that accesses Andromeda. Instead of applying my Nibiruan temple technology, I sat for twenty-nine days and nights tuning into what is beautiful on planet Earth. The true beauty of Earth comes from the ability to live without fear of death and from enhancing life to the maximum.

On Nibiru, we are obsessed with death because our cycles are so long. Periodically, there are galactic catastrophes. Because we live thirty-six hundred years to one of your solar years—thus seeming to be "immortal" to you—these catastrophes are things we have actually experienced. During a life on Earth, the chances of experiencing such violent change is rather remote. Thus, we gods have projected on you the idea that death is negative. Your personal deaths are the same as cosmic catastrophes are to the gods! The constant presence of life and death on Earth upsets us so much that it never occurs to us that it might not bother you! *Our divine judgment about how you feel about death is a primordial projection and you cannot escape it unless I—as Goddess—release that desire for immortality*. For this reason, I came to create a temple that will teach the gods how you *really* feel about dying. We gods must see that life and death are harmonious and a source of ecstasy on Earth. Then you can let go of the *desire for perfection* that we have projected on you.

To do this, begin by imagining how to create a temple in which life and death are harmonized. Then I bring in the symbols that will help people with this issue. First, I offer the wisdom of the Brahma bull: attunement to sexual power and the eternal planting cycles. The bull's integrated sexuality is the key to emotional freedom and the ability to be in the present moment. This is Pleiadian wisdom. In this solar system, from an Earth perspective, the Pleiades lie in the shoulder of the Bull in the Sky. The bull teaches how to transcend fear, even fear projected by the Nibiruan gods: the Pleiades radiate love, compassion, and sexual intuition.

The second symbol I bring in is the vulture, which teaches that decay and death are in the same circle as creation and life. I bring this wisdom into form so that when death occurs, the people in this culture will meditate deeply on the decay process and use this to let go of attachment and their desire for control of life. They will be able to see that all life on this planet is part of a cycle of creation and decay, and they will not be saddened by it.

Enki also insisted on placing a temple teaching here, a painting of the hunt before the domestication of animals. This painting represents the energy of this culture before it moved from hunting and gathering to planting and growing. It was used to teach that men are the activators of change, while the birthing and planting done by women were only passive activities. Later, my priestesses will paint over this mural.

Women are mistresses of the beasts and guardians of the animals. When we attune to the powers of the beasts, we are fearless. We are also concerned about male control of the animals, since the beasts first trusted *women* when they agreed to live with humans. The new relationships we created with animals made it possible to move beyond the survival mentality — to elevate the hunt to the level of an initiation. Because of us, hunting did not have to be done so frequently, and it could also be used as a great opportunity to move beyond fear. The fact is, keeping the grain and creating a safe haven for birthing was a gift from women to men. It was an invitation to become *partners*.

Attuning to the animals rather than controlling them is the pathway to the stars. This is why the zodiac is a pathway of animals in the sky — a doorway to cosmic connection. Likewise, working with the growing cycles is a way to feel the pulse of the Earth. This is why I have attuned myself to this sacred land, rather than just superimposing temple forms from my home planet.

Now it is time to walk into the temple and see what I have created with my thoughts. I go with the statuette of Ereshkigal, Goddess of the Earth, leaving the people outside. I walk through a square doorway into the temple, which is made of adobe mud and rock with four great beams over the doorway. It is square with a large, empty space inside. I am carrying Ereshkigal, and I am Inanna, Goddess of the sky.

First I stand in the center, looking toward the east wall to an engraving of a great bull. Then I turn to the north to see an altar below a square wall space. I cannot see what is painted there, but I know it is a mural. Above the mural are three bull skulls with jutting horns.

Now I begin to see the mural below the bull skulls. It is is composed of cosmic geometric designs, and below it is a panel of hand impressions, meaning that this is guarded by the Order of the Red Hand. I become excited because I know that soon I will see the keys of the Keepers of Time. To gain this knowledge, I face the east and contemplate the engraved bull. The east is where the Sun rises, and the key to correct contact with the solar culture comes through attunement to the rising Sun.

First I receive an astonishing revelation from my home planet, Nibiru. I see that we are confused about Earth because we do not orbit around the Sun, as the rest of the planets do when entering the Solar System, since

Nibiru orbits through the Asteroid Belt. Next I see that the Sun is actually the eighth star in the Pleiades, and therefore the Pleiadians have more potent influence on Earth than the Nibiruans. I am amazed by the implications of the knowledge this Bull of the East is offering me: eventually the love teaching of the Pleiades will prevail because the Sun is one of its stars. I stand quietly hoping that my brain circuitry can access this spiralic information.

The correct understanding of solar consciousness for Earth people is to always orient toward the rising Sun. Because I inadvertently followed that law here, I am being showered with Earth secrets. I feel my heart opening. We have come to your planet for hundreds of thousands of years hoping for such revelations. My third eye is suddenly illuminated with light as my heart courses with joy.

Like a zombie, I walk into another room in the temple, into another dimension. It seems a later time in this temple, but all I am interested in is *seeing* as much as I can. Again I, Inanna, orient my vision first to the east, where I see a raised relief of a goddess who represents both the Earth and myself. I am about to be given the story of my origins! I can barely breathe as I focus my eyes. I see that the hands and feet of the goddess are raised as though she were flying toward the Earth, as if she were returning to her home. Her body is decorated with the veils of time and other cosmic patterns, and in its very center is the symbol of Atlantis as home on Earth: a pattern of three concentric rings.

My eyes instinctively begin to travel the lines painted on the goddess body. In those of her upper chakric system is my story, the story of the eternal female. The lines in her body represent the web of life, the net of creation.

Before she draws me into the oblivion of her blank face, the goddess says, "Beloved Inanna, I now tell you a secret that will carry you through the pain of the next eight thousand years. We are all goddesses—creators of life itself. The seeds are already in place for a plan to forget home, forget cosmic bliss, forget the powers of our wombs. But a time will come when this temple will be found. As soon as it is opened, the cycle of remembrance of divine birthing will begin again, and the animals, children, and the City of the Goddess will again be supreme."

Suddenly I find myself in another room in another time, and again I strain my eyes to see. My body senses that I must not face eastward, so I turn in almost the opposite direction, to the southwest wall. There, I am amazed to see rows of red hands connected with strange, webbed, red-and-black lines. These lines are the same as those in the body of the God-

THE VEILED GODDESS

dess. I stare, wondering if my brain circuitry can handle this. It gives me the same sensation as traveling through the time tunnel that we use to access Earth. *I am seeing how matter materializes in time!*

My eyes peruse the mural. First I notice that there are seven hands in the lower row, meaning that this panel is for Earth initiation. I know this because I have traversed the seven gates of the underworld, and because I have seduced men seven times in order to capture them into this world. The upper row contains twelve hands, meaning that this panel is also for initiation into twelve-strand-DNA forms. I know this because I am the goddess who first created the twelve-strand-DNA human.

But, this is impossible! We limited humans to two-strand DNA when Atlantis fell. Yet this temple was built after the fall of Atlantis. How could humans have had this information? Nervously, I begin to study the lines and discontinuities in the mural to see how much the Earthlings really did know.

Let us investigate this sophisticated time calendar divided into three phases, beginning on the right and reading left.

Phase One: This is the previous Age of Aries (29,000 to 26,800 B.C.) to the end of the previous Age of Aquarius (24,200 to 22,000 B.C.), showing the initiation of Homo sapiens into self-reflective powers at the beginning of the Mayan Calendar around 25,000 B.C., during the previous Age of Pisces. At the beginning of the previous Age of Aquarius, there is shown a great lightning bolt to the left of the third hand in the uppermost row. This bolt indicates great cosmic rays coming from the Galactic Center. There is also a radical discontinuity—a blank space—at the end of the previous Age of Aquarius, exactly when twelve-strand DNA was reduced to two-strand DNA in the physical body. With only two receptor systems, it was calculated, human beings would be able to survive the coming cosmic rays; otherwise, the species would be obliterated.

In this section there are three hands above and three below, reflecting the time of balance when the twelve-strand-DNA human achieved full initiation before the discontinuity. The DNA manipulation is seen in the line patterns above the blank space that represents the discontinuity. The orbital patterns of Nibiru in the Solar System—a sort of "planetary clock"—are drawn in detail between the six hands. Always the lower hands of Earth initiation are woven into the orbital patterns, but the hands representing Nibiruan guidance are suspended slightly above the planetary clock. The hand in black shows that Nibiru ruled Atlantis during the previous Age of Aries, the last phase of the Nibiruan hegemony until we returned during the previous Age of Sagittarius.

The wavy lines during the previous Age of Aries indicate intense electrical activity in the skies. The bull hindquarter, the central symbol of the Denderah zodiac (an Egyptian zodiac that is painted on the ceiling at Denderah Temple—a zodiac that was drawn when this mural of the hands was painted), lies in the transition zone into the previous Age of Pisces. This symbolizes the influences from the Pleiades and Orion at this time. The Earth hand below the hindquarter is filled with lines, indicating a remarkable infusion of stellar implants. There is even a doorway into Earth, as can be seen by the line next to the hand that runs to the next hand. The circular form in the Age of Pisces just below the first and second Nibiruan

TIME CALENDAR

hands symbolizes the incarnation of a female avatar who controls the DNA alteration later, seen in the similar forms just to the left of the great lightning bolt.

Phase Two: The second phase covers the Age of Capricorn (22,000 to 19,800 B.C.) through the Age of Libra (15,400 to 13,200 B.C.). The Age of Virgo, to the left of the web of lines, is mostly a blank discontinuity. This shows the time of radical Earth changes when the planet was cleansed and Atlantis sank beneath the sea. This section shows a completely new formation of Earth cultures during the ages of Capricorn and Sagittarius, with great creativity and complexity during the ages of Scorpio and Libra and much involvement by Nibiru in Earth affairs. Notice the forceful, loose, and simple matrix of the planetary orbits during Capricorn, when all the creativity comes from Nibiru. The absence of a hand for Earth during this time shows that denizens of the planet were like little children following the advice of elders. Sagittarius was a time of partnership between Nibiru and Earth, and then Nibiru dominated Earth under Scorpio. This section is walled in on each side, as if representing a phase all its own.

Phase Three: Civilization begins again in the next section, which covers the Age of Leo (11,000 to 8800 B.C.) to the Age of Taurus (4400 to 2200 B.C.) The lines between the hands showing planetary positions are quite regular, but they end abruptly around 6600 B.C. This indicates the date of this mural, since its creators could not predict the Solar System orbits beyond their own time. Interestingly, the mural shows the previous Age of Gemini (6600 to 4400 B.C.) with a black hand of Nibiru above, followed by the previous Age of Taurus with a red hand, but there are no hands below. These hands are signs of initiatic orders, and the fact that there are no hands in the Earth zone shows how overwhelming the sky factor was expected to be during these times, as it was during the formative Age of Capricorn.

Take careful note of this mural, for it shows how deeply involved we Nibiruans are with your solar system. The mural ends with the end of the

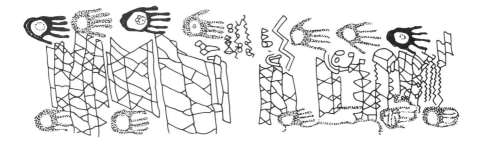

Age of Taurus. It is also instructive and fun to look back into the previous ages of Aries and Pisces (29,000 to 24,200 B.C.) and compare them to the most recent such ages, from 2200 B.C. to A.D. 2160. For one thing, Christ incarnated from the Pleiades along with a number of other remarkable avatars at the same point in these times as the bull hindquarter, denoting 26,800 B.C. in the mural. And the female avatar Hildegard of Bingen entered the cycle at the same point as the entry in about 25,000 B.C., symbolized by the circular symbols.

I, Inanna, cease studying this mural of the ages of time. It is an astounding record left on the Earth by the Keepers of Time, and it awaits future discovery. Now I am about to witness the birth of a child on Earth. As I begin to observe, I note that my first initiatic gift was to be able to see the symbol of Atlantis imprinted on the womb of the Goddess in this temple. Having read the mural of the ages of time, I realize that her body fully comprehends all the cycles of Earth.

Suddenly I am in the room of the flying vultures. A baby is about to be born. The expectant mother is on a birthing table attended by three nude women. The baby is born into the hands of one of the women, beside a large, stone basin of warm water. The woman immerses the baby in the water, washes it, then wraps it in a clean, white calfskin. Then she hands the baby to a nude priestess standing in front of a wall covered with paintings of red vultures.

The priestess is in an altered state, completely tuned into the vulture energy. As she takes the baby, she is aligned with the powers of life and death, and she imbues the infant with trust in these forces. She holds the spiked core of a seashell. Carefully holding the baby's head in her right hand, her fingers put pressure on the hypothalamus, behind the baby's skull. Then she presses the sharp shell into the area of the baby's third eye, piercing the skull bone. Holding the baby up so its head lies on her heart chakra, she daubs the wound with a clean cotton cloth. She holds the baby until the bleeding stops. Then the baby opens its eyes, stares into the eyes of the priestess, and sees the vultures behind her.

Next, the other priestesses take the baby and put a blue cotton headband around its head. Finally, they take the baby back to the mother, who is ready to breastfeed. By having been opened at birth in this way, the baby will live a life of cosmic connection without fear of death or the underworld.

Now I turn to see an altar with large bull horns. Behind it, there is a painting of the Garden of Eden with the Tree of Life in the midst of an idyllic scene of birds and flowers. There is also a crystal skull with luminous light around it in the root system of the tree. This is the skull of a male. I am amazed to see it here because it is the skull of Spica, which was originally carved on Nibiru. Spica is the divine architect of Atlantis, the supreme master of geomancy, who later became known as Imhotep of Saquarra in Egypt.

This skull is the only object my people brought to Earth that still remains here. We brought it as a gift in 10,800 B.C., and we would like to know where it is in what is known as your *now*. When it is discovered, a new time of bringing in the child will begin. This will be a time when all children will be chosen by their mothers and fathers. When that time has arrived, the baby will be birthed into the arms of its father. This skull holds the key to the male being able to totally integrate the female in himself and participate in birthing as well as insemination.

None of these people at Çatal Hüyük has seen this skull, but finally I see how they could have known about the great ages of time. They honor the skull by having it in this mural, in the room of the women's birthing ceremony. This crystal skull holds the records of Atlantis when Atlantis was a Goddess culture and men and women lived in harmony. It is a Keeper of the Frequency. As I stare at the mural, I realize that the skull is now located in Turkey, below the Black Sea. It is underground in a cave, and since it is still on this planet, it can be tuned into at any time. In later times, it will be the focus of a desperate journey that will occur after a great cataclysm, and that journey will be called "The Search for the Golden Fleece."

What would it be like to live in a world in which the "chosen people" would be the chosen children? *This would be a group not of people given power by a god who established male control over the planet, but of* all the children— *each child desired and loved by its parents. Just thinking about this possibility makes me feel sad. I realize that my capacity to imagine it is almost gone. Carried away by sadness for my ancestor grandmothers, for my daughter and her daughters, and for all the men who will never experience relating to women as equals, my consciousness begins to search for a time when my earthly female powers were intact. As fascinating as Inanna is, she is from another planet. She is a great teacher—she is part of me—but what about a time of empowerment as an Earth woman? There was such a time, and I return to it now.*

I am the seven-year-old Aspasia. It is 1576 B.C., and I am with three women wearing hooded capes walking in a line up the side of a mountain through fog. This is the mountain that I have often stared at through the bull-horn symbol in the south courtyard of Knossos. Inside this mountain is the crystal cave, a cave that feels like a huge pit of emptiness in my solar plexus. This mountain is composed of crystalline rock covered by a layer of earth, rocks, plants, and trees.

Back in the ancient days, the original mountain was a huge quartz-crystal cluster. This great crystal grew underground in the midst of a huge cave system of dripping water and minerals. At the time of the Flood, the layers of earth over the crystal cluster were washed away by the deluge. There is no mountain like this anywhere else on planet Earth, and Knossos was built right next to it because of its power. We did not build on the mountain itself because we knew it must be able to freely radiate light to the sky. Instead, we built next to it, and we placed one of our most important altars there. We used blocks of crystal rock for the construction. The crystal cave inside the mountain contains a huge inner sanctum with a sacred spring. Springs are sacred to the Goddess, and this one runs into the river behind Knossos, where we do our purification rites. The cave is a natural entrance into the mountain.

I am walking into the crystal cave with my three grandmothers. As we go deeper, the light begins to diminish. I feel as though I am walking into my innermost self. This is a pathway into the higher self that exists in my body. We do not understand the higher self as something outside ourselves. My higher self was encapsulated in my physical body at birth. Now, seven years later, I cannot even imagine being separate from it. As I enter the crystal cave, I feel like I am walking into my own solar plexus. We are silent as we penetrate further into the cave; the only sound is the plinking water dripping into pools.

As the water drips, it makes musical sounds in the deep reaches of the cave, and in my head I can hear the millions of voices of those who have been part of all my lives. As we go deeper, I hear music in the crystals vibrating to the sounds of the dripping water. These high-pitched sounds are like the music of the stars singing in the night sky over the sea. I look around and am entranced by the clear quartz-crystal formations everywhere—on the walls, on the pathways, and on the ceiling of the caves.

The pathway we are following was made of gold dust by the ancient ones. All we can see now is this gleaming path and the little flecks of light from the crystals, which look like fireflies on a moonless night. As we walk, I am increasingly hypnotized by the music of the crystals and the dripping water in the pools. The sounds echo in my chest like my own heartbeat.

I put my consciousness in my heart. Every time my it beats, it makes sound waves in the blood cells coursing through my veins, just like the dripping water makes sounds in the crystals in the inner cave. I feel fluids moving inside my body. It is getting darker and darker; the golden pathway provides the only light.

As we continue, the grandmothers are observing me. They are waiting for me to encode all of the teachings I am receiving. They are teaching me as we walk along that nothing can be understood by identifying it. All is known simply by walking on the golden thread to the center of the Earth. This initiation is deeply encoded in my being. This golden pathway has been passed down through time as "Ariadne's Thread." Like the labyrinth, it is outside of time; there is no beginning or end to it.

These grandmothers are the three wise teachers of the three phases of the Moon. They have brought me to walk this pathway only after much deliberation. They were careful about choosing me for this teaching because of the responsibilities that it would carry throughout my life as Aspasia and beyond. The grandmothers are selfish. They are the guardians of *all* women on planet Earth, and they do not wish any female to carry more burden than is necessary for the collective. However, they are having me walk much further than usual today because they know that my soul will return as Barbara at the end of the twentieth century to bring these teachings. At that time, I will know how to keep from getting caught in the confusions by simply moving down the golden path.

We have reached the end of the path. The grandmothers have accompanied me just far enough for me to be able to walk safely and securely in the future modern world.

We are now in the very center of the crystal mountain. It is here that the secret teachings of the grandmothers will be communicated. They take me to the center room, an egg-shaped chamber about fifteen feet high whose crystalline walls are riddled with small caves. In the middle of the floor is a pool of clear water. This is ancient water, rainwater that has seeped through the runnels and fissures of the mountain over aeons of time.

The grandmothers lead me to a throne carved out of crystal, an exact duplicate of the throne in the palace at Knossos. It is slightly above and on the edge of the pool. They put me on the throne, then sit in front of me. Crystal clusters glisten under the mirrorlike surface of the pool. The grandmothers meditate, focusing their vision simultaneously into the center of their heads and mine.

My head feels energized, like it is opening up and spinning, and an inner red flame begins to flicker. In the center I feel a ruby star. This is not solar or lunar light; it feels like a place in me that just *knows*—knows that there is no end or beginning.

Next I see images that begin as tiny specks of light. Gradually, they expand into exquisite creations of animals, people, babies, trees, temples, and even a forest. The light undulates, wave, and twists into form after form. A fetus begins as a speck in the womb and grows into a beautiful young woman, then into an old woman. An old man with a cane travels backward in time, getting younger and younger. The Temple of Knossos begins as a primitive encampment by our sacred spring, then grows into a large one-story village with gardens in the center; finally it becomes a magnificent, multistoried, elaborate structure.

All the while, the eyes of the grandmothers glisten, reflected in the water. My breath creates musical notes in the crystals as my beating heart makes the cave pulsate. In this moment, I know that in my future lives, I will birth and birth until I discover how to choose a child as the grandmothers have chosen me. And then I will be as happy as I once was deep in the Earth, in the crystal cave called Magic Land.

Chapter Seven

DECODING THE PRINCIPLE OF TWELVE

"There were these giant black animals, something like giant bats, longer than the length of this house, who said that they were the true masters of the world."

"Oh, they're always saying that. But they are only the Masters of Outer Darkness."

—Michael Harner, *The Way of the Shaman*

I shine a light into my pineal gland and place a gem inside to reflect that light through its crystalline matrix. At this time, the gem is a ruby. When full spherical consciousness has been activated, that gemstone will become an emerald. I ask Sekhmet, the lion goddess of Egypt who rules human courage, to guide me on an exploration of the male side of consciousness. But Sekhmet is not allowed to release this teaching without the permission of Horus, who is the teacher of correct timing. Horus speaks:

"I am Horus—the guardian of time. You asked for spherical consciousness, so now you must act in accordance with this request. Watch in your reality and notice each time a stone calls out to you. The original Mantle of Atlantis contained twelve sacred gemstones. Now that you have asked for the keys to twelve-strand DNA, remember that the thirteenth stone lies in your throat chakra just where Sekhmet always wears an emerald.

"Remember to move into feeling whenever you achieve more knowledge, and you *will* activate the twelve stones of the Mantle of Atlantis. The only gateway into the knowledge of twelve is the feeling powers of Earth. When you begin the quest for this full spectrum, you are venturing into the initiatic temple records of Nibiru. *This is an unattainable goal without feeling* for without feeling you will be caught in desire.

"The way to keep from getting caught in desire is to hold your knowing in your heart. Whenever you dare to speak of this knowledge, do so with feeling in your throat—or, like the angels, you will fall from the heavens. Beware when you discover anything that you cannot *feel*, when you find yourself captivated by the powers of knowing the big truth. When that cold, steel knife of obsession comes into your mind, extract it from yourself as though it were the most loathsome reptile. Move everything into your heart by attuning yourself to the Moon, the filter of cosmic knowledge on Earth.

"You will relearn and master the fifth-dimensional keys of the twelve stones, the twelve solar angles, the twelve planets, and the twelve cosmic teachers. But then you must transit to the principle of thirteen—knowing intuitively at a cellular level. Who of you knows about choosing the heart above all powers of materialization? Consider this information carefully because in the end, the open heart will be your final test."

Horus is the teacher of perspective as well as the chief spirit guide for astrologers. When he spoke, he offered some keys to cellular knowledge, but I still felt like there was something I did not understand. My answers came in May of 1991, when I traveled with some friends to Tana Toraja, one of the more remote Indonesian islands. Like the Balinese, the people of Tana Toraja say they came from the Pleiades, and they are famous for the wood carvings of their ancestors called tau taus. *These small effigies are set up in high niches carved into sheer rock faces on the edges of mountains, while caves in the base of the mountains are filled with the skulls and bones of the ancestors.*

While on Tana Toraja, I visited a number of ancestral villages with two other companions. As we drove along with our Indonesian guide, Benjamin, I kept seeing megalithic stone circles in the jungle near each village. I repeatedly urged Benjamin to stop so that I could explore them, but he kept putting me off, commenting that these rantes *(circles) were everywhere, and he would show me the better ones later. He was correct. As we drove along, I kept seeing black, phallic standing stones through the trees near each village.*

I trusted Benjamin. From the moment I first saw him, I knew he was my twin soul. All of this lifetime I had been feeling this man's presence in some remote jungle location. His Christian name suggests that he comes from my own Semitic root through Isaiah—the Tribe of Benjamin. He is one of the 5 percent of Tana Toraja's indigenous people who had recently become Christianized, so I could not share this awareness with him. But I could see in his eyes that I was part of his story, too. For me, Benjamin was a male side of myself that existed in a parallel reality filled with the Stone People. Now, for the first time, I discovered why I had been so obsessed with standing stones ever since I was a small child.

We spent a wonderful day walking from village to village on footpaths through rice paddies. The ancestral houses in the villages of Tana Toraja are swaybacked houses made of reeds. Resembling boats, they are symbolic of the ships that the ancestors from the Pleiades arrived in long ago. These dwellings are hoisted up on stilts and braced in front with gigantic tree trunks that are nailed with rows of water-buffalo horns culled from sacrificial ceremonies over hundreds of years.

These days, in each village young boys tend the sacred water buffalo. They spend the whole day walking, watering, and feeding them. Then they lead them into the rice paddies to fertilize the water with their waste. Each boy gives a year of his life to attend a sacred buffalo. This ritual indicates a profound connection to the Pleiades—located in the Constellation of the Bull—just as the tall tree trunks nailed with water-buffalo horns reach for the skies in the ancestral villages.

We stopped at many stone circles, and in each one of them I meditated and prayed, asking for illumination about the meaning of the circles and the sacredness of the water buffalo. After a day of trekking, Benjamin could see that I was really searching for something. To me, Tana Toraja was a living laboratory of intact genetic information—the sacred story of the people from the Pleiades—and I was a participant in this story.

The next day, Benjamin took us to an active stone circle where visitors are rarely taken, a circle where ancient ceremonies are still conducted. When we arrived, I was stunned. The circle, or rante, *lay at the end of a great valley of lush rice paddies surrounded by sheer cliffs that contained* tau taus *and ancestral bones. It consisted of about fifty upright stones, each weighing between twenty and fifty tons. Some of them were even carved obelisks. In the center of the circle were four trees marking the four sacred directions, and within the trees, an elevated bamboo platform was suspended about ten feet above the ground. Like the geographic layout of Atlantis, the circle consisted of three concentric rings. And beyond the outer circle was a wide pathway of small, black, river-smoothed stones.*

Benjamin indicated that he wanted to be alone with me. He led me away from our companions back into the jungle behind the circle. This was very strange behavior in his culture, so I knew he had something important to say or do. Passing a wooden ancestral house filled with tau taus, *we came to a giant basalt rock the size of a sixteen-foot-square monolith. It had been painstakingly flecked into the shape of a human head but without eyes and ears. This rock undoubtedly weighed at least several hundred tons, and I wondered if it had been moved here. On the "brow" of this head was carved the head of a huge water buffalo, and beneath this was an elegantly carved, closed door. Benjamin showed me a little window into the interior. I looked through it to discover that the boulder had been hollowed out and contained ancient bones and ornately carved boxes.*

Looking into my eyes, Benjamin asked, "Are you a Christian?" I became deeply thoughtful and said, "Benjamin, I am one of the old people of my own country. In my land, before the white men came, we also had stone circles, temples in rocks, and teachings of the sacred buffalo. When the white man came, my people were driven from the land, and our sacred teachings were driven underground. In Tana Toraja, you still have the stones of your ancestors, the ancient ceremonies, and the medicine ways of the stars. But now the Christians are coming into your land, and unless they have changed, they will try to destroy your stone ancestors and your ceremonies. No, Benjamin, I am not a Christian."

Benjamin looked down at the deep black jungle soil, then we walked back into the center of the circle. Luckily, we were still left alone. He began to describe in detail the ceremonies that are still performed in that sacred place. Beginning after sunset, he said, the priestesses come from the village bearing torches. They walk around the pathway just outside the last circle of standing stones all night long.

In the morning, the priests and other villagers gather in the circle to observe the rising Sun. At the same time, a cockfight begins inside the *rante* under the raised platform inside the four central trees. As with all Pleiadian cultures, birds are sacred to the people of Tana Toraja. The cock, of course, crows just before the Sun rises.

Next, either pigs or water buffalo—which and how many depending upon the occasion—are brought into the circle and sacrificed. The pigs are decorated with garlands, as though they were gods, and they are imprisoned in little square decorated houses on stilts and carried into the circle. The water buffalo are simply led into the circle by the men—led to their death as these men once led them in life. The buffalo walk without fear. As all this goes on, fish divination is being carried out in the rice paddies, and occasionally old women in ecstatic states dance into the middle of the circle carrying flopping fishes. The sacrifice continues all day. Late in the afternoon, the rains come, and the dark red blood seeps into the rich soil and runs into the rice paddies.

When I asked Benjamin why his people sacrifice the animals, he said he did not know. But he said that he was always told that there was the skull of a young boy at the base of each one of the large raised stones and that each stone represented one of the great ancestors. These days, he said, the spirits of these same boys enter the boys who tend the water buffalo that are eventually sacrificed, as the spirits who live in the mountain caves live again in the daily lives of the villagers. Again I asked him why the sacrifice, and again he replied that he did not know. He said that nowadays the priests cannot even remember how to raise the stones. When the last king of Tana Toraja died in 1979 and his stone was to be raised in the royal *rante*, it fell over after a crane lifted it into place. It still lies there on the ground today.

Benjamin was summoned by my companions, who had gone to the village adjacent to the *rante* to examine the ancestral houses. He went to join them. After he left, I went right into the center of the stone circle and put my hands

on the big flat stone that was used for sacrifice. Again I asked, "Why sacrifice?"
And a great vision came over me as the waves of sound from a voice swept down
through my body.

I see a figure standing on a cliff on an arid mountain, wearing the skin
of a spotted jaguar. The figure is Teshub, Hittite god of storm and thunder.
He appears to me like a deva spirit—more as a primordial Earth guardian
than a thunderbird god. He is not at all like the angry sky god described
in Hittite mythology, the one who rides a bull and slays the sky serpent,
Yanka.

As he stands on the edge of the cliff, Teshub draws rays of light into
his belly from all directions. These beams seem to radiate out hundreds
of miles, but they are actually radiating *inward*. Just below Teshub's
diaphragm, I see a mass of red balls generating power. They are the size
of golf balls, and together they look like a mass of huge red atoms. The
incoming rays of energy are connecting to these red balls, making them
glow like red coals with yellow auras. From the mass of red balls, I see
a glowing yellow energy beam going straight down into the center of the
Earth. This beam glows more and more intensely as the mass in Teshub's
solar plexus gets hotter and redder.

Teshub is taking the pulse of the Earth. His energy feels extremely
foreign to me, and it is hard to feel him, even though I am able to see him
quite vividly. I know that he has knowledge about the center of the Earth
that is critical to human beings at this time. I want to *know* him; I want
to experience his power. Sadly, this power feels alien to me, but I sense
from some place deep in my soul that I must connect to this force. We are
supposed to resonate with the Earth, but we do not remember how to feel
these pulses in the "civilized" world. Humans read only Earth *surface* information such as storms, earth movements, tides, migration patterns,
and species health. But if we were truly grounded and in tune with the
planet, we would also be able to connect with the *center* of the Earth. This
root connection, the key to male attunement with the Earth, does not exist for me because I have not accessed it in this life. I want to know it, and
I am deeply stirred by this unfolding mystery.

As I watch Teshub connecting to the center of the Earth, I shake myself
and let go! Wildly, I move into the streams of his red-hot, pulsing body
in order to feel what he feels, and instantly I am flooded with visual images of what he is seeing.

Through Teshub, I see that there is another world in the center of the
Earth—a world of water, mountains, forests, creatures, and plants. It is

exquisite, like the Garden of Eden. Existing in natural harmony and balance, this realm is the inner consciousness of the Earth, just as the realm of the subconscious is the inner human world. This world is the creation matrix that cannot be penetrated or altered. The center of the Earth is a complete universe, a microcosm of perfection, like a self-sustaining ecosystem sealed in a bubble. When surface cultures attune themselves to this microcosm by means of ceremonial techniques, they naturally create harmony in their lives.

This closed system has everything the surface world has and much more. Here there is no destruction of species, no interference in the original genetic patterns, and no fouled emotional patterns. Nor will there ever be such destruction, interference, or fouling. I can see that when anything threatens to penetrate this holographic world, the cosmos reacts by destroying the threat. The surface world of the Earth has experienced many invasions and influences by outsiders, but its inner harmony has always remained undisturbed. This is the center within which Teshub communicates—the perfect, undisturbed being called Gaia.

As I meditate in this sacred *rante* in Tana Toraja, I see that this stone circle is a tool for communication with the center of the Earth. For the first time, I see the real reason for the stone circles after dreaming about them since I was a child. I saw those stones in my dreams and visions as Benjamin participated in his ceremonies on Tana Toraja before he was Christianized. I now realize why I have always known that megalithic technology must be one of the keys to recovering Earth's harmonic resonance, its basic survival knowledge.

Since there is no scientifically measurable access to this place in the Earth's center, what is measurable to us about the status of Earth's ecosystem is available only from readings on the surface. Scientifically, the Earth's core behaves like a single crystal of pure iron lined up on a north-south axis. The electromagnetic field on the surface of the Earth is in alignment with this crystal center. Though the deeper truth of this core is not available to science, it is totally accessible psychically. In fact, the ancient, indigenous Earth sciences were all created to assist in this communication link. Due to the degeneration of psychic skills in "civilized" humans, access to this center has been extremely limited for thousands of years, though remnants of this knowledge still exist in various shamanic cultures.

As I tune into Teshub, I feel his engrossing pulsation with the Earth, and I understand how powerful feelings must be in order for someone to attune to the Earth. Teshub's appearance in my vision is now a sign that my male side is going to begin to feel the Earth, and this is very exciting to me. My female side has always intensely felt the Earth, but that has been only half of me. Also, I have felt caught on the planet, as though nailed on a divisive cross when I incarnated. I wonder if this vision of the center of the Earth is a sign that men will begin to feel from their male side.

The ability to feel the Earth is critical for the survival of all life. A person who dumps oil and chemicals into the waters, who slaughters the animals and indigenous people, or who destroys the forests cannot access the central core. This great insensitivity has pushed us farther and farther away from resonation with the Earth frequency. But anyone who lives on the Earth who fearlessly feels real pain about the degradation of the planet can access the core.

Now we are being pushed to the wall by the pain of the Earth. One by one, people are opening their hearts to the suffering of the planet. This process will accelerate, especially for men. We need to disseminate indigenous teachings and perform ceremonies *immediately*—ceremonies that will help people to cry and grieve and release their deep cellular feelings about the planet's suffering. The reason for this is that when the complete teaching about the core of the Earth—the *Heart of the Mother*—is revealed, there must be as many people as possible who have the ability to respond fully to its power.

Now, as I stand in this *rante* of Tana Toraja, I am being flooded with information on sacred sites—information that will decode the mechanics of the relationship between the surface and the core of the Earth. This central closed system includes balanced harmonics and a power module that resembles the structure of an atom, a molecule, a solar system, or a galaxy. This is the holography of ecosystems, just as stars are the holography of light. It supersedes all other Earth forms, and it is the *pregnancy of the male*. This creative pregnancy is the way the male can discover the geomancy of the Earth's surface—feeling her pulse: by means of his own kundalini energy. This sexual union between Earth and the stars is aborted by the male lack of creative participation.

In ancient times, when the Keepers of Tradition guided humankind, the harmonics on the surface of the Earth vibrated with the Heart of the Mother. In those days, it was easier for people to tune to this core, which was remembered as the Garden of Eden. Even today, some indigenous people still live in this garden. And anytime humans are in resonance with the Heart of the Mother, the harmonics of surface reality resonate with the Earth pulse.

There came a time came when invaders from Nibiru arrived and wished to "improve" Earth. Yet the Nibiruans could not penetrate the Earth's center—not even psychically. They could only manipulate the systems on the surface by *rearranging matter*. They gave much to the surface cultures with their advanced technology, but whenever they attempted to alter the vibration of the central core—for example through nuclear technology, crystal technology, or genetic manipulation—Earth harmonics were disturbed due to lack of feeling for Gaia. This interference has always resulted in surface destruction. So beginning thirty-six hundred years ago, the Nibiruans were allowed to incarnate so that they could learn to love the women of Earth in order to learn to feel Gaia. The time has arrived for them to feel, and the present moment is unique because the male vibration—heavily imprinted by the Nibiruans—is realizing that disharmonic penetration of Gaia always results in destruction.

Most importantly, because the Nibiruans entered the incarnational cycle, it was inevitable that they would participate in the destruction. Some still believe they will ascend and avoid this, but that is not true. Now males are poised to choose creation over destruction, and their teachers are their female counterparts. You can see how close we are to the shift as the abuse of the female rises in exact proportion to the increasing abuse of the planet.

In the mind of the Creator, it is necessary to have certain perfect, immutable forms from which all matrices of being and morphogenetic fields emanate. These forms, which live in the center of the Earth, are *models of materialization*, and nothing would exist without them. Sacred sites are portals to these *libraries of perfect forms*. The morphogenetic fields of all the kingdoms—mineral, insect, plant, animal, and human—exist there. When the portals are open at sacred sites during equinoxes and solstices, we can receive the Earth's teachings. Humans were created for this purpose, and suddenly the triggers of our evolution—the Nibiruans—have figured this out after becoming part of us for thousands of years!

A rock, a spider, a bird, a priest, or a priestess can turn the keys to these doors just by existing, but alien visitors can get access only through *feeling*—which unfortunately is an atrophied sensation for them. However, when a solar system is coming into holographic knowledge, as ours is at this time, its planetary civilizations learn to consciously attune to these perfect forms. Since Nibiru is a planet of our solar system, the Nibiruans participate and benefit from this evolution right along with humans. And since Nibiru orbits way out of our solar system and accesses star knowledge, it is time for its stellar consciousness to infuse our solar system.

Just as the core of Earth is a perfect ecosystem, Andromeda Galaxy is a perfect galactic system. It also cannot be penetrated or disturbed by any other energy form, and it can be resonated with only by means of higher-dimensional feeling. All these teachings are hidden from those, such as the Nibiruans, who would take power and control. This cosmic law exists to protect the morphogenetic fields of the central Creator's mind—the source of manifestation itself. If these fields could be accessed without feeling, the primordial galactic-center form could be pierced and altered or destroyed.

When the Nibiruans first came to Earth, we humans were not "developed" in their eyes. They paid no attention to our shamanistic teachings in the forests and caves. To them, we were ignorant animals. As a result, we had time to see that they did not *feel* anything. These cold-blooded aliens amazed us—they seemed like reptiles. As soon as the Keepers of Tradition identified the problem, they created time just so the visitors could learn how to feel. The visitors were given calendars that delineated the time frame of their Earth schooling, and the Keepers of Frequency were put in charge of blocking access to the knowledge of Earth until the new students *felt* the answers. Toward the end of a calendar cycle, such as the ends of the Mayan and Hebrew calendars, the visitors would wake up and realize that Earthlings were running the whole show. And what was the reason for the show? Simply that Earth runs according to the "Law of Home": that anyone who wants to visit is welcome, but the treasures—the sacred sites and sacred knowledge—are managed by the natives.

In 3600 B.C., one of the times the visitors came to Earth (and the beginning of their most recent schooling cycle), they brought their own temple teachings—Nibiruan astrology and divination. The Keepers of Tradition were fascinated withthese teachings, just as they are fascinated with all knowledge from the mind of the Creator, and they began to study this wisdom. But the most interesting parts of this time calendar were planned for the last twenty years of the cycle—A.D. 1992 to 2012. In August of 1992, the male energy would align with the female Earth energy sufficiently to create a fusion between the Keepers of Tradition and the Nibiruans. Fascination would overtake both sides as both would awaken simultaneously to stellar wisdom. Just as the visitors could learn only through feeling, Earthlings could learn about the stellar realms only through *thinking*.

Thus, the Nibiruans brought their own temple teachings to Earth and freely offered them. They were masters of astrology—how the cosmos "thinks." Meanwhile, the ancient shamanistic societies—the Keepers of Tradition—offered to teach and initiate by means of the heart. Now the calendars of time are ending, and the indigenous people are returning to the Dreamtime as the visitors have awakened and begun to realize that the Earth people were considerably wiser than they had thought. The Dreamtime is where the stellar DNA of the Andromeda Galaxy communicates with the perfection of the center of the Earth. This reality is *eternal*. Since the Fall, when materialization first began, the Nibiruans have tried to raid both sources because they want to be able to create as the Creator does. However, that level of creation is outside of time.

Still standing amidst the towering stones in the *rante*, I am reminded of obelisks in Egypt, and I wonder if they access the Dreamtime as this *rante* does. In the Egyptian Eighteenth Dynasty, the Keepers of Frequency decided to hide access to the Dreamtime—the Blue Nile—because they were afraid of the skill and technology of the Nibiruans. Since these Egyptians were from the Sirius star system, they did not trust the Earth to protect herself. They believed that if invaders had access to their star communication channels—the Sekhmet teachings—they would somehow be able to pierce the primordial egg. The invasion by the Hyksos and their takeover of the temples caused the Egyptians to fear the visitors, and they became obsessed with guarding the portals.

Egypt is unique because some of its portals lead right to the center of the Earth, and these can be pierced by ceremonies performed during specific stellar and planetary alignments. These portals were ceremonially aligned with the temple system during the Pharaonic line of the Amenhoteps. Similarly, at Teotihuacan in Mexico, direct access to Andromeda opens to the west of the courtyard in front of the Temple of the Moon. Teotihuacan was shut down in A.D. 200 to block Nibiruan access to this portal.

In my life as Ichor, I participated in closing these portals and burying the ancient teachings that are now being brought back by the star teachers. I now see that fear complexes were behind each shutdown and that distrust of the unique protective powers of the Earth has resulted in a massive knowledge starvation. Those of us who tried to protect Earth in previous lives have been *Keepers of Portals*, and we have returned in this life to open all the knowledge keys we once blocked. As these portals open, many of these teachings will be available through Egyptian and Mayan consciousness after 1996, when the pyramid of Giza in Egypt and the Pyramid of the Sun in Mexico will begin to vibrate once more. This vibration will easily open the inner brain centers that allow humans to be totally trusting and fearless. These feelings will in turn open the Dreamtime of ecstatic communion between Andromeda Galaxy and the central core of Earth.

Now is also the time for teachers to reawaken the ancient knowledge of Earth astrology. We must teach people to tune into the Earth again by observing the angles between the planets and correlating these with their own personal experience and that of the Earth. The key formation time occurs each month at the New Moon. As this divination work unfolds, people will be able to feel that certain planetary alignment systems create energy fields on this planet. Then, if these energy fields are accessed at a sacred site, or portal, the sacred information of that site will become available. Through such divination, we can tune into those influences that help us to balance our bodies and souls, just as they harmonize the surface of the Earth with the central core. And with our new alignment to the lunar cycles, we can remember how to attune to the stellar influences as well.

I sense that this *rante* also reads star patterns. I know that Aspasia understood stellar patterns and connections. She was constantly calculating where the stars were located by observing where they rose over mountain ridges and correlating their positions with stone markers. I know that, for some reason, the information she got was of critical importance. Even now, I can feel that she was deeply concerned about some great event going on in the sky in 1500 B.C. Likewise, the people who erected these giant stones on Tana Toraja were deeply concerned about some celestial event— but what? In order to find out, I create an explosion of white light in the center of my head, and I send it out like a laser beam to the Galactic Center.

I see a sarcophagus painted with complex star patterns. In it, I see a mummified pharaoh, and I know that the mummy—the maintenance of the physical body after death—is the key to Egyptian stellar astrology. In my vision, the body of the pharoah flies through the sky, surrounded by stars and deep blue night. This body, this eternal speck of Earth, has become a supernova, a new star. This is the stellar purpose and destiny of all human souls.

Only humans can observe divination teachings such as those of the snake and the jaguar. Only humans can perform sacred ceremonies at geomantic power points and construct temples and standing stones to help awaken other minds to Earth resonance and stellar vibrations. The function of humans on Earth is to gain access to teachings that connect Earth and sky—to make a cosmic connection between the primordial egg and the centers of galaxies. Once they do this, they will find themselves flying amidst the stars. As I stand meditating in this sacred *rante*, for the first time since early childhood I am flying again in the night sky.

By means of such pure, ecstatic, and fearless connection, we have the ability on Earth to revert *completely* to our original perfection. As we imagine such wildness, we must not forget that Sekhmet, the lion sky goddess, rules courage. She is the guardian of the gates to other realities, and her Earth partner is Anubis, the guide through the portals of the Earth. As we attempt to awaken this deep knowledge, we must allow Anubis and Sekhmet to guide us. Sekhmet will help us to increase our vibrational frequency as we assimilate more light, and Anubis will guide us through all the dark portals into the Earth.

The vision in the *rante* on Tana Toraja continues to feed me with extraordinary sight. It is apparent to me that the Nibiruans interrupted Earth's natural evolution because of problems on their own planet, which does not possess a perfect holographic ecosystem. Consequently, they manipulate lifeforms instead of trusting creation because there is cold, inert rock in their planet's central core. Our relationship with them has been one of primordial fratricide, caused by their attempts to invade us for the warmth and knowledge to be found in the center of the Earth. We must survive their raiding and manipulation so that we can finally offer them what they really want—trust in creation. This is our present objective, and therein lies the meaning of the "War in Heaven Bypass." However, it is hard for us to see what is going on, because *the whole battle is occurring within male/female relationships.*

The critical time is now, because we are about to graduate from school. The calendars are ending, and our brothers and sisters in the sky have finally discovered the treasure of Earth. Gradually, through their experience with us, the Nibiruans have begun to realize that *we* remember the perfect form of the cosmic egg. They now realize that Earth-born humans have the keys to the natural functioning of the planet. At first they thought they could attune to it, then they wanted to penetrate it. But the Keepers saw that if the Nibiruans could gain access to the egg, they would apply their old control paradigms on Earth rather than respecting its natural evolution. So the temple shutdown in 1537 B.C. was the correct move by the Egyptians when faced with Nibiruans who wanted to access the central Earth. Sekhmet locked up the portals, making the locks accessible only through feeling. But that shutdown also installed blocks that would have to be removed at the end of the calendars. Now we must trust the Earth to protect herself as the male vibration begins to feel and to regain access to her portals.

The next level of this communion—this War in Heaven Bypass —has been happening since Harmonic Convergence. In August 1987, after thirty-six hundred years of dormancy, the Earth's power points were reactivated. As soon as the sacred sites began to awaken, individuals all over the planet who were attuned to these vibrations woke up and began remembering the sacred teachings, the Heart of the Mother. The cosmic egg is an energy of exquisite perfection. It is more powerful, more creative, more sexual, and more wonderful than anything we can imagine. As time fulfills its calendar of experience, the cosmic egg begins to hatch. And its contents—nothing less than attunement between the Earth and the cosmos—will allow us all to break through the chaos of our lives and spiral into ecstatic wonderment. I see this now because I can *feel* it, right in the center of this stone circle.

The Nibiruan mind-set that has poisoned planet Earth has most recently manifested as the reptilian attitude that American political leaders call the "New World Order." This is a mind-set that believes in scarcity and limitation when the Earth is actually abundant and unlimited. This is a mind-set that would throw all the people into crocodile pits. The world's power brokers are gluttons who control more resources than they need in order to protect themselves against the scarcity they fear.

When our separated brothers and sisters first came here, they were amazed by the perfection of Earth. But like greedy thieves, they raided the planet instead of respectfully seeking its knowledge from the Keepers of Tradition. They came here with a scarcity mentality—with a belief that things can be used up and that people must always be afraid of running out of the resources they need. This entire behavior was directed toward the *control of reality*. And in the present age, that tendency could ultimately destroy this planet, which holds the master disk of genetic creativity.

Control is the exact opposite of the Dreamtime creation described by the ancient jaguar shaman. The fear of scarcity is the main reason for destruction of the ecosystem. It creates hoarding and selfishness, and resources are not circulated. It is a mania driven by individuals who are determined to grab the last bite of food before the famine. It is the primary obstacle to universal attunement and trust in the perfect cosmic egg, the very alignment that makes it possible to grow food and care for all people on the planet.

As time collapses and we attune to eternal perfection toward the end of the twentieth century, we will also face the shock of realizing that we are not alone and that we have *never* been alone on this planet. Very soon, we will receive scientific verification of the fact that many other beings inhabit the universe with us. Among the most important of these beings—at least to us—are the Nibiruans, who have drastically influenced our life and thought over the aeons because they are part of our solar system. In these times, it is just as critical for us to understand their galactic thinking as it is for them to learn to feel the pain of the Earth. In order to shed more light on this situation, I project myself into a Nibiruan lifetime on Earth centuries before the birth of Christ.

The guardians of the process of Nibiruan incarnation on Earth are Jeroboam and Jezreel, who appear as classic Sumerian bird gods guarding the entrance to the Hebrew Temple of Solomon—a holographic insert of a Nibiruan temple on Earth. The guardians are posted at the temple gate because no one is allowed to investigate this issue, but I plan to do it anyway. The guardians hold small Sumerian seed bags filled with corn. In fact, they hold these bags out to me so I can see that the corn is their gift to the Earth; they seem to be extremely eager to be recognized as givers of sacred corn.

I decide to pass by the guardians, and as I walk into the entrance, I feel columns on each side. It is like walking between rods in an electrical cell—the one to my left is like the negative charge, the one to my right like the positive charge. They are very tall and massive, and they cause the angel-wing points in my clavicles to activate. Resistance in my body to the power of the Nibiruans melts away as I feel the power of my own wings, my bird self, my life as an angel. The two columns become magnetic vibrating trees of aqua-blue light. I begin to embody the visitors and hear a highpitched humming sound in my left ear. In a flash, I *become* a Nibiruan.

I am wearing a wide mesh collar that covers the entire front of my body; it is made of light copper chain with many jewels set in it. The central jewel is a large ruby. The surrounding stones include sapphire, yellow topaz, emerald, green peridot, amethyst, light aqua turquoise, lapis lazuli, and green chalcedony. In the center of the collar above the ruby is a large circular diamond. This is the Atlantean collar of the alchemist—the collar worn by those who have mastered the art of mind over matter.

This collar is my Nibiruan emblem of authority over the relationships between worlds. One of my jobs is to create electromagnetic fields. I have been an alchemist for aeons, and magnetism is the force we use to create forms on Earth. We were first attracted to this planet because of the powerful magnetic fields generated by the great iron crystal in its core. This core—the alchemical "Philosopher's Stone"—is what makes the creation of life possible on the Earth, and it is very precious in the universe.

Our experiences on Earth are personal ones. When we visit, we experience time, personal relationships, and cultures. When we travel into the stellar realms of consciousness, we are free from these personal levels of experience, and we experience other dimensions. I have requested entrance to the Temple of Solomon in order to travel into the stellar realms. To do this, I must first understand the astrology of these realms; otherwise, we will be unable to locate them. Just as mathematics is needed for space travel, astrology is needed for travel in consciousness.

Stellar astrology—galactic exploration—is a form of psychic mapping that makes it possible to explore various archetypal realms such as lion, reptile, bird, and bear. This is why the zodiac is understood to be a river of animal images. We Nibiruans need this astrological knowledge in order to complete our experience, and it can be accessed only through the Temple of Solomon. That is why so much secrecy envelops Hebrew mysteries. This secrecy is very intense, but it must be penetrated when the end of the current Nibiruan Great Cycle, the end of the current Mayan Great Cycle, and the precession of the equinoxes into Aquarius converge around A.D. 2013. Humanity is contemplating the end of linear time, and *astrology is the key to going beyond time*. There is an urge to finish materialization, to create, and to understand these hidden forces.

Consumed by desire to access astrological records, I suck all my force into my heart. Even if all that I know would cleave into a massive earthquake, I ask for access *now*! So doing, I flash into the center of the Temple of Solomon to stand in front of the central throne of the judge. There, I see a great being who holds a gigantic crystal ball.

Suddenly I realize that this crystal—the key to the psychic realms—was made by *ourselves*, the Nibiruans. It is a highly polished asteroid that we picked out of the Sirius star system long ago. We removed layers of burned incrustation and polished it, brought it to Earth, and placed it in the center of the Temple of Solomon in order to give Earth access to stellar astrology. How ironic that we ourselves have forgotten its teachings!

My brain feels fuzzy. I see that this is a diamond ball, a polished sphere of star matter. It was brought to Earth from the Sirius system, when the Temple of Solomon was built on Earth, and later it will be transferred to a vault below the Vatican.

Now I see that I have come here not so much to access the star teachings as to find *myself*. We Nibiruans brought this galactic diamond to Earth in order to discover for the first time how to truly share ourselves with Earthlings. Up until then, we had no intention that Earth people would become our brothers and sisters. But then we realized that Earth would birth Christos—the healed male vibration—and, as visitors, we needed this healing more than we knew. The search by Mary and Joseph for a room to give birth in the Holy Land is actually an allegory of our need to give birth as males on Earth! Something in our destiny prompted us to offer this gift, that we might learn from the Earth people and they from us, and this created *polarity*.

All this learning is ruled by the *Principle of Twelve*, and this principle is experienced by means of polarity—the full exploration of the male and female aspects of consciousness. The meeting point between Earth and Nibiru exists in the ability of both sides to evolve into *twelve* sides of awareness simultaneously. This will be accomplished by the mastery of the male/female confusion when we learn to stretch the polarity to the maximum and become our opposite sides. As we travel to our own solar system after leaving yours, we navigate through space by dividing our journey into twelve sections. This is the *stellar horoscope*—a plane that bisects your consciousness and opens you to awareness of our journey. It is exactly the same as your Earth horoscopes being divided into twelve solar angles, which help you understand your personal energy fields while you are "alive."

You are only now beginning to understand the Principle of Twelve in Earth astrology, and you must stretch yourself to imagine this division of stellar astrology. To keep it simple, the stellar field divided into twelve is the field in which your higher self operates, and greater knowledge about it will help you embody your higher self more completely.

The easiest way to understand anything is to journey through it, so come with me as I journey from the field of the Sirius star system into your solar system and then back out in the direction of Sirius. If these orbital systems seem impossible to imagine, remember that your astronomers report that your galaxy is composed of spiral arms that maintain their position as the galaxy spins in space. The truth is, distances between stars and galaxies are *dimensional*. You are multidimensionally linked to the Sirius star system by devices called "light years."

I am departing Sirius carrying the crystal ball on my journey to Earth. The first stellar angle I pass through that creates a stellar ray of consciousness to Earth is the constellation Orion. The energy in this sector of space is especially influenced by the star Betelgeuse, which sends powerful and constant messages to Earth. This energy is infused with the belief that societies on Earth need armies to protect themselves, that bureaucrats must create orderly social structures, and that people must have political and religious leaders. This energy is the source of hierarchy and the belief in killing in order to maintain it.

Next I pass through the field of the star Ophiucus. The thoughtform here is that esoteric orders must be founded on Earth so that the cycles and patterns on Earth are controlled by initiates—"benevolent angels" who will utilize their warrior powers when necessary. This belief is called Ka-Ba-La, and a great mind, Melchizedek, controls this section of stellar input, and he is very powerful. He is also the source of hierarchy, often playing a supportive role to kings, but his main interest is in male secret societies. Melchizedek creates these control systems in order to elevate certain people and protect them from possession and evil. These control systems are always based on the idea—"Merkabah"—that these chosen people can ascend from Earth whenever the battle gets too thick. However, this control will break down when the secret societies break down, and then males will cease to be fascinated with the lord of secrets and will discover women. Then they will not want to leave the Earth.

Next I pass through the ray of Regulus. Regulus is a transpersonal pattern. It promotes the belief that things must always revolve around a center and that kings are needed to rule the people. This archetype is called the "divine right of kings," and it is heavily infused into human history. Humans will let go of the need for kings when each person on Earth accesses his or her own powers of self-sufficiency and creativity.

After I leave the zone of Regulus, I pass through the zone of the Pleiades. Here, I begin to feel the power of the heart—the source of human rootedness on Earth as well as the access portal to the stellar realms. By activating their heart chakras, Earthlings can synchronize their own cycles with the natural spin of the Earth, which results in unconditional love.

Now I pass through the ray of Alpha Centauri. From this ray, humans learn that when one focuses healing consciousness into a particular form, that form can influence any other reality through meditation. This is called holographic healing, and its energy can be transmitted to any location.

At this point, I enter the Solar System. There is so much activity it feels like going into a pinball machine. I rush past Pluto, where I receive an imploding sense of darkness as my stellar identity is stripped away, allowing me to feel the spinning planets. I soar past Neptune, hearing violins and flutes and feeling a loving attraction to the Sun. I pass by Uranus, feeling an electrical force that repels any incongruous vibration. I feel like I could spin out of control, but I shoot ahead.

Next I enter a zone of emptiness traversed by a wild little body called Chiron. It is so tiny that I can't see it, but I can feel it like a jester creating magical realities. I am amazed to see that energy is being rearranged here so that vibrations from the outer planets and stars can be transmitted to the Sun. Wanting to penetrate this mystery, I go deeper into intuition, where all is known. And there I see light and feel wonder as I suddenly realize that Chiron's function is very much like that of Sirius B orbiting around Sirius A. Just as Sirius B expresses the consciousness of Sirius A, Chiron expresses the mystery of the Sun by weaving the web of creation. Chiron lives out the legend of the wounded healer, fusing species, just as the Sun lives in the cosmos fusing light and darkness. Chiron is the rainbow bridge between Sirius and the Sun.

Next I pass by the great planet Saturn. Here, something amazing happens to my energy field. I become self-reflective, and I test myself about what I have to offer. Why have I come here? Who am I to think I can visit here? Before coming to Earth after such a long journey, I assess myself and my plans. I congeal into time and space for my visit. I become my own identity.

As I pass by Jupiter, I feel an amazing pull. I am grabbed, spun, and captured by a circular force field. I blast through it as the Jupiterian moon, Io, watches me being thrown off my elliptical orbit and I move around the Asteroid Belt and out past Jupiter again. At this point, I receive a sense that Jupiter, with Io's assistance, has just judged me, just assessed my agenda very carefully. I see it in a flash: Jupiter holds all the records of how much all of us have progressed. Jupiter is like a library of evolution and mastery that records the progress of all beings in the Solar System. But where am I going? What time is this?

My time sense of this visit to Earth is A.D. 0. I will slow time down in an attempt to decode the influence of this orbital journey. What was I doing then as I passed through the Asteroid Belt and visited Earth? Compelled to know, I blast energy from my heart through my throat and into my third eye. This slows the passage of time, just like retro rockets slow a spacecraft. Suddenly I am navigating through a sea of spinning asteroids, and I see that I am not alone. I have come with other Nibiruans.

We Nibiruans have plans to land on Earth with the crystal, but we are very concerned that it could shatter as we spin through the Asteroid Belt. Though we deeply desire to give this crystal to Earth, we seriously doubt that we can land and bring it into the physical dimension. Thus we send a message—a deep, desperate sound that communicates with the iron crystal in the center of the Earth. The message is passed from the computer system on Io that we cannot land on Earth without shattering the crystal. What shall we do?

We quickly realize that we can give the Sirian crystal to Earth only if the Earth herself can somehow "give birth" to it. This is the only way to get it into the physical plane. The crystal is star matter; it would shatter in the atmosphere, but its vibration can be shifted from the fourth dimension into the third. That is, its fourth-dimensional attributes can be used to create a "diamond body," much as a shaman can become a lion or an eagle.

The Earth Goddess responds to this creative idea by shivering, which informs us that she can now receive the crystal. She understands that this crystal will forever alter the experience of the planet itself, and she also lets us know that she has prepared the Earth for the arrival of this diamond body. This diamond child, this "cosmic egg," will manifest as all children during this time. And when time is finished in A.D. 2013, all Earthlings will become this child.

In the past, when we Nibiruans were involved in actual gestation and birthing on Earth, we accomplished it through various implant procedures, interference in the womb, and even through gods who mated with human females. But this time we have created a new way for Earthlings to become star people: cellular attunement to the corridor between Earth and sky through resonation with the galactic diamond.

This resonation from the iron core of the Earth crystal— a humming—occurs when a man and woman achieve mutual orgasm. In that moment of perfect resonation, the crystal becomes organic, forming into a fertilized egg of carbon essence. The cover-up—the "Immaculate Conception"—was written into the records in order to make certain that Earthlings would not realize that Christ was the first human to incarnate with a diamond body through the natural processes of the Earth. At the time of his actual conception, the humming enlivened his cells with the vibration of stellar light.

Christ was born when a star was visible in the sky. This was the night when the Sirian crystal was holographically inserted into his cells. The Temple of Solomon, which later became the Vatican, thus became the womb of the Mother, the Temple of the Diamond Body. Christ was born from all dimensions and realities, but the stellar ray that he carried personally was Pleiadian. On the night when the star passed across the sky, the Magi—the astrologers and record keepers of the Temple of Solomon—knew exactly where to go to visit and protect the child against the powers who controlled bloodlines on the planet.

This sharing of the child gifted by Nibiru represented a new form of kingship on this planet. It marked the beginning and also the eventual end of the reign of priests and kings—a reign that would cease completely by A.D. 2013. This birth of the first human being from all dimensions was the beginning of a new Earthling who would lead the way to star communion. It would mean there could be no war in heaven because thereafter the children of the stars would be born on Earth until the end of time.

These incarnations will be completed in A.D. 2012 when a great star will appear as the fiery Feathered Serpent in the sky. Ancient records report that astonishing bodies have appeared in the sky about every eighteen-hundred years, but we still do not have all the information on the sources of these appearances. According to Zecharia Sitchin, who based his research on Sumerian clay tablets, Nibiru orbits into our solar system every thirty-six hundred years. His research on Sumerian records indicates that its most recent visits were 3600 B.C. and A.D. 0. However, there was a great, fiery body in the sky around 1500 B.C. that Aspasia saw; this event is also reported in most ancient records. Whatever the source, these periodic visitations always cause great infusion of cosmic awareness on Earth. Since the Mayan Calendar ends in A.D. 2013, it is likely that another visitation is coming soon.

At the end of time, the arrival of the star will be like the return of yourselves. By A.D. 2012, all the cover-ups will be exposed just as all the Dead Sea Scrolls—the Nibiruan records of the A.D. 0 teaching—are translated. Other records and artifacts will also help to awaken the Earth. With the reentry of the star into the

Solar System, the actual encodement of Christ consciousness will shift the planetary consciousness, just as Christ shifted it in A.D. 0.

Make no mistake, Christ was a multidimensional human who incarnated on Earth with twelve-strand DNA. He said humans would one day do all that he did and more, and that time has arrived. From 1987 to 2013, all individuals born on Earth will be imprinted with the multidimensional self. In their adoration of the Christ, the Magi astrologers created a longing for the knowledge that you have just begun to witness since 1987. They saw who he really was, and now humans are seeing it en masse.

Now, after presenting the Nibiruan gift to the Earth, it is time to resume my journey. I shoot back out past the planets of the Solar System. As I emerge outside the orbit of Pluto, the first stellar ray I encounter is the Andromeda Galaxy. This ray activates the knowledge that there are other solar systems and galaxies with the same species and genetic diversification as those of planet Earth. This is the teaching that the source of Earth's genetic coding is the cosmic morphogenetic field. The species on Earth exist in many other places and will always exist in many other places. The Solar System is beginning its transfiguration: its Sun is preparing to become a supernova, and its lifeforms will exist eternally in the cosmic morphogenetic field, regardless of species extinction on Earth.

It is interesting to note than in A.D. 1054, there was a supernova that brought great teachings to the indigenous people of Earth. It was recorded as an Anasazi petroglyph on the walls of Chaco Canyon, New Mexico, and the Anasazi culture attained great heights at that time. Native people teach that resonation with supernovas is a key to dimensional shifts—that is, by attuning to a supernova, you can shift your soul essence to another dimension if you choose. Most recently, Supernova 1987, seen during late February 1987, marked the beginning of Harmonic Convergence.

As I travel in the field of Andromeda Galaxy, I take all the energy that has been vibrating in my third eye and blast it out the top of my head. Suddenly I find myself sitting in a lush canyon. Around me, deer chew on plants and clear water trickles by. Rays of light beam down, holding glistening dust from space. Staring into the dust, my eyes perceive great spaces of dark matter. I move my essence into those spaces, and I am invisible to all who know me. I have transited to another world—a world where I will receive teachings from Sirius.

These Anasazi canyon people left a spiral behind to remind Earthlings of their knowledge about what occurs when a star explodes: that those who are totally in the light simply transit to another planet. If they require magnetic fields, they come to a planet with an iron crystal in its center. These canyon people came to Earth in 1054 from an exploding star called Hope. They were the first kachinas, spirit beings who taught star dances, to visit Earth, and they became the star *teachers of the clans. They brought these star dances to Earth so that the people would learn to dance their energies and let go of their desire for control. These spiralic ceremonies, which carry human consciousness to the Dreamtime, have been danced by the people since Hope first burned into light. This is Hopi, and the Hopi also say the end of time has almost come.*

Finally, I leave the Andromeda ray and pass through the ray of the Galactic Center, which exists to remind all beings that there is no beginning or end—only movement. Beings become denser as they move into the Solar System, and they become formless as they spiral back at the end of time.

After passing out of the ray of the Galactic Center, I move into a zone of very deep space. This feels like a zone that comes to the Solar System from a black hole. This black hole is Cygnus, which teaches about vacuums, about the feeling of being sucked into nothingness. It teaches people about trusting in life, even at the moment of death. It teaches about letting go of ego.

I travel past the ray from Cygnus and enter a zone called Nereids. This is a place of dolphins and fish swimming in the sky, of creatures that swim in electromagnetic fields. This is the zone Earthlings contact when they channel, allowing themselves to dance in the fields and not get caught in form. This is the place of letting go into being, the zone between sexual desire and materialization.

Next I am propelled through a zone that feels like the whole Milky Way Galaxy. This is a wide zone that is in synchronicity with the ecliptic points on Earth—the points that make it possible to perceive other realities by observing the pathways of stars in the sky. This is the zone that integrates the outer spatial reality with the perceptual fields on Earth. Here, one knows how to be in the present moment by becoming a master of perception. As I move out of this zone, I am filled with love as I realize once again why we Nibiruans gave the Earthlings our sciences. We wanted you to feel the same creative excitement that we feel.

Now I am approaching the Sirius star system, where my people are waiting for me. They can't wait to tell me that when the Christ was born on Earth, they saw a beautiful blue light; that when they saw this light, they knew that someday there would be a fusion of stellar and Earth realms; and that there would come a time when we would be welcome on Earth. But since I have made this great circuit through space, I already know this. I have already seen the gift we Nibiruans gave to Earth, and I have seen how it will soon come back to us. We will learn to love.

WERNEKE © 1992

Chapter Eight

CITY OF THE GODDESS

The body has been there for all of human history, and the body forgets *nothing*: all of human history is engraved within each cell and sinew of human embodiment. All of the ancient and continuing abuses of patriarchal culture are carried forward in each living body to be passed along as blood and breath to every new body conceived and born. Our efforts to understand and positively affect the flow of history will be greatly enhanced by our ability to understand and positively affect our own bodies.

—Michael Sky, *Sexual Peace*

Many writers have explored the patriarchal and technological Atlantis, and the conclusion is always the same: that it was a "man-caused" apocalypse. In contrast, perhaps the only way to imagine an ideal world that results in life and creativity is by means of a feminist, child-centered focus. What would such a world be like?

It would be a world in which the concept of a "chosen people" would be the chosen children—*each child desired and exquisitely nurtured by its parents. Such a world would put an end to the "chosen people" who demand male control of the planet. In our patriarchal world, children are "owned" by their fathers because they carry their bloodlines. The end result is always violence, racism, and control; only the agreeable child is supported or has any value, and women and all other species are valued only if they are "useful"—that is, available to be fully used by men.*

To create a world where every child is chosen and every species is honored, women with a strongly developed male side and men with a strongly developed female side must be our primary leaders. In this book, I have been deeply immersed in Atlantis as a Goddess culture, and I feel a personal need to explore how we might reattain the Goddess harmony on Earth.

As I ask for insight into how this could happen, I am propelled right into more knowledge about the needs of my own male side. First, I see a star called

Spica in the constellation of Virgo. Spica encourages success, renown, riches, and love of art and science on Earth. But its influence can also create injustice or unscrupulousness toward the innocent ones, the children. Spica rules emeralds and removes scarcity, and its medieval, magical seal star number eighteen denotes erotic sexuality. Could it be that the chosen child must always be conceived amidst great passion and eroticism? The Goddess has said that it is so.

As my inner knowing opens, I see that this vision has come forth because Spica is the source of Atlantean male technology. Its star trainers were sent to Earth to help establish technology. During this development, it was always important to have a teacher from Spica on hand to determine whether a particular system might cause disharmony among the plant, animal, mineral, or spirit kingdoms. If so, it was not allowed. These teachers were—and still are—called the Keepers of Systems. *They, I realize, must be the key to male nurturance. I am amazed. I see that we are on the verge of finding the missing link to earthly harmony. It is time for me to return to Earth as a Spican to discover how to create a safe world for the chosen child.*

I am Argolid. I incarnated in Atlantis from Spica. I am very tall and extremely straight like an Aryan, and my muscles are tight but not bulging. I use ropes to fly through the air, and I do acrobatics to keep my muscles lean. I don't want lots of hormones like testosterone in my muscles, since they create excess energy that I would then have to dissipate. Such dissipation of male energy on Earth creates war, control, and abuse. By keeping myself lean and fit, I am very healthy and I feel good all the time. The energy in my body is very balanced.

I am not in any way part of the incarnational soul cycle of Barbara, who lies on the table. She does not have the proper magnetic, cellular, or metallic structures to bring this teaching through. Therefore, I have come through today by arcing my energy between her heart and the body of the male facilitator who is in the room with her. It would be damaging to her physical vehicle to bring in my full imprint.

To Barbara, I feel like a bee. From me she can hear a very high, resonant sound that makes it possible for her to access the information I wish to transmit. As you listen to my story, do not be confused by my ability to report from extremely ancient times concurrently with what you call your *now.* My sense of time is totally spherical.

Confusions and intense fear about Atlantis are coming from the time when the last Atlantean theocracies were destroyed by the great eruption of Santorini, or Thera, around 1500 b.c. That huge cataclysm reimprinted the fall of Atlantis that had occurred in 10,600 b.c. As we move into the male harmonic from *before* such cataclysms, respect the inner blocks and fears you still hold. The remnants of these theocracies came to an end during those great traumatic upheavals. Thera was an original Atlantean temple form, just as drawings of the Cretan labyrinth are Atlantean temple forms. The island described in the *Critias*, by Plato, is an accurate description of this basic temple form. This perfect geomantic form is the eternal secret to cultural harmony on Earth.

About twelve thousand years ago, a huge Atlantean temple on an island in the Atlantic sank in a gigantic cataclysm. People think this was Atlantis. But the temple form and the complete culture of Atlantis also existed in many other places on the planet. One of the most perfect Atlantean ruins is on Malta, but those are subterranean parts of the temple form. The description that has come down through Plato from Solon, the Greek priest who studied in Egypt, is a map of the *surface form*. This form is primarily masculine, while the subterranean form is primarily feminine. Like the inner womb, it is rarely seen.

When the surface form exists along with its female subterranean structure, the result is perfect harmony between males and females. Where the two structures meet, there is a sacred spring grounded with an Earth/sky crystal. Then there must be circles of land around the crystal, alternating with circular canals. The land beyond the last circle of water may be farmland, grazing fields, wild plains, or jungles. Beneath the great crystal are sacred caves where smaller crystals grow. Lacking these, caves are constructed to access the telluric forces.

The star and Earth teachings meet at the power point in the central crystal, and the communication to the center of the Earth goes from the sky through this crystal and circulates through the water to all the land. The concentric circles of water radiate the emotions of the inhabitants out to the stars, and the inhabitants are taught to meditate with checkered designs of red and white, which balance feelings of dark and light. These constructions can be almost any size, as long as the essential form is honored. In a large complex, dwelling places or even a whole city can be contained in the land circles, with great surrounding farms to feed the population.

Because desires manifest realities, the main crystal must be kept completely free of human desires. Instead, the people create with *intent*, and they are the *Keepers of Intention*. All creations are a direct result of the clarity and purity of the lives of the people: they do not attempt to control realities with crystals. The central confusion about Atlantis comes from the Nibiruan visitors, who did not understand the inherent clarity of these people. They arrived and assumed that the harmonic creativity of the Atlanteans came from their crystal. Then the Nibiruans placed their own thoughtforms in the crystal by means of laser beams, creating an interference pattern. Thus, the cycle turned from creation to chaos, and Atlantis became third dimensional and dense.

When the Spican teaching was pure, the Spican crystal was the interface between Earth and sky, and it circulated knowledge and harmony of all cosmic cycles. The sacred spring circulated feelings from the Earth through the waters to the land, and the people attuned to these pulsations as they soaked in the golden rays of the Sun. As long as the proper intention was maintained, the form functioned correctly, and the people were fourth dimensional—not caught in time.

This living temple form I have just described is the source of all the legends about the central crystal of Atlantis. It is also the source of great fear about crystals, as well as respect for their power, thus making them two-edged swords for many people. It is possible to make a very small model of this form for personal meditation in order to access teachings from the stars, and it must be used with clear intention and unconditional trust.

Remnants of this form still exist in places like Avebury. That is why many megalithic sites have henges or moats around them, and Glastonbury was once surrounded by rings of water. Many churches were built over such sites, their sacred springs gushing under altars built over subterranean Goddess caves. In ancient Egypt, this form radiated from the central temples on the Nile, and its canals circulated the water during the inundation.

When this form is in place, people are very happy, peaceful, and creative. It is like a womb, a central emergence point for celestial energies. Great stellar souls were first drawn to life on Earth by this form, and they will return again when it is recreated on the planet after A.D. 2013. With this form, there is no problem with water access for planting.

Now, with this explanation, let us go back to the time when I, Argolid, first created this Atlantean temple form. It is 27,000 B.C., during an Age of Aries. There are almost no archaeological remains of the form from that time because the last ice age scoured much of the planet down to bedrock, and great waves destroyed many Atlantean islands. Nevertheless, I was here—a stellar source of new technology for planet Earth. Each stellar source such as I comes to Earth to work with her elements—time, cycles, and species—in order to create technology. Technology, the practical creative use of materials in the cosmos, is the same everywhere, but the individual location is unique because it affords perspective. I came to Earth to experience your particular creative field, just as you take a trip to a foreign country to experience its unique creations.

In my particular case, I incarnated on Earth, which was a brave act in 27,000 B.C. I was birthed by a woman who was as similar as possible to my own body type. I chose what you now call an Altamira woman, living in a cave in what you now call the Pyrenees. I chose this group of individuals because they were about eight feet tall. We Spicans were about thirteen feet tall, which made us appear to Earthlings as great, towering beings, or "gods." We had long, angular bodies that seemed to wave in the wind, and we were filled with great light.

I can remember the preparations for my arrival. The sacred Earth Goddess who was ready to accept my essence became pregnant during an intense, erotic ceremony. It was necessary for the people to create a great orgasmic force in order to attract a child from the stars. There is no other way to attract beings from other dimensions to Earth.

In order to achieve this, they first spent much time in their caves listening to the water, which caused their inner minds to vibrate to the spin of the planetary and star orbits. They also vibrated with kundalini energy, which activated the water in their bodies and caused electromagnetic activation in their brains. Most important, they *maximized their sexual force*. While one couple made love, the rest of the clan surrounded them and drummed to the stars, calling for great beings to come to Earth.

The intention of these people was to give birth to beings from every star in the sky. Each person made love to no more than a few persons in his or her life because the fusing of kundalini energy during sex was so intense that personal identity tended to be lost. These people knew they could be lost forever by merging with too many others, and it took them a whole lifetime to learn to fuse while still retaining their sense of self. Also they discovered that it was easier to maintain personal identity when they joined amidst clan support. At a minimum, it was essential for the father of a woman and the mother of a man to be present in meditation when they fused with another for the first time.

The ceremony that was created around my mother is what attracted me to Earth. She loved male erections, so for her mating ceremony, she asked to go into the deepest reaches of the cave with fourteen young men. There, these men formed a circle around her and brought phallic power into their bodies. When my mother saw a blue light above one of them, she chose that man to make love to her. The other thirteen men stood around the mating couple continuing to hold their erections while I was conceived; so, in a sense, they are all my fathers. The Temple of Saquarra in Egypt, which still remains on Earth, represents this ceremony, and it will be activated again when male erections are no longer hidden.

Months later, just before my birth, the cave filled with my light from Spica. This pleased and delighted the people, because they then understood that a divine child would arrive to be their teacher. In your now, when someone comes in with star teaching, it is not acknowledged at birth, and the information the child carries is usually not given to the world. In the next phase of evolution, all children will be recognized at birth, and the people will learn from all of them.

When I was born, I was much longer than a normal baby. I was also shining—a sign that I had come from the stars. I came to the Altamirans because their feelings about sexuality were very pure and powerful, but they had not yet developed systems for community harmony. These people were to become my "clay," so first I needed to gain their special knowledge. For example, they could see that I was fascinated with the Dreamtime because it was my only access to my stellar source. But I did not have the ability to tune into my dreams. This left me feeling lonely and separated from my origins. So they put me in a cave, which they kept lit by means of an inner fire in their heads, and they sat around me in a circle while I was sleeping. They tuned into what I was dreaming by vibrating with the cells in my brain, and accessed visions of the images in my brain. Then, on the cave wall all around me, they made paintings of what they saw in my head. Whenever I woke up, I saw imprints on the walls that were images of my own dreams. Gradually, I developed the ability to see what I was dreaming as I dreamed it.

Next, the people initiated me into the crystal teachings of Earth. On Spica, we knew how to meditate with crystals and how to use them to create power and energy. The memory of crystal activation came into form on Earth with my arrival here, and later that knowledge was the reason for the fall of Atlantis. When a being incarnates on Earth from another location, such as Spica, the memories and teachings of that place eventually manifest in the new home.

Geomancy—the ability to read Earth energy—can help to determine the effects of bringing such techniques into a new location. The Atlantean geomancers, for example, knew all about the seismic consequences of control and power meditation with crystals. The real trouble started when the Atlantean scientists took over. The problem was that they thought of Earth simply as a colony—they refused to respect the knowledge of the original people, who kept the vibration of quartz in the stones in harmony with the central iron crystal of the Earth. Colonization of any place will always be destructive unless the indigenous energy complexes are the primary forms that guide the new culture.

The Atlantean concentric circular form made it possible for star technology to develop on Earth. Beings from other stars besides Spica came to Atlantis—beings who understood atomic structure, solar energy, elemental energies, and space-travel technology. You are fascinated by Atlantis because Earth is again developing all these same technologies. But your disinformation system denies the reality of Atlantis; it is usually said to be fiction, for if you allowed yourselves to believe that it *was* real, then you would have to look at why it ended in catastrophe. And in looking, you would have to conclude that you have been creating a similar catastrophe—colonies on Earth that are not in balance with its natural systems. You would be forced to see that you are attempting to colonize space with shuttle programs such as *Atlantis* that destroy ozone as they are fired off. You might also be forced to notice that *Atlantis* is being sent up periodically to get a good look at the atmosphere so that those in power can go underground *in time* to save themselves from the expected catastrophe.

At any rate, I was initiated into the Earth crystal knowledge, and the living Atlantean temple form that I created fit the geomantic needs of Earth. It provided adequate water and open land to grow plants to support life. It also provided a cohesive circular form for social interaction. Most importantly, the structure circulated the vibrations of the Earth in its spin around the Sun into the cosmic fields. If you walk from the outside to the center of this form, you cross its waters by means of bridges to the four directions. Or you can travel by means of water from the center to the outside without encountering any barriers. The center has the most concentrated energy, while the outside realms have more diversity. This allows individuals to activate various kinds of energy in themselves during various cycles of their personal lives. In short, the system is a maze that offers mystery, integrity, intention, centering, exploration, and challenge. *It activates people on Earth.*

In many cases, this living temple form was built over already existing caves that had been the sacred sites during the early years of the Great Cycle. The most powerful Atlantean temples were built over such caves—as at Teotihuacan, Tenochititlan, Malta, Abydos, Knossos, Santa Fe, and Atlanta. These caves were repositories for Earth intelligence—portals to the crystal core. They were used for birthing, sacred sex, meditation, accessing the Dreamtime, and teaching. They also facilitated the removal of outside influences so that a meditator could access his or her inner center and connect with the Heart of the Mother. In those days, it was known that connection between the center of the Earth and the Galactic Center created harmony on this planet because it kept open the natural human wisdom.

The temple form also controlled population because everyone understood that it was not to be enlarged beyond the original three circles. First a sacred temple was built in the center over the sacred caves; then the first people—the "ancestors"—developed the first circle of land. Then *their* children moved out and built the second circle. When the grandchildren of the first people became adults, they developed the third circle.

The first circle then became the home of the grandfathers and grandmothers, who in turn became the wisdom keepers of the temple. The second circle became the home of the parents with grown children and the adults with no children. (Adults had plenty of time for creativity because they gave birth to so few children.) The third circle was home for the young families. This outer location enabled the children and young parents to

ATLANTEAN TEMPLE FORM

roam the outlying forests, commune with the animals, and do their vision quests. By the time these people matured and moved into the middle circle, they had found their purpose: work for the village and personal spiritual direction. Then they played and stretched their creativity to the maximum, and they spent great amounts of time learning from their children.

The second circle was also used for theaters, community forums, schools for job training, and buildings for making products and doing art. Structurally, this was the densest section of the village. Fear of difficult weather and catastrophe was nonexistent because the inhabitants of the outer circle could always find shelter in the middle circle. This constant availability of shelter encouraged the families in the outer circle to live very simply, which allowed them the greatest amount of time for creativity.

Likewise, the center circle of the elders was a place of meditation for all the villagers. Here, both adults and parents could come to recharge and reattune their spirits through the elder wisdom, and children spent a great deal of time there being instructed by the elders. Inhabitants of the outer circles could always seek shelter in the temples.

The wise elders were always revered and cared for. They conducted all initiations and spiritual instruction in the temples. The population was naturally stable, since no young family wished to produce a child who would crowd out a beloved elder. Often, after an elder went to the spirit world, a new child was a rebirth of that elder. And birthing was ruled by the principle of "welcoming to Earth." Each child was chosen as a gift to civilization, and each decision to have a child implied knowing that the child would have space to grow, become an adult, and express its creativity—and that someday it would be taken into the circle of elders.

As long as children are chosen, initiated, and taught, there can be no serious disharmony between male and female, Earth and sky, or young and old. The child is our creative self, and when it is unwanted or abused, the denial of self begins. When we are old, we become like children again, and just like little children, we must be cared for. This form creates joy, creativity, pleasure, and enjoyment of service. It is not necessary to be unhappy on planet Earth. Unhappiness is an illusion.

In those days, the temple form was unique in each location due to climatic differentials, diversity of tribes, surface ecology, and telluric forces. Even so, it was the perfect Earth form for community order and efficient use of resources. And it still is. Imagine one such form on an ocean peninsula with the surrounding sea for harvesting; another in the jungle where the forest is harvested; and another next to a river meandering through a savannah. Since water and sustainable Earth were the first requirements, this form was not used in deserts except where springs could be accessed. Since the center was always the most powerful point, it could not decay. Since the children required nature for growth, the outer areas could not be polluted, overpopulated, or turned into garbage dumps. Thus, all resources were recycled, the unit was self-sustaining, and the form was womblike, protective, and fully open to the sky and the elements. This form naturally circulates energy. Though it has not been used for some time, the Earth will recreate it again.

The real teaching behind this living Atlantean temple form is correct birthing within an enlightened culture led by elders. Keepers of Tradition hold the respect and power necessary to protect knowledge for seven generations beyond themselves. This was how societies first evolved on Earth, and the indigenous records on this law are still protected by the elder traditions. Meanwhile, however, something in time has malfunctioned as souls have entered this plane, and those souls have broken down the Earth traditions. You are now poised at the apex of confusion, world violence, pollution, and overpopulation threatening all life. Your societal structures are rotten to the core, collapsing under the weight of resource annihilation. Never have humans been so totally confused.

How did this malfunction occur? You must ask the Pleiadians, the *Keepers of Harmony*. They can take you right to the Galactic Center, where these records are available.

I am Allini, a Pleiadean teacher from Alcyone, and I can read the Galactic Center records. From these records, I see that the primary being who was involved in genetic manipulation on earth was called Inanna. I see her now as a winged goddess holding up two replicas of the symbol for the North Node of the Moon—the omega symbol—which give information on the karmic reasons for incarnation. Inanna stands on the backs of two lions, smiling, and on each side of her are two great owls. I am intrigued by why she holds these nodes as she stands as mistress of the animals of Atlantis. Let us go into these symbols.

As I contemplate them, I am catapulted to the point in the Solar System where the orbit of the Moon crosses the plane of Earth's orbit around the Sun—the ecliptic. This intersection is the location of the lunar nodes for each person in his or her birth chart, and these nodes explain a person's real purpose—the incarnational choice. I am suspended at this nodal intersection, exactly where consciousness of the Galactic Center enters the human at birth. I, Allini, am the goddess of love, beauty, and harmony, and I am always present when the galactic

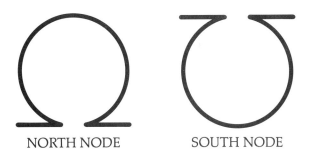

NORTH NODE   SOUTH NODE

codes imprint the soul. I encode all babies with a feeling that they are loved by the Source, and I cause all beings on Earth to search for love throughout their lives. On Earth, I am called the "Blue Lady."

However, something malfunctions in most births, and babies forget about me. When attempting to elucidate the original malfunction, we must understand the mechanics of the flash of energy from the Source that imprints the nodal axis on the ecliptic—when the *feeling potential* is directed to a given lifetime.

Inanna had an especially strong influence on Earth during the time of the Goddess culture. During that time, between five and ten thousand years ago, the atmosphere of the Earth was thicker, more enveloping, and more oxygenated, and the climate was most hospitable. It was a time of much creation, especially in water. When the planet warmed up after the last ice age, all was greenness and swarming energy. The Earth was very soft and very safe—it especially favored the feminine influence—and Inanna saw that the people were ripe for a spiritual connection to Nibiru, her home.

Referring to the node intersections on the ecliptic, Inanna could see beings incarnating from many dimensions, many galaxies, many different places in the universe. But once they came into matter, their sense of self became of Earth. She saw that most souls had difficulty integrating their multidimensional experiences into the physical, and she wished that this cosmic knowledge could become known in the Earth dimension, the physical, the realm of time. To actualize her wish, Inanna incarnated several times. She lived on Earth periodically from 7200 to 3600 B.C. and was a primary teacher for the Goddess culture; a great deal of her teaching had to do with birthing. As a result of her work, cosmic connection became a potential for indigenous humans.

It is 7200 B.C., Nibiru is in the Asteroid Belt about ready to orbit out of the Solar System back toward Sirius, and Inanna is watching that point where the North Node of the Moon intersects the eliptic. She examines its potential. Can she use this power point to learn more about how to feel? And if she learns to feel more as Earthlings do, can she evolve more spiritually? With this thought, she contemplates the surrender of her Goddess self. She knows that the more she can feel, the more she can infuse her higher self into form—which will benefit both herself and those on Earth. She sees that the birthing dynamic of Earth is potentially more fruitful for her than any other experience in the universe. At this moment of realization, she is metamorphosed by a flash of blinding light as I, Alinni, fuse with her. We have both seen that we can evolve more by immersing ourselves in Earth experience. Thus, her brilliant mind becomes heightened by my intense feelings. Inanna becomes me, and I become Inanna.

I am Inanna, and I wish to speak to you of my Earth experience. My desire to enter more deeply into Earth life created the idea of giving birth to children of my lineage who would remain on Earth—that is, to create Earthlings who were also Nibiruan. Thus, the age of the great Goddess culture had arrived—gods and goddesses walking the Earth while still being connected to the cosmos.

First, I created birthing temples such as Çatal Hüyük. Then I began experimenting with sex and gestation. My struggle to allure an Earthling into sex with me is immortalized in the ancient Sumerian tale of Inanna (Ishtar) and Dumuzi (Tammuz). Before this time, many male gods had joined with Earth women who had then given birth to demigods, but my work was the reverse: I was the first Nibiruan female to give birth to the child of an Earth father. In fact, at the time, this was the only way to ensure that the children of Nibiru would remain on Earth. Their Earth fathers would force them to remain and build families. Unfortunately, though, this need also created the patriarchy. And the patriarchy would later destroy the very Goddess culture that had created it.

It was tricky to bring multidimensional beings into solid form. Another problem—also unforeseen by me—was that many DNA memory codes had to be shut down. If the Earth children from Nibiru remembered how to ascend to the fourth dimension, they would not want to stay. As you can see, the work of anchoring the fourth dimension into the third—*the ultimate purpose of linear time*—has been very traumatic, and I would never have tried it if I had seen how difficult it was going to be.

I, Inanna, worked on conception by utilizing light meditation as the sperm pierced the egg. I created light codes of genetic perfection that would help the Nibiruan and Earth genes to fuse effectively. This vibration also infused the zygote with a memory of the Source, the Galactic Center.

The previous hundreds of thousands of years of genetic manipulation by Nibiruans had created many aberrations. In fact, all of the diseases known to humanity were originally triggered from conception between

Nibiruans and Earthlings who fused with insufficient erotic vibration. During conception, I also worked to charge the erotic potential of the Earth, which opens human cells to an infusion of cosmic light. Eventually, my work will bring an end to disease. Even in your time, babies conceived in the midst of high erotic vibration have enhanced genes.

Today, you are on the verge of global transmutation—the same reinfusion of light into matter that I was working with nine thousand years ago. The return to genetic clarity will be the next evolutionary stage of the Earth/stellar bond. In fact, this process has already begun, and it is accelerating rapidly. Now, just as I once surrendered myself to matter, the time has come for you to surrender yourselves to the enlightenment.

That same light infusion is entering the Solar System again, and it will be building up until 2012. As a result, all the old diseases and genetic aberrations are being triggered now. These aberrations must be burned out of your genetic codes, but you can allow this to happen only by opening your consciousness to the light of knowledge. Let us look into how this functions regarding disease.

When Nibiruan genes were first united with human genes, the sexual force of humans was stronger and the mental ability of the Nibiruans was greater. The immune system is vitalized by sexual energy, and the brain is synchronized by mental force. However, in humans, *the immune system is strengthened by sex combined with feeling*; this is what differentiates humans from animals. Therefore, sexuality without love became dangerous to the human immune system.

Conversely, the mental superiority of the Nibiruans did not mix easily with the evolving Earthling. This created diseases such as Alzheimer's, which is triggered by too much left-brain activation, and heart disease, which tends to arise when the feeling center is ruled by the mind. The Nibiruans possessed fabulous left brains, but the development of their right brains had been stunted. Now, as we struggle to synchronize our brains, peculiar diseases are manifesting.

Already a series of early waves of light from the Galactic Center have been correcting DNA mutation and activating brain synchronization. These early waves are preparation for the complete light infusion. If the synchronization were to occur too quickly, human beings might cease to exist. The new genetic code will be in tune with the Source, free of disease, and protected by a strong immune system. Now you must enhance your sexuality by using it only with love, and you must quickly synchronize both sides of the brain.

The second stage of my work as Inanna involved the birth process on Earth, and through many lifetimes I learned a great deal from which modern women—and men—could benefit. One of the most basic of my teachings is that a genetically valuable fetus should not be aborted. It is important to understand that the soul does not enter the fetus until the exact moment of birth but that, nevertheless, the fetus has inherent biological value from conception. When humans learn to value the biology of Earth—to respect the exquisite and perfect power of Gaia—then there will be fewer abortions.

Another area that I explored was the fetal environment. I discovered that if a fetus is given proper nurturance, it will imprint very few, if any, negative patterns. However, if the fetus is not nurtured during development, it can carry severe negative emotional and cellular imprints at birth. Such imprints can also occur during the birth process. Notice that emotional and etheric imprints can occur in the fetus even before the soul fuses with it. These imprints are the most difficult ones to identify during later life by an individual seeking healing.

After the fetus has matured and the time of birth has arrived, it is ready to receive a soul. The way this works is that a soul assesses the Earth realm, searching for a means to gain experience on Earth. There is much misunderstanding about this moment. For example, some people say that the soul does a scan of the parents, including a review of their bank account, future plans, and housing. The idea of such analyses is ridiculous and very funny, illustrating how little humans understand about multidimensionality and the cosmic synchronicity principle. The soul simply attunes to the cellular matrix of the fetus, and the solar magnetic field calls the soul into time. That calling into time is triggered by the power of the lunar nodal axis—the gateway into Earth that I, Inanna, guard. The soul's entry is not a rational, third-dimensional scan of possibilities. *It is lured into life by genes that love it.* Matter is very creative. Magnetism rules the patterns of life, and they function at their optimum in a climate of deep feeling and love, the real energy of the Sun.

Thus, the soul searches for and is drawn to a fetus that carries a vibrational attunement to its essence, its creative life in the Sun. Then, exactly when it enters, there is an electromagnetic field imprint—the astrological chart—which offers all of the possibilities for advancement of that soul's karmic pattern.

Usually a soul of very exquisite resonance will be drawn to a similar fetus. For example, parents who are very spiritually advanced can actually draw a being to them who shares their developmental level. They can create a fetus that will be a teacher for them, a vehicle for a life of intense spiritual advancement.

Such parenting will become more and more common on planet Earth—*if* Earthlings can manage to avoid eradicating their biology altogether.

In your time, more and more children are coming in with fewer and fewer negative imprints. Regarding the future of Earth, look to these children. If there is no emotional-body trauma in a fetus and if there are no negative imprints on the child up to age seven, then the negative, past-life emotional-body memory bank of the soul is not activated. *Activation of negative memory shuts down twelve-strand DNA!* On the other hand, activation of positive memory awakens and enlivens it.

During my lifetimes of research, I also discovered that in the child's early life or in the womb, traumatic events can trigger negative memory patterns. Of course, one of the reasons the soul incarnates in the first place is to activate negative imprints in order to clear them and progress. But ideally, these imprints are activated after age seven when the child becomes conscious of itself. The conscious child is able to learn from its experience as it is occurring. This is called *being in the moment,* and the child can clear those imprints the soul has chosen to eliminate.

A memory activated in a child before age seven tends to feel *eternal.* In this case, the child tends to scatter the memory into the past or future and cannot respond to present-moment opportunities to clear it. The younger the child, the greater the scattering. And when this occurs in the womb, the child has no idea where to look for the problem. It is like coming into a world with trillions of little notes waiting to be deciphered.

Since the body holds memory of the scatter point, bodywork can take you right back into the original event and decode it, even if it is a prebirth memory! Your emotions can work with divination systems that create bridges to the little notes that are actually magnetized pieces of your inner self waiting to be recognized. Mysteriously, you find yourself feeling a resonance with an animal, a tarot card, or a planetary archetype that reminds you of a lost part of self. The urge to remember drives you to go into feelings in your body and clear imprints until you find yourself feeling in the present time. These blocks are the key to *all* psychological growth in life, so clearing them catapults you into the present moment.

In your time, much progress is being made clearing blocks through past-life regression. Since you have scattered them into the past, that is where you need to go to access them. But what you are really tapping into is much more than past lives—you are tapping into your biological records and your actual soul memory bank, which is cosmic. The multidimensional self contains all these things. Such imprints can also be explored by means of dream work. Journeying into these memory banks with any technique that acknowledges their reality offers you the opportunity to see what your soul wants you to learn.

The way you work with your blocks is the key to your evolution up to A.D. 2012. You can explore this best by being willing to consider that you create your own reality. Once you decide to become a creator in the moment, you can start *choosing which block you wish to play with next*. You have more power and intention because *you decide* when you are ready to tackle a soul agenda, and this aligns your free will with your soul growth. This concept is gravely misunderstood because its exploration has centered on disease, but it is impossible to explore conscious creation of reality through disease. You must study it by observing individuals who have successfully removed blocks. Disease is always based on an old block, and you may or may not move through it in a given lifetime. In order to understand future evolution, study of individuals who are not evolving will get you nowhere. It is time to carefully observe individuals who are busy creating joyful, productive, nonlimited, healthy, and brilliant lives.

If you continue to go into the blocks you feel and clear them by consciously experiencing them, then one by one you remove them and your vibration begins to resonate more and more closely with the present moment. Always the body must work with the mind. When you clear your body, you move back to the conception point when the Source flashed into biological form. When you clear your mind, you begin to see the agenda of your soul. If you allow your soul time to resonate in your body during meditation, gradually that light of conception fills your cells.

I, Inanna, would also like to tell you that in spite of my past mistakes, Earth is moving into a vibration in which more individuals will be accessing the Source. You are coming to the end of a long phase of learning many lessons, but you still cannot imagine getting out of school. The Goddess is returning because she remembers life on Earth *without* school. This is the shift in emphasis that you are all feeling now, but at this point you find it difficult to imagine a new reality. Ironically, your imagination is the tool you need most, since with it you can create images of new realities. As the soul moves out of fields that generate lessons and into fields of pure creativity, those who have blocks to the new fields are driven to clear them. This is why there is so much disease in your time and why so much therapy is necessary.

It is time for you to become smarter about genetics, pregnancy, and early childhood. Earth is now a popular destination for souls who are ready to birth and move back into perfect resonance with the Source. If it seems like you are on the verge of disaster, remember that the light is already shining at the end of the tunnel, and the evidence of this light is the huge effort people are making to learn their lessons.

If a negative imprint occurs after birth, one can return to the original trauma and clear the imprint. It is prebirth imprints that are very difficult to clear. The new teaching of using acupuncture needles for emotional-body clearing is the best method available for this. Prebirth imprints are buried deep in the cells of the body, and there is almost no other way to access and clear such blocks. You will come to a time soon when many teachers working with emotional-body clearing will use acupuncture needles in their therapy.

Another technique that can clear prebirth cellular records is ceremonial healing. Many cultures thousands of years ago understood this need. They knew instinctively that ceremony means reattuning people to the Source. For example, if a village had been engaged in a very traumatic war, a ceremony was done afterward to clear the tribal members of such negative imprinting. War was understood to *always* be a failure, and clearance of the resulting anger was possible only after confession of the errors. No sexual intercourse or conception of new life was allowed until the clearance ceremony had been completed; otherwise, the fetus would be imprinted with anger.

Healers in your time are now learning to combine ceremony and therapy, and this will become more common in the future. During a healing, a resonant field of correct order is established in the body, and ceremony with that field can permanently rearrange the cellular prebirth imprints. The deeper the imprint in the body, the deeper the healing. Someday you will even learn how to heal your DNA.

Now, before I leave you, let me give you a brief glimpse into one of the many birthing temples that are dedicated to me, Innana. The goal in all such temples was to bring a child to Earth with minimal separation from the Source. Sex was sacred and engaged in only under circumstances of joy and peace, never between angry people. A man had a right to a woman only if he was prepared to be the sacred protector of the hearth where that child would live. During pregnancy, a woman's body was considered the temple of the Source, and pregnancy was an ecstatic experience. The unborn child was viewed as the mother's teacher, and she communed with it as much as possible. The child taught the mother how to prepare for its arrival. Thus, the mother was deeply in tune with the fetus, and as the birth time arrived, both mother and father called for the soul that would be most perfect for the happiness of the family. This often resulted in the return of a beloved parent or grandparent.

The priestesses who assisted with the birth first went into a room next to the birthing temple. This room, painted with wall reliefs of red vultures, served as a purification chamber. There the priestesses meditated and breathed deeply, moving out any fear. Then an erotic force would rise in their bodies. Only when the priestesses were free of all astral disturbances could they enter into the birthing chamber. They would come into the birthing room in high states of meditation—ecstatic states of consciousness that are very hard to attain while in the body.

These priestesses would then attune to the soul of the arriving child. As they did so, often they could see the Blue Lady from the Pleiades merging with me, Inanna, as I held the North Node of the Moon in my hands. Even in your time, some people who attend births attain these ecstatic states as the soul comes in, and some even see blinding light and the Blue Lady.

My birthing temples were equipped with basins of water placed under openings to the sky. Often the surface of the water reflected the light of the Moon or the stars, or glistened in the bright sunlight. At the moment of birth, a metal bowl was struck that resonated with the Earth, and a crystal bowl was struck that rang the tone of the incoming soul. The bowls were struck simultaneously by two priests who stood tall and blindfolded so they could not see the actual birth; they struck the tones when they heard the child's first breath. Then they went into an adjacent room to cast a chart for the exact moment of birth in order to determine the choices of the returning soul.

The mother usually felt little pain from the birthing, but in difficult cases hypnosis was used. After the birth, the baby's skull was restructured in order to restablish its natural harmony with the cosmos after passing through the birth canal. Then the baby was massaged in warm water and swaddled very gently. Finally, the priestesses worked with the baby in a state of pure meditation until the body relaxed with the power of its soul. This was always a source of joy for the mother as well as for the priestesses.

The imprinting of the child during the first weeks of life was also considered extremely critical. The vibrational relationship between the soul and fetus is formed by means of magnetic imprints from the planetary cycles during the first three lunar cycles. This perceptual phase is extremely intense, establishing a pattern for the gradual ripening of this body with its soul.

In this lifetime as Barbara, I have been offered great wisdom by Avebury Circle about the Atlantean circular form. Avebury's inner circle contains stones that are like a council of elders to me, as the original elders of the inner circle of the Atlantean form were to the inhabitants of Atlantis. In fact, I strongly suspect that Avebury Circle is a central temple for the elders of an ancient Atlantean city form. The male control forces have invaded and blocked this portal for more than two thousand years, and I feel deep inside that, at one time, Avebury must have been a birthing temple for correct entry of the soul. Following my intuition, I return to Avebury again, to a lifetime in which I helped encode the circle and the primordial egg of creation with the wisdom of the cosmos.

I *become* Avebury Circle, as if every one of its great stones were a part of my body. The tallest stone in the southernmost circle corresponds to my throat

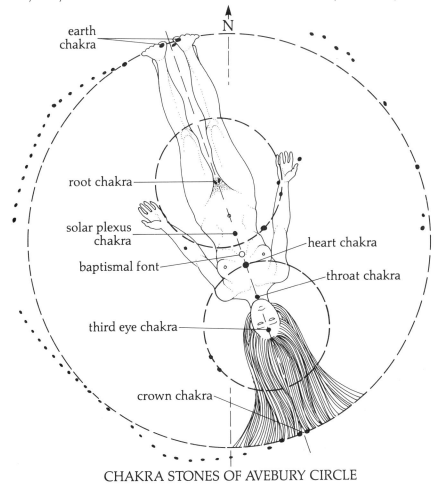

CHAKRA STONES OF AVEBURY CIRCLE

chakra. It is twenty feet tall, like a thin knife reaching for the sky. It receives intense electrical shocks, and the crystals in the caves below it intensify its magnetic field. In order to help charge this stone, I ask for the master key to the throat chakra.

Like the genitals, the throat is a major source of human energy exchange. We must learn to merge our light bodies through the throat. We must learn how to have maximum fusion *without* the sexual act. This can be accomplished through orgasmic levels of communication, which we can achieve when we understand that we do not need to control ourselves all the time. We can learn how to connect on other levels, how to be close without sex.

This circle informs me that our ideas about how to break down separation are being transformed. One of the major areas of breakthrough today is in regression and psychospiritual work, where we are allowing ourselves to play with each other in other dimensions and times, in so-called "other lifetimes." Through these other-dimensional experiences together, we are *feeling* that we are not all separate from each other. There are many ways in which we can merge with others now—many paths to orgasmic fusion without sex.

Several paths to such orgasmic fusion are electromagnetic intensification, kundalini rising, and new heights of spiritual excitement. These new ways of relating to others transcend the limitations of human sexual relationships, or they can be added to mutually orgasmic sex. They also create a level of play that is exquisite: through them, we begin to realize that we might have "created" somebody else who has also "created" us. We feel free to enter into mystery plays together and to explore significant curiosities. As we do so, the energy field around us intensifies, and other dimensions of knowing, such as the Dreamtime, are activated.

The only things that retard such exploration are control patterns from negative experiences in the past: we are afraid of what others might think of us. But we are also so tired of limitation that we are beginning to play with emotional divination—fusion with the energy of another as we feel our own life force within another being. Think of how little we have enjoyed the people we have been traveling with for so long! The place to shift all this is in the throat chakra. Now we are ready to *feel* with the throat chakra, to discover new forms of spiritual ecstasy through new forms of communication.

This tall needle stone, this throat-chakra receiver in the southern circle, is like an antenna, accessing information on weather cycles and human activity. But it is also a broadcasting antenna. Throughout the ages, there has been much suppression of the throat chakra—for example, through hanging, choking, and strangulation. There has been a conspiracy to shut down the throat because it can communicate with and project to all dimensions. It is also a creative force par excellence that often threatens the powers that be—including the vested interests of our own self-imposed limitations.

Next, I tune into the third-eye stones. This is a set of two huge black stones that angle inward toward the throat-chakra stone. Behind these are the two stones that form the south gate that leads out of the southern circle. From the south gate, there is an alignment of stones heading north; from the third-eye stones, a straight line could be drawn through the throat-chakra needle stone, the heart-chakra stone at the intersection of the south and north circles, the solar plexus flat rock, and the three cupping stones of the root chakra in the north circle. The center point of both circles is the heart-chakra stone, where the baptisms once occurred. This is a fantastic form to work with because it corresponds exactly to my physical body, and it teaches the lessons we need to know about the powers of the chakras.

The two flat third-eye stones are angled toward the center throat-chakra stone, and they pick up signals from the heart and throat. The throat-chakra needle stone receives from all directions; then it beams rays to the third-eye stones, causing those stones to deflect information and power back through the whole system. The third eye is constantly informing the lower chakras of a higher level of available information. The backs of the third-eye stones are like the bones in the skull where the medulla oblongata is located, and they are tremendous attractors of information from the dimensions beyond the third.

This system pulls information into the back of the head, which corresponds to the back of the stones. The throat chakra vibrates and resonates, sending out a great force, which is also sent back through the lower chakras. This process informs the whole system, but the information being broadcast is also the key to interference and possession. Therefore, people with very receptive third eyes can pick up a lot of information. If their throat consciousness is not extremely acute and doesn't send energy down to the solar plexus to feel its qualities, they may unknowingly broadcast information that could draw in energies that they may not be prepared to handle.

As the time of the end of the Mayan Great Cycle draws nigh, the key to subtle discernment of potential possession by the visitors lies in the throat and solar plexus chakras. Forget watching the skies for silver ships, and take a closer look at your neighbor. The apprehension of invasive energies teaches people about how their words reflect what is in their minds and about how the information they receive is distorted by their own interference factors. Nothing will be more important in the 1990s than the development of discernment about what is really going on. For now, let us say that no one or no thing can invade you if you know how to read its vibrations.

The throat is most invested in protecting the heart, and if you listen very carefully to who or what is signaling, you will feel in your solar plexus what is harmonious with the Earth. Your solar plexus contains the complete record of every invasion of consciousness since the beginning of time, and it can read every energy ray coming into it. The only thing that interferes with its clarity is lack of feeling. This system we are describing in Avebury Circle, which mirrors the energy system of our own bodies, is now ready to become a receiver and sender of unblocked cosmic light energy.

Avebury Circle teaches that the third eye is an efficient receiver and sender from the fourth dimension and higher. It receives no information in the third dimension, although it does read synchronicities having to do with third-dimensional activities and events. The throat and all the lower chakras receive information in the third dimension. The crown chakra, however, is the entrance to the Nibiruan gateway. From the south gateway stones in Avebury Circle, in fact, there is a snaking pathway of stones that leads to another stone circle, now called Overton Hill. This circle was once called Silla, and it corresponds to the Galactic Center.

As I walk through the south gateway, tremendous energy buzzes from one stone to another and rushes through my body. Here, the avenue snakes, and I can see that the four gates of Avebury mark the four directions. The avenues leading out of these gates were constructed of great pairs of male and female stones about thirty feet apart. Back in 3000 B.C., these stones, weighing a few tons each, were placed upright in long lines extending for at least twenty miles in all four directions. In fact, the avenues reached all the way to London, which also contained great stone circles. This Earth medicine wheel, the largest ever built on the planet, is the most important teacher about the powers of Gaia.

The first major point to the south of Avebury Circle is Silbury Hill. If you keep going south on the avenue of stones that passes by this hill, you would eventually come to Stonehenge. As I pass down the snaking pathway, I notice that the stones on my right are female—decidedly round and magnetic—while the stones on my left are male—more phallic and electric. A bit farther along, the pattern begins to switch from left to right, but each pair always consists of a male and a female stone.

As I pass slowly between the pairs, I become supercharged with both male and female polarities. I can feel my cellular sexual memory opening, and the energy begins to intensify, propelling me back into the distant past. The farther I travel back in time, the stronger become the etheric plane and the density of the planet. I am getting excited because I can feel that I am about to access an amazing erotic power.

I am now approaching an intersection. To my left lies the pathway to the galactic stone circle of Overton Hill, and to my right lies Silbury Hill. Here I cross a river called Cunnit. Once on the other side, I move rapidly back through the veils of time, arriving at the site of Silbury Hill as it appeared in 23,562 B.C.

Before me, I see a cleared area about a thousand feet in diameter. This area includes two circles: an outer circle of tree stumps about fifty feet in diameter and an inner circle of flattened straw over a smooth, chalk surface. These circles were created by the Eye Goddess, and there are many owls flying around them, symbolizing the magnificent powers of the eye. The outer circle of tree stumps delineates the outer rim of the iris, while the inner circle represents the pupil. This "eye" has the ability to see into the third dimension from all other dimensions. Its totem keeper is the owl. The owl assists the survivor, the wolf, during its night hunting, and the hawk assists the wolf during the day. This eye in particular is the "lens" through which all of the beings who take an interest in Earth can see how things are functioning in the third dimension.

There is a woman sitting in the center of the circle—Grandmother Seven Macaw of the Pleiades—and she is myself. I am meditating with an obsidian egg, the egg of creation from the Goddess. This egg changes form according to the consciousness with which one meditates. I have not accessed this moment before, and I am amazed. It is 23,562 B.C., and I am encoding the primordial egg with information from the stars—information that it will need in order to hatch between A.D. 1996 and 2011. I encode the egg with the fifth-dimensional galactic time cycles, then I bury it and return slowly through the layers of time.

As time passes, the tall tree stumps of the outer circle become the foundation posts for a temple covered with animal skins. Later, I see, the posts are replaced by stones that contain energies from thousands of years of meditation and storytelling.

I move forward in time to the beginning of the Fifth Mayan Great Cycle—3125 B.C.—when Avebury Circle, just north of here, was first constructed. It was at this time that the great henge was dug, the outer stone circle was constructed, and the snaking avenues to the four directions was completed. After that came the chalk formation of Silbury Hill, the hill of the womb of the Goddess, which was placed right over the spot where Grandmother Seven Macaw buried the primordial egg. As with all of the most important sacred sites on the planet, this place embodies layer upon layer of time.

Now I move forward in time to witness the chalk construction. I see that the people have cut great blocks of white chalk. The first circle of chalk blocks is eight feet high, and it has no ceiling. (Eventually, progressively smaller circular layers above this center circle will close it to the sky.) This is the original inner circle, the pupil lens of the Eye Goddess, which is always open to the sky during the first phase of construction.

Now priestesses are cutting blocks of virgin soil from the place where the Cunnit River flows from the crystal cave of Swallows Barrow (now called West Kennet Barrow)—the emergence cave of Spider Grandmother. One by one, the women cut the blocks. Each block has a bottom layer of fine gravel that filters water; next, a layer of clay; next, a layer of rich Earth; and above that, a layer of Earth filled with roots and mosses. The soil by the sacred spring is moist and fecund, and these blocks are filled with snails, bugs, nematodes, and worms.

As the blocks are cut, they are charged by the sacred spring that is filled with crystals and gemstones. No males are allowed to visit this spring, and as the priestesses cut and remove the soil, they are in a state of deep meditation.

This ceremony is done to teach about all the years it takes the Earth to create her surface. The priestesses cut away the blocks and remove the soil in a sacred manner, just as it was done by the grandmothers when the first solar circle was created for the harvest of the grain. In those days, the grandmothers removed all the soil where Silbury Hill was later located. They cut down to the original chalk layer, and the surface was smooth like a baby. Over thousands of years, grain was winnowed in that circle, making its surface look like a golden sun from the sky. That yearly circle of golden grain would make it possible for the crop circles to manifest thousands of years in the future.

Now, as she works, each priestess asks the Mother Earth for permission to cut away her skin and use it to help create a chamber for the sacred son. The priestess then walks slowly along the pathway of stones, carrying a single block of soil to the circle of the golden Sun, the iris of the future hill of the Eye Goddess. None of them know exactly why they are doing this, but all of them were called for this ceremony in the Dreamtime. With the help of the priestesses, the Goddess is dreaming her temple into form. Going through the opening into the chalk circle, each priestess places her block of live soil onto the chalk floor of the chamber, which is still open to the sky. Eventually, these blocks of earth transform the floor into a green carpet of life. I see the chalk layer glistening in the night moisture of a soft Full Moon rain.

Now the layer of chalk blocks that will form the next level of the hill has been brought to the circle. The time is coming for the temple to be activated before the final level of blocks is put into place that will cover the inner center and close it to the sky. As the Full Moon rises, the nine priestesses remove their robes, enter the chamber, and sit around its edges with their backs against the chalk wall. In the center, there is space left for only one person to lie down on the soft green carpet.

Now priests wearing robes of many colors are leading a naked young man along the avenue of stones from Avebury Circle. He has just experienced the *hieros gamos* (sacred marriage) fire ceremony in the north circle of Avebury, and he is filled with sexual power. This ceremony was one of the most exquisite Goddess initiations ever experienced in Avebury Circle, the culmination of twenty thousand years of women training men about sexuality. As he walks along, this young man is reexperiencing this ceremony in his mind, so I can tune into what has just occurred.

A young priestess had dreamed of a golden child wandering through the fields of grain, and she shared her dream with the grandmothers. They had her lie on the grass within the cupping rocks of the root chakra of the north circle, and herbody coursed with light as she watched energy and blue light sparking on the surfaces of the ancient stones. Meanwhile, the young man stood facing north in the south circle in front of the throat stone as two concentric circles of people rushed around and around in opposite directions.

The outer circle of men and women inside the henge stones ran counterclockwise with torches, making lines of red fire in the night. Around them in the surrounding hills, sacred barrows were lit by a rising Full Moon. The inner circle of men ran clockwise. Their torches cast light into the circle where the young man stood in front of the electrified needle stone, which was sending arcs of electricity in all directions. His phallus pounded as a group of five priests sat on the ground in front of him, taking his force into their hands to create healing energy for the people. Next the young man felt an explosion in his groin. Hot juice shot up his spine and burst into his head. He became obsessed with the desire to possess the young priestess. At the same moment, the priestess felt a wavelike pulsation in her inner groin, and the edges of her cavity began glowing with yellow light that instantly drew the soul of a golden child into the north circle.

The women in the north circle, who were also running clockwise with torches, gasped with joy as they saw the child glowing above the cupping stones. The grandmothers began crying with exaltation, for many of them remembered seeing the same light the first time they welcomed a male priest in this way. However, never before had the child been visible to all the people.

The circles of fire continued rotating as the young man began walking north, his erect phallus leading his feet into the dark center point; he felt an overwhelming magnetic draw toward the priestess. His spine of blue light filled his head with invisible power. He embraced the heart-chakra stone, left it, and then stood in the dark power center encoding the planet with knowledge about the power of male and female uniting to bring in the sacred child. Little did he know then that more than five thousand years of confusion would pass before the people would remember his magnetic attraction to the Goddess.

The young man stood inside the gate of the inner circle as the women ran behind him, making his whole body shiver with electricity. Then he saw the priestess lying on the ground in a bed of grain covered with soft moss and flowers. All of the juice in his spine returned to his phallus, and he was pulled forward as if possessed. As he approached the priestess, blue light crackled all around her and on the surface of the cup stones. He knelt and raised her full hips to his phallus. She shivered as he entered her virginal body. Moving in and out, he felt as though he were making waves in an ocean as she sucked him in deeper and deeper.

The circles of people moved in a frenzy. Meanwhile, hundreds of owls were dropping down into the deep outer henge, feasting on thousands of mice and rats released by the villagers; the rodents had been captured to feast the owls just for this moment. The owls had been called in to watch for interference from any other dimension during the entrance of the golden child. This baby was a star child, created in perfect love between man and woman, and the owls had come to observe his entry onto the Earth.

The young man had been taught by the priests to hold his seed until he felt the magnetism of the woman's orgasm rising. As he plunged in and out of her soft body, the fire reflected his pumping body, wet with perspiration.

Then the priestess began to sink into an inner wildness such as no one had ever spoken of. As she was thrust and moved about, she saw animals in her mind, faces of the ancestors, and spiraling diamonds of starlight. Then her body engulfed her like a Full Moon tide rushing over great boulders. The power rose from the base of her pelvis and blasted blue light up her spine and into her brain as an orgasm of hot sperm exploded through the young man's phallus. Through the channel from his skull to the base of his spine and out his male organ, the man gave the golden child all his knowledge of the Earth. The people circling with torches sang in a high-pitched wail to the stars, encoding the planet with joy. . . .

Now, coming down the pathway between the stones, the young man is amazed to feel the kundalini rising in his spine again. But this is a different kind of kundalini, created by the charge between the powers of the female and male ancestorstones—it is more mental and less physical.

His phallus rises as he crosses the river. He is approaching the opening into the first chalk layer of Silbury Hill. Inside, the priestesses sit in a circle awaiting the young man who has created the golden child. As he comes into their circle, he feels drugged, as though by hallucinogenic mushrooms. He feels possessed by orgasmic waves of time and space, as if he were the immaterial center of an energy vortex. He lies down in the center of the circle as the women sit around him on the soft soil. The chamber is open to the sky, and he can feel them receive him totally.

This ceremony is to be the beginning of the new cycle—the creation of the conscious male side for both men and women. Until now—3113 B.C.—the Goddess has ruled the planet, and the male principle has been in service to the Goddess. This is that exquisite point when a new seed is germinated—a seed that will produce a balance between male and female. These nine women and one man have entered into an agreement whereby they will hold this ceremony in total trust for the planet. No matter what experiences are required for the activation of the male principle, this ceremony is to be secreted away to make it possible for the entire five-thousand-year cycle to be lived out. These people are followers of the Dreamtime, and this ceremony will one day return as the activation of the phallus by the Goddess.

As the young man lies on the soft grain, the women begin to teach him how to lie with them during this conjunction of Moon and Jupiter with the Pleiades. The Pleiades rules the Dreamtime, and this night is an ideal time to create life. The women are meditating on the quality of this lunar conjunction, contemplating ways to manifest its powers into the material world, and they are transferring their thoughts to the man's brain. The women charge their own bodies with kundalini energy and send it into him, generating a series of erections that feel to him like rising and falling waves in the sea. By lying there and freely allowing his body to respond to this subtle energy, he is forming bonds of trust with the priestesses that cast out fear and judgment—bonds that will eventually fuse male and female.

This total trust is needed to survive the difficult, five-thousand-year activation of the male principle. This phase will be complete in 1992. Then the memory of the fire ceremony and the circle of women will reawaken in the male his natural allurement to the magnetic female. Once again, he will melt down inside. Trust will return, and the magnetism will intensify twenty-four hours a day all through 1993.

The young man now lets go completely, opening himself as the energy rises up through his body. The nine priestesses are charging the soil in the chamber with the full force of magnetic activation. The man begins seeing blue lines to the stars and planets as he lies on the sacred earth, and he travels out into the universe while they charge the soil. Thousands of years later, when this male activation is complete, all men will finally remember to travel in the sky only while they are in harmony with the vibration of the Earth.

Meanwhile, the soil within the chamber becomes so charged with power that its lifeforms will remain alive until the chamber is opened near the end of the cycle. This opening of the central chamber of Silbury Hill in the early twentieth century will possibly result in the greatest shock ever encountered by archaeologists. When they open the chamber, its lifeforms will still be fresh and vital after five thousand years without sunlight, rain, or fresh air.

This chamber is the power chamber that holds the knowledge that the electromagnetic attraction between male and female creates absolute protection in all species. It is this joining that attracts children who have no negative imprinting, who live on Earth in a multidimensional state of consciousness, and who share with all species. There will be no war in heaven when the signet of Atlantis creates an Earth on which every being is loved.

> And there was a war in heaven: Michael and his angels fought against the dragon. And prevailed not; neither was their place found any more in heaven. And the great dragon was cast out, that old serpent called the Devil, and Satan, which deceiveth the whole world; he was cast out into the earth, and his angels with him.
>
> —Revelation 12: 7–9

SELECTED BIBLIOGRAPHY

Adams, W. Marsham. *The Books of the Master of the Hidden Places*. New York: Samuel Weiser, 1980.

Adkins, Leslie and Roy A. *A Thesaurus of British Archeology*. London: David and Charles, 1982.

Aldrid, Cyril. *Egypt to the End of the Old Kingdom*. London: Thames and Hudson, 1965.

Allegro, John. *The Dead Sea Scrolls*. Middlesex, England: Penguin, 1964.

Angus, S. *Mystery Religions*. New York: Dover, 1975.

Apollonius of Rhodes. *The Voyage of Argo*. New York: Penguin, 1959.

Argüelles, José. *The Mayan Factor: Path Beyond Technology*. Santa Fe, NM: Bear & Company, 1987.

Arochi, Luis E. *La Pyramide de Kukulcan: su simbolismo solar*. Mexico: Panorama, 1988.

Ashe, Geofrey, ed. *The Quest for Arthur's Britain*. Chicago: Academy Chicago Publishers, 1987.

Asher, Maxine. *Ancient Energy: Key to the Universe*. Palm Springs, CA: Ancient Mediterranean Research Association, 1979.

Augustine, Saint. *Confessions*. Translated by R.S. Pine-Coffin. New York: Dorset Press, 1961.

Bachofen, J.J. *Myth, Religion and Mother Right*. Princeton: Bollingen, 1967.

Baer, Randall N. and Vicki V. *Windows of Light: Quartz Crystals and Self-Transformation*. New York: Harper & Row, 1984.

Baigent, Michael, Richard Leigh, and Henry Lincoln. *Holy Blood, Holy Grail*. New York: Dell Publishing, 1983.

————. *The Messianic Legacy*. New York: Henry Holt, 1986.

Bancroft, Anne. *Origins of the Sacred: The Spiritual Journey in Western Tradition*. London: Arkana, 1987.

Baran, Michael. *Twilight of the Gods*. New York: Exposition Press, 1984.

————. *Insights into Prehistory*. Smithtown, NY: Exposition Press, 1982.

Begg, Ean. *The Cult of the Black Virgin*. London: Arkana, 1985.

Bensinger, Charles. *A Mayan Initiation Journey to Tikal, Quirigua and Copan*. Private paper. Santa Fe, NM: 1990.

Blackman, E.C. *Marcion and His Influence*. New York: AMS, 1978.

Blair, Lawrence. *Ring of Fire: Exploring the Last Remote Places of the World*. New York: Bantam, 1988.

Bord, Janet and Colin. *The Secret County*. London: Granada, 1976.

_____. *Earth Rites*. London: Granada, 1982.

Boulay, R.A. *Flying Serpents and Dragons: The Story of Mankind's Reptilian Past*. Self-published, 1990.

Braghine, Colonel A. *The Shadow of Atlantis*. Wellingborough, England: Aquarian Press, 1980.

Bramley, William. *The Gods of Eden*. San Jose, CA: The Dahlin Family Press, 1989.

Branston, Brian. *The Lost Gods of England*. London: Thames and Hudson, 1984.

Brennan, Martin. *The Stars and the Stones*. London: Thames and Hudson, 1983.

Brindel, June Rachuy. *Ariadne*. New York: St. Martin's Press, 1980.

Brunton, Paul. *A Search in Secret Egypt*. New York: Samuel Weiser, 1980.

Budge, E.A. Wallis. *Babylonian Life and History*. New York: Copper Square, 1975.

_____. *The Book of the Dead*. New York: University Books, 1960.

_____. *The Egyptian Heaven and Hell*. La Salle, IL: Open Court, 1905.

Burl, Aubrey. *Prehistoric Avebury*. New Haven, CT: Yale University Press, 1979.

Campbell, Joseph. *The Mysteries*. Vols. 1 & 2. Princeton: Bollingen, 1955.

Caesar, Julius. *The Battle for Gaul*. Boston: David R. Godine, 1980.

Castleden, Rodney. *The Knossos Labyrinth*. London: Routledge & Kegan Paul Inc., 1990.

_____. *Minoans: Life in Bronze Age Crete*. London: Routledge & Kegan Paul Inc., 1990.

Cayce, Edgar Evans. *Edgar Cayce on Atlantis*. New York: Paperback Library, 1969.

Ceram, C.W. *The Secret of the Hittites*. New York: Alfred A. Knopf, 1956.

Chan, Roman Pina. *Chitzén Itzá: La Ciudad de Los Brujos del Agua*. Mexico: Fondo de Cultura Economica, 1980.

_____. *Guide to Mexican Archeology*. Mexico: Minutiae Mexicana, 1970.

_____. Quetzalcoatl: *Serpiente Emplumada*. Mexico: Fondo de Cultura, 1977.

Childress, David Hatcher, ed. *Anti-Gravity and the Unified Field*. Stele, IL: Adventures Unlimited Press, 1990.

Chopra, Deepak. *Quantum Healing: Exploring the Frontiers of Mind/Body Medicine*. New York: Bantam, 1989.

Churchward, James. *The Cosmic Forces of Mu*. New York: Paperback Library, 1968.

Clow, Barbara Hand. *Eye of the Centaur: A Visionary Guide into Past lives*. Minneapolis: Llewellyn, 1986.

_____. *Heart of the Christos: Starseeding from the Pleiades*. Santa Fe, NM: Bear & Company, 1989.

Coe, Michael D., and Richard A. Diehl. *The Land of the Olmec*. Austin, TX: University of Texas Press, 1980.

Coe, William R. *Tikal: A Handbook of Ancient Maya Ruins*. Guatemala: Associación Tikal, 1986.

Cohen, A. *Everyman's Talmud*. New York: Schocken, 1975.

Cory, L.P. *Ancient Fragments*. Minneapolis: Wizards, 1975.

Cottrell, Leonard. *The Bull of Minos*. New York: Grosset and Dunlap, 1953.

Craine, Eugene R., and Reginald C. Reindorp. *The Codex Perez and The Book of Chilam Balam of Mani*. Norman, OK: University of Oklahoma Press, 1979.

Crossan, John Dominic. *Four Other Gospels*. Minneapolis: Winston, 1985.

————. *Eden, the Forgotten Books of and the Lost Books of the Bible*. World Publishers, 1927.

Cumming, Barbara. *Egyptian Historical Records of the Later Eighteenth Dynasty*. Fascicles 1, 2 & 3. Warminster, England: Aris and Phillips, 1982.

Cumont, Franz. *The Mysteries of Mithra*. New York: Dover, 1956.

Dames, Michael. *The Silbury Treasure*. London: Thames and Hudson, 1976.

Däniken, Erich von. *According to the Evidence*. Great Britain: Souvenir, 1970.

————. *The Gold of the Gods*. Great Britain: Souvenir, 1973.

————. *Miracles of the Gods*. New York: Delacorte, 1974.

Davidovits, Dr. Joseph, and Margie Morris. *The Pyramids: An Enigma Solved*. New York: Hippocrene Books, 1988.

Davies, Nigel. *The Ancient Kingdoms of Mexico*. Middlesex, England: Penguin, 1987.

————. *Voyagers to the New World*. Albuquerque, NM: University of New Mexico Press, 1979.

Davis, Theodore M. *The Tomb of Queen Tiyi*. San Francisco: KMT Communications, 1990.

Donnelly, Ignatius. *Atlantis: The Antediluvian World*. San Francisco: Harper & Row, 1971.

Doreal. *The Emerald Tablets of Thoth—the Atlantean*. Sedalia, CO: Brotherhood of the White Temple, 1939.

Doresse, Jean. *The Secret Books of the Egyptian Gnostics*. New York: Viking, 1960.

Dorland, Frank. *The Mystery of the Crystal Skull*. Taos, NM: Wisdom Books, 1984.

Doumas, Christos G. *Thera: Pompeii of the Ancient Aegean*. London: Thames and Hudson, 1983.

Drake, Raymond. *Mystery of the Gods—Are They Coming Back to Earth?* Self-published, 1972.

Eisler, Riane. *The Chalice and the Blade*. San Francisco: Harper and Row, 1987.

Eliade, Mircea. *Death, Afterlife, and Eschatology*. New York: Harper and Row, 1974.

————. *Myth of the Eternal Return*. Princeton, NJ: Bollingen, 1954.

————. *Rites and Symbols of Initiation*. New York: Harper Torchbooks, 1958.

————. *Sacred and the Profane*. New York: Harcourt Brace Jovanovich, 1959.

Eogan, George. *Knowth and the passage-tombs of Ireland*. London: Thames and Hudson, 1986.

Eusebius. *The History of the Church from Christ to Constantine*. Translated by G.A. Williamson. Middlesex, England: Penguin, 1983.

Faulkner, R.O. *The Ancient Egyptian Book of the Dead*. New York: Macmillan, 1985.

Fell, Barry. *America B.C.* New York: Simon and Schuster, 1976.

————. *Bronze Age America*. Boston: Little Brown, 1982.

Ferro, Robert, and Michael Grumley, *Atlantis: The Autobiography of a Search*. New York: Bell Publishing, 1970.

Finegan, Jack. *Archeological History of the Ancient Middle East*. New York: Dorset Press, 1979.

Fontenrose, Joseph. *The Delphic Oracle: Its Responses and Operations With a Catalog of Responses*. Berkeley: University of California Press, 1978.

_____. *Python: A Study of Delphic Myth and its Origins*. Berkeley: University of California Press, 1980.

Fox, Hugh. *Gods of the Cataclysm*. New York: Dorset Press, 1981

Fox, Matthew. *Original Blessing*. Santa Fe, NM: Bear & Company, 1983.

Freidrich, Otto. *The End of the World: A History*. New York: McCann & Geoghegan, 1982.

Galanopoulos, A.G., and Edward Bacon. *Atlantis: The Truth Behind the Legend*. Indianapolis: Bobbs-Merrill, 1969.

Gallenkamp, Charles. *Maya*. New York: Viking, 1976.

Gimbutas, Marija. *The Language of the Goddess*. San Francisco: Harper & Row, 1989.

Gordon, E.O. *Prehistoric London: Its Mounds and Circles*. Thousand Oaks, CA: Artisan Sales, 1985.

Graves, Robert. *The Greek Myths*. Vols. 1 & 2. England: Penguin, 1955.

Graves, Robert, and Raphael Patai. *Hebrew Myths*. New York: Greenwich, 1983.

Graves, Tom. *Needles of Stone*. London: Granada, 1978.

Griaule, M., and G. Dieterlen. *The Pale Fox*. Chino Valley, CA: Continuum Foundation, no publication date.

Griffiths, J. Gwin. *The Conflict of Horus and Seth*. Liverpool, England: Liverpool University Press, 1960.

Grof, Stanislav and Christina. *Beyond Death*. London: Thames and Hudson, 1980

_____. *Spiritual Emergency: When Personal Transformation Becomes a Crisis*. Los Angeles: Jeremy P. Tarcher Inc., 1989.

Guignebert, Charles. *Christ*. New York: University Books, 1970.

_____. *Jesus*. New York: University Books, 1956.

_____. *The Jewish World at the Time of Jesus*. New York: University Books, 1959.

Habachi, Labib. *The Obelisks of Egypt: Skyscrapers of the Past*. Cairo: The American University in Cairo, 1984.

Haich, Elizabeth. *Initiation*. Palo Alto, CA: Seed Press, 1974.

Halifax, Joan. *Shamanic Voices: A Survey of Shamanic Voices*. New York: Dutton, 1979.

Hall, Nor. *The Moon and the Virgin*. New York: Harper and Row, 1980.

Hammond, Norman. *Ancient Maya Civilization*. New Brunswick, NJ: Rutgers University Press, 1988.

Hansen, L. Taylor. *The Ancient Atlantic*. Amherst, WI: The Amherst Press, 1969.

Hapgood, Charles H. *Maps of the Ancient Sea Kings: Evidence of Advanced Civilization in the Ice Age*. New York: E.P. Dutton, 1979.

Harleston, Hugh. *The Keystone: A Search for Understanding*. Self-published, 1984.

Head, Joseph, and S.L. Cranston. *Reincarnation: The Phoenix Fire Mystery*. New York: Julian Press, 1977.

Heinberg, Richard. *Memories and Visions of Paradise*. Los Angeles: Jeremy P. Tarcher Inc., 1989.

Herodotus. *The Histories*. Translated by Aubrey de Selincourt. Middlesex, England: Penguin, 1982.

Heschel, Abraham. *The Prophets*. New York: Harper Torchbooks, 1962.

Hesiod. *Theogony and Works and Days*, Translated by M.L. West. Oxford: Oxford University Press, 1988.

Heyerdahl, Thor. *The Maldive Mystery*. Bethesda, Maryland: Adler & Adler, 1986.

Hitchin, Francis. *Earth Magic*. New York: William Morrow, 1977.

Hoffman, Michael A. *Egypt Before the Pharoahs*. New York: Dorset Press, 1979.

Hope, Murry. *Ancient Egypt: The Sirius Connection*. England: Element Books, 1990.

Horning, Derk. *The Valley of Kings: Horizons of Eternity*. New York: Timkin Publishers, 1982.

Jalandris. *The Hall of Records: Hidden Secrets of the Pyramid and Sphinx*. Self-published, 1980.

Jaynes, Julian. *The Origins of Consciousness and the Bicameral Mind*. Boston: Houghton Mifflin, 1976.

Jonas, Hans. *The Gnostic Religions*. Boston: Beacon Press, 1963.

Joseph, Francis. *The Destruction of Atlantis*. Olympia Fields, IL: Atlantis Research Publishers, 1987.

Josephus. *Antiquities of the Jews and Histories of the Jewish Wars*. Translated by William Whiston. Philadelphia: David McKay, no publication date.

Jung, C.G. *Aion: Researches into the Phenomonology of Self*. Princeton: Bollingen, 1959.

————. *Psychology and the Occult*. Princeton: Bollingen, 1977.

————. *Synchronicity*. Princeton: Bollingen, 1960.

————. *The Visions Seminars*. Books 1 & 2. Zurich: Spring Publications, 1976.

Kerenyi, C. *Goddess of the Sun and Moon*. Irving, TX: Spring Publications, 1979.

Lamy, Lucy. *Egyptian Mysteries*. New York: Crossroad/Continuum, 1981.

Laurence, Richard. *The Book of Enoch*. San Diego: Wizards, 1973.

Lemesurier, Peter. *The Armageddon Script*. England: Element Books, 1981.

Le Plongeon, Augustus. *Sacred Mysteries Among the Mayas and the Quichés*. Minneapolis: Wizards, 1973.

Levi. *The Aquarian Gospel of Jesus the Christ*. England: L.N. Fowler & Co., 1907.

Lerner, Gerda. *The Creation of Patriarchy*. Oxford: Oxford University Press, 1986.

Lichtheim, Miriam. *Ancient Egyptian Literature*. Vols. 1 & 2. Berkeley, CA: University of California Press, 1973.

Luckert, Karl W. *Olmec Religion: A Key to Middle America and Beyond*. Norman, OK: University of Oklahoma Press, 1976.

MacMullen, Ramsey. *Christianizing the Roman Empire AD 100-400*. New Haven, CT: Yale University Press, 1984.

————. *Paganism in the Roman Empire*. New Haven, CT: Yale University Press, 1981.

Mahan, Joseph B. *The Secret: America in World History before Columbus*. Columbus, GA: Self-published, 1983.

Maltwood, K.E. *Enchantments of Britain: King Arthur's Round Table of the Stars*. Cambridge: James and Clark and Co., 1982.

Maspero, G. *The Dawn of Civilization: Egypt and Chaldea*. London: Society for Promoting Christian Knowledge, 1896.

Masters, Robert. *The Goddess Sekhmet: The Way of Five Bodies*. New York: Amity House, 1988.

Matthews, Caitlin and John. *The Western Way: A Practical Guide to the Western Mystery Tradition*. Vols. 1 & 2. London: Arkana, 1985.

Matthews, John. *At the Table of the Grail*. London: Routledge & Kegan Paul Inc., 1984.

————. *The Grail: Quest for the Eternal*. New York: Crossroad/Continuum, 1981.

Matthews, W.H. *Mazes and Labyrinths: Their History and Development*. New York: Dover, 1970.

Mavor, James. *Voyage to Atlantis*. New York: Putnam, 1969.

Mazar, Benjamin. *Recent Archeology in the Land of Israel*. English edition by Hershel Shanks. Washington, DC: Biblical Archeology, 1985.

McMann, Jean. *Riddles of the Stone Age: Rock Carvings of Ancient Morrow, Europe*. London: Thames and Hudson, 1980.

Men, Hunbatz. *Los Calendarios Astronómico Mayas y Hunab K'u*. Juarez, Mexico: Ediciones Horizonte, 1983.

————. *Mayan Initiation Centers of Tik'al-Quilighua-Copán*. Private paper. Mérida, Mexico, 1990.

————. *Secrets of Mayan Science/Religion*. Santa Fe, NM: Bear & Company, 1990.

Mertz, Henriette. *Atlantis*. Chicago: 1976.

Meyers, Carol. *Discovering Eve: Ancient Israelite Women in Context*. Oxford: Oxford University Press, 1988.

Michailidou, Anna. *Knossos: A Complete Guide to the Palace of Knossos*. Athens: Ekdotike, 1989.

Michell, John. *The Earth Spirit*. New York: Crossroad/Continuum, 1975.

————. *The New View Over Atlantis*. New York: G.P. Putnam & Sons, 1983.

————. *Secrets of the Stones*. London: Penguin, 1977.

Moore, Marcia, and Mark Douglas. *Reincarnation: Key to Immortality*. New Harbor, Maine: Arcane, 1968.

Moscati, Sabatino. *Ancient Semitic Civilizations*. New York: Putnam, 1960.

Musaios. *The Lion Path: A Manual of the Short Path to Regeneration for Our Times*. Berkeley: Golden Sceptre Publishing, 1987.

Negev, Avraham. *Archeological Encyclopedia of the Holy Land*. NJ: S.B.S. Publishing, 1980.

Newham, CA. *The Astronomical Significance of Stonehenge*. Wales: Moon Publications, 1972.

Noorbergen, Rene. *Treasures of the Lost Races*. New York: Bobbs-Merrill, 1982.

Nyssa, Gregory of. *The Life of Moses*. Mahwah, NJ: Paulist Press, 1978.

O'Brien, Christopher. *The Genius of the Few: The Story of Those Who Founded the Garden in Eden*. Wellingborough, England: Turnstone, 1985.

Ochoa, Lorenzo. *Olmecas y Mayas en Tabasco*. Villahermosa, Mexico: Gobierno del Estado de Tabasco, 1985.

Ogilvie, R.M. *Early Rome and the Etruscans*. Glasgow: Fontana, 1975.

O'Kelly, Michael J. *Newgrange: Archeology, Art and Legend*. London: Thames and Hudson, 1982.

Oppenheim, A. Leo. *Ancient Mesopotamia*. Chicago: University of Chicago, 1977.

Pagels, Elaine. *Adam, Eve, and the Serpent*. New York: Random House, 1988.

_____. *The Gnostic Gospels*. New York: Vintage, 1979.

Patten, D.W. *The Biblical Flood and the Ice Epoch: A Study of Scientific History*. Seattle: Meridian Publishing Co, 1966.

Pendlebury, J. *The Archeology of Crete*. New York: Norton, 1965.

Perera, Victor, and Robert D. Bruce. *The Lost Lords of Palenque: The Lacondon Mayas of the Mexican Rain Forest*. Berkeley: University of California Press, 1982.

Petrie, W.M. *Religious Life in Ancient Egypt*. Boston: Houghton and Mifflin, 1924.

Petronius. *The Satyricon*. Translated by J.P. Sullivan. Middlesex, England: Penguin, 1965.

Pettinato, Giovanni. *The Archives of Ebla: An Empire Inscribed in Clay*. New York: Doubleday, 1981.

Phillip, Brother. *The Secret of the Andes*. Bolinas, CA: Leaves of Grass, 1976.

Phillips, Graham, and Martin Keatman. *The Green Stone*. London: Grafton Books, 1984.

Piggot, Stuart. *The Druids*. London: Thames and Hudson, 1975.

Pogacnik, Marko, and William Bloom. *Leyline and Ecology*. Glastonbury: Gothic, 1985.

Pritchard, James. *The Ancient Near East*. Vols. 1 & 2. Princeton, NJ: Princeton University Press, 1958.

Ragette, Friedrich. *Baalbek*. Park Ridge, NJ: Noyes Press, 1980.

Rawlinson, George, *Ancient Egypt*. New York: G.P. Putnam & Sons, 1904.

Recinos, Adrian, and Delia Goetz. *The Annals of the Cakchiquels: Title of the Lords of Totonicapan*. Translated from Quiche by Dionisio Jose Chonoy. Norman, OK: University of Oklahoma Press, 1979.

Redford, Donald B. *Akhenaton: The Heretic King*. Princeton: Princeton University Press, 1984.

Reed, Bika. *The Field of Transformations: A Quest for Immortal Essence of Human Awareness*. New York: Inner Traditions, 1987.

_____. *Rebel in the Soul: A Sacred Text of Ancient Egypt*. New York: Inner Traditions, 1978.

Renault, Mary. *The Bull From the Sea*. New York: Vintage, 1975.

Riordain, Sean P., and Glyn Daniel. *New Grange*. London: Thames and Hudson, 1964.

Robinson, James M. *The Nag Hammadi Library*. San Francisco: Harper & Row, 1977.

Rostovtzeff, M. *Rome*. New York: Oxford University Press, 1960.

Russell, Jeffrey Burton. *The Devil: Perceptions of Evil from Antiquity to Primitive Christianity*. Ithaca, NY: Cornell University Press, 1977.

_____. *The Prince of Darkness: Radical Evil and Power of Good in History*. Ithaca, NY: Cornell University Press, 1988.

Rutherford, Ward. *The Druids: Magicians of the West*. Wellingborough: The Aquarian Press, 1978.

Sanders, E.P. *Jesus and Judaism*. Philadelphia: Fortress, 1985.

Schele, Linda and David Freidel. *A Forest of Kings: The Untold Story of the Ancient Maya*. New York: William Morrow, 1990.

Scholem, Gershom G. *Major Trends in Jewish Mysticism*. Jerusalem: Schocken Books, 1941.

Schwaller de Lubicz, Isha. *Her-Bak: Egyptian Initiate*. New York: Inner Traditions, 1978.

_____. *Her-Bak: The Living Face of Ancient Egypt*. New York: Inner Traditions, 1978.

_____. *The Opening of the Way*. New York: Inner Traditions, 1981.

Schwaller de Lubicz, R.A. *The Egyptian Miracle: An Introduction to the Wisdom of the Temple*. New York: Inner Traditions, 1985.

_____. *Esoterism & Symbol*. New York: Inner Traditions, 1985.

_____. *Sacred Science*. New York: Inner Traditions, 1982.

_____. *The Temple in Man: Sacred Architecture and the Perfect Man*. New York: Inner Traditions, 1977.

Scrutton, Robert. *Secrets of Lost Atland*. Jersey: Neville Spearman, 1978.

Sejourne, Laurette. *El Pensamiento Nahautl Cifrado por los Calendarios*. Mexico City: Siglo Vientiuno, 1981.

_____. *Pensamiento y Religion en el Mexico Antiguo*. Mexico City: Lecturas Mexicanas, 1984.

_____. *Supervivencias de un Mundo Magico*. Mexico City: Lecturas Mexicanas, 1985.

Settegast, Mary. *Plato Prehistorian*. Cambridge, MA: Rotenberg Press, 1987.

Sety, Omm. *Abydos: Holy City of Ancient Egypt*. Los Angeles: LL Company, 1981.

Sharkey, John. *Celtic Mysteries: The Ancient Religion*. New York: Crossroad/Continuum, 1981.

Shearer, Tony. *Beneath the Moon and Under the Sun*. Santa Fe, NM: Sun Books, 1975.

_____. *Lord of the Dawn: Quetzalcoatl*. Happy Camp, CA: Naturegraph, 1971.

Sheldrake, Rupert. *A New Science of Life*. Los Angeles: Jeremy P. Tarcher Inc., 1981.

_____. *The Presence of the Past: Morphic Resonance and the Habits of Nature*. New York: Times Books, 1988.

Shorter, Alan. *The Egyptian Gods*. Routledge & Kegan Paul Inc, 1983.

Sitchin, Zecharia. *Genesis Revisited*. Santa Fe, NM: Bear & Company, 1990.

_____. *Lost Realms*. Santa Fe, NM: Bear & Company, 1989.

_____. *The Stairway to Heaven*. Santa Fe, NM: Bear & Company, 1992.

_____. *The Twelfth Planet*. Santa Fe: Bear & Company, 1990.

_____. *The Wars of Gods and Men*. Santa Fe: Bear & Company, 1992.

Smith, Morton. *Jesus the Magician*. San Francisco: Harper & Row, 1978.

Spanuth, Jurgen. *Atlantis of the North*. London: Sidgwick & Jackson, 1979.

Spence, Lewis. *Atlantis Discovered*. New York: Causeway Books, 1974.

_____. *The History and Origins of Druidism*. New York: Rider, 1942.

_____. *The History of Atlantis*. New York: Bell, 1968.

_____ *Myths and Legends of Ancient Egypt*. New York: Farrar & Rinehart, 1811.

_____. *Myths of Babylonia and Assyria*. London: George Harrap, 1916.

_____. *The Occult Sciences in Atlantis*. New York: Rider, 1978.

Steiner, Rudolph. *Egyptian Myths and Mysteries*. Spring Valley, NY: Anthroposophic Press, 1971.

Swimme, Brian. *The Universe Is a Green Dragon*. Santa Fe, NM: Bear & Company, 1985.

Szekely, Edmond Bordeaux. *The Discovery of the Essene Gospel of Peace*. International Biogenic Society, 1977.

Talbot, Michael. *The Holographic Universe*. New York: Harper Collins Publishers, 1991.

Taylour, Lord William. *The Mycenaeans*. London: Thames and Hudson, 1983.

Tella. *The Dynamics of Cosmic Telepathy*. Aztec, NM: Guardian Action Publishers, 1983.

Temple, Robert. *The Sirius Mystery*. New York: St. Martin's, 1976.

Thompson, William Irwin. *Islands Out of Time*. Santa Fe, NM: Bear & Company, 1990.

_____. *The Time Falling Bodies Take to Light*. New York: St. Martin's, 1981.

Tompkins, Peter. *The Magic of Obelisks*. New York: Harper & Row, 1981.

_____. *Secrets of the Great Pyramid*. New York: Harper & Row, 1971.

Trench, Brinsley Le Poer. *Forgotten Heritage*. London: Neville Spearman, 1984.

_____. *The Sky People*. London: Neville Spearman, 1963.

Turner, Frederick. *Beyond Geography: The Western Spirit Against the Wilderness*. New Brunswick, NJ: Rutgers University Press, 1983.

Tyler, Larry. *Mayan Cycleology: The Secret of the Ages and the Key to Survival in Time*. Self-published, 1987.

Ulanov, Ann Belford. *Receiving Woman*. Philadelphia: Westminster, 1981.

Velikovsky, Immanuel. *Ages in Chaos*. New York: Doubleday, 1952.

_____. *Earth in Upheaval*. New York: Dell, 1955.

_____. *Mankind in Amnesia*. New York: Doubleday, 1982.

_____. *Oedipus and Akhnaton*. New York: Pocket Books, 1960.

_____. *Peoples of the Sea*. New York: Doubleday, 1977.

_____. *Ramses II and His Time*. New York: Doubleday, 1978.

_____. *Stargazers and Gravediggers: Memoirs to Worlds in Collision*. New York: William Morrow & Co., 1983.

_____. *Worlds in Collision*. New York: Dell, 1973.

von Franz, Marie-Louise. *Alchemy: An Introduction to the Symbolism and Psychology*. Toronto: Inner City, 1980.

Wasson, R. Gordon, Carl A.P. Ruck, and Albert Hoffmann. *The Road to Eleusis*. New York: Harcourt Brace Jovanovich, 1978.

Wentz-Evans, W.Y. *Cuchama and Sacred Mountains*. Chicago: Swallow Press, 1981.

West, John Anthony. *Serpent in the Sky*. New York: Harper and Row, 1979.

_____. *Traveler's Key to Ancient Egypt*. New York: Alfred A. Knopf, 1985.

Whitworth, Eugene E. *The Nine Faces of Christ: Quest of the True Initiate*. San Francisco: Great Western University Press, 1972.

Wilhelm, Richard. *The Secret of the Golden Flower*. New York: Harcourt Brace Jovanovich, 1962.

Wilson, R. McL. *The Gnostic Problem*. New York: AMS, 1958.

Wood, David. *Genisis: The First Book of Revelations*. Turnbridge Wells, England: The Baton Press, 1985.

ABOUT THE AUTHOR

Barbara Hand Clow is a noted astrological counselor, ceremonial leader, writer, and editor. She received her master's degree in theology and healing from Mundelein College in 1983 after writing a thesis on "A Comparison of Jungian Psychoanalytic Technique and Past-Life Regression Therapy." *The Mind Chronicles* trilogy is based on this thesis, as it explores the collective unconscious through deeply probing her subconscious mind.

Clow believes that everyone on Earth possesses the memories of all times and places within their cellular matrices and that anyone can remember everything they have ever known if they have the courage to go deep within the experience themselves. She feels, as do many Native American and Mesoamerican spiritual teachers, that the purpose of the late twentieth century is to go beyond time, and beyond history. Therefore, her *Mind Chronicles* series is a journey through time and history calibrated to trigger her readers into clearing memories.

As a result of her extensive personal work with ceremony at sacred sites and its role in the evolution of consciousness, Clow wrote the first volume of *The Mind Chronicles* trilogy, *Eye of the Centaur: A Visionary Guide into Past Lives*, in 1986. Next, her continued work on clearing the emotional body and emptying the contents of the subconscious mind through shamanic journeying compelled her to write the second volume, *Heart of the Christos: Starseeding from the Pleiades*. In *Signet of Atlantis: War in Heaven Bypass*, the third and last volume of the trilogy, Clow accesses multidimensional consciousness and travels in the most celestial realms of experience.

Clow is also the author of *Stained Glass: A Basic Manual* (Little Brown, 1976), *Chiron: Rainbow Bridge Between the Inner and Outer Planets* (Llewellyn, 1987), and *Liquid Light of Sex: Understanding Your Key Life Passages* (Bear & Company, 1991). She travels widely teaching workshops based on her various books, and she is not currently available for astrological readings.

Clow is married and the mother of four children: Tom, Matthew, Christopher, and Elizabeth.

ABOUT THE ARTIST

Angela Werneke is a designer/illustrator who sees her work as a way of healing and nurturing the Earth. Her visionary artistry appears in the first two volumes of this trilogy, *Eye of the Centaur* and *Heart of the Christos*, as well as in Nicki Scully's *The Golden Cauldron* (Bear & Company, 1991). She has received professional recognition for her book design and illustration, which includes Bear & Company's *Medicine Cards* as well as *Keepers of the Fire* and *A Painter's Quest*. Angela is art director for Bear & Company and lives in the high juniper desert of northern New Mexico.

BOOKS OF RELATED INTEREST
BY BEAR & COMPANY

BRINGERS OF THE DAWN
Teachings from the Pleiadians
by Barbara Marciniak

ECSTASY IS A NEW FREQUENCY
Teachings of The Light Institute
by Chris Griscom

EMERGENCE OF THE DIVINE CHILD
Healing the Emotional Body
by Rick Phillips

THE GOLDEN CAULDRON
Shamanic Journeys on the Path of Wisdom
by Nicki Scully

THE LOST REALMS
Book IV of The Earth Chronicles
by Zecharia Sitchin

THE 12th PLANET
Book I of The Earth Chronicles
by Zecharia Sitchin

THE WARS OF GODS AND MEN
Book III of The Earth Chronicles
by Zecharia Sitchin

Contact your local bookseller or write:
BEAR & COMPANY
P.O. Drawer 2860
Santa Fe, NM 87504